"PERHAPS YOU'RE GROWING UP AFTER ALL," HE TEASED.

Star slammed her glass down on the coffee table so hard that it was in serious danger of shattering.

"You really are the most insufferable, unbearable, arrogant . . ." She didn't trust herself to continue. With as much dignity as she could muster, she got to her feet. "I'm going now."

With one movement Max was out of his chair and across the room, reaching the door ahead of her, blocking her way. "Don't go," he said.

She tried to push past him. He grabbed hold of her wrists. She struggled to release herself but his grip was firm and determined. The feel of the strong, hard hands that held her captive sent a thrill of excitement through her body.

Max lowered his hungry gaze from Star's bright eyes to rest on her lips. Slowly he leaned forward and gently brushed her lips with his own. This was not something to be hurried. . . .

QUANTITY SALES

Most Dell books are available at special quantity discounts when purchased in bulk by corporations, organizations, and special-interest groups. Custom imprinting or excerpting can also be done to fit special needs. For details write: Dell Publishing, 666 Fifth Avenue, New York, NY 10103. Attn.: Special Sales Department.

INDIVIDUAL SALES

Are there any Dell books you want but cannot find in your local stores? If so, you can order them directly from us. You can get any Dell book in print. Simply include the book's title, author, and ISBN number if you have it, along with a check or money order (no cash can be accepted) for the full retail price plus $2.00 to cover shipping and handling. Mail to: Dell Readers Service, P.O. Box 5057, Des Plaines, IL 60017.

Lucky Star

Betty Paul

A DELL BOOK

Published by
Dell Publishing
a division of
Bantam Doubleday Dell Publishing Group, Inc.
666 Fifth Avenue
New York, New York 10103

ISBN: 0-440-20600-6

Reprinted by arrangement with
Judy Piatkus (Publishers) Ltd.

Printed in the United States of America

Published simultaneously in Canada

February 1990

10 9 8 7 6 5 4 3 2 1

KRI

LUCKY STAR

1

Somewhere a shutter was banging in the wind. A Santa Ana had blown up in the last hour, that hot, dry wind that local Californians say makes people nervous and jumpy. Even a little crazy.

Star Merrick lay on the vast, ornately carved wood-framed bed, staring up into the darkness. No wonder she couldn't sleep—that racket would rouse a deaf mouse—but it wasn't the only reason for her wakefulness and Star knew it.

The luminous hands of her digital traveling clock stood at twenty minutes past three when she finally gave up her attempt to sleep and flicked on the bedside lamp. A gentle, rosy light filtered through the silk shade, barely illuminating the heavy Spanish-style furnishings of her bedroom.

Blast that shutter! Better check it wasn't one of hers that had broken loose.

Star swung long, slender legs off the bed and stood tall—high breasted, slim hipped, skin glowing the color of ripe apricots from three months of sunshine—and stark naked. Sleeping in the buff was a new experience for Star, one of the many changes that had taken place in her life during her stay in Los Angeles. Not important in itself but still a long way from cozy school pajamas. She picked up the pair of oversize glasses from the bedside table and put them on. No use going on a tour of inspection if she couldn't see. She shrugged on the hint of a negligee that she'd bought only that day from one of the chic boutiques on Rodeo Drive and padded across the tiled floor to the window.

The night was clear, the wind having blown away the ubiquitous smog. Stars shone ferociously bright in the black velvet sky. She checked her shutters. They were firmly secured. She looked across the patio and saw that a shutter of her father's bedroom was unlatched and banging noisily. How could he stand it? Vernon said that the sound of flowers growing kept him awake. Star sometimes suspected that in fact he slept like a babe and that his "insomnia" was just a way of emphasizing the burden of being so brilliantly creative in his waking hours. For as long as Star could remember he had been one of the top British film and television directors—right up until two years ago, when suddenly everything seemed to collapse for him, including his marriage to Laura Denning, Star's mother, the famous TV actress of the ever-popular soap, *Harringtons*. After their breakup Vernon had decided to leave England and give Hollywood a try. It was a wise move. Here things had really taken off for him and now, with one television serial successfully launched, he was busy setting up other projects.

A figure appeared at the window of Vernon's room. It was Charlene, his current girlfriend. She flung open the window and, with her long blond hair blowing wildly in the gale, struggled with the shutters, finally managing to close them. Star smiled a little wryly. Vernon seemed to have Charlene well trained. With Laura he would have got up and closed the shutters himself. Not Laura. Never Laura.

Thinking of her mother, Star's smooth brow creased into a worried frown. How, she wondered, was Laura going to react to what she'd done? Say she was too young? She knew her mother still thought of her as a schoolgirl. Well, she certainly wasn't one anymore. She was an adult. Old enough to vote, so certainly old enough to make her own decisions about her own future. And she'd made the right one about Gary. No question. He was the sort of man any girl would be happy to love and share her life with. Of course he was. So why was she pacing round her room at three-thirty in the morning? Being plain stupid, that's why.

But marriage? The total commitment? Till death us do part?

She picked up a small Cartier jewel box from the dressing table, opened it, and took out a ring. Her ring. A perfect aquamarine surrounded by diamonds. Gary said he'd chosen it to match her eyes. She looked up at her reflection in the mirror. Her eyes were indeed a quite startling blue-green and, now that she'd lost so much weight, seemed larger than they used to, especially when she wore her new contact lenses. And she'd discovered too that high cheekbones and a well-defined chin had been hiding under all those chubby folds.

Even so, she couldn't lose the feeling that the girl she saw in the glass wasn't Star Merrick at all. The real Star Merrick was thirty pounds overweight, wore her hair in a scruffy ponytail, dressed in baggy jeans and sloppy T-shirts, and looked out at the world through unbecoming granny glasses. The inexplicably unremarkable daughter of the most remarkable parents whom she could never hope to emulate—especially her brilliant and beautiful mother. The eternal schoolgirl safe and even happy in the noncompetitive confines of an English boarding establishment for young ladies, where academic excellence was not considered top priority, but character and fair play were. Star had enjoyed the undemanding atmosphere and had hidden behind a façade of being fat and funny and fairly dim. But you can't stay at school forever. As it was she had stayed an extra year under the pretext of getting A levels. She'd managed a pass in Eng. Lit. but the rest were in her usual form of nonachievement. When the results arrived in L.A., Star had responded with a self-deprecatory joke: "You know me. Thick as a dozen oak planks."

If Vernon was disappointed he didn't show it. "Never mind, darling," he'd said absently. "Brains aren't everything." Then, glancing at his watch as always, he'd said he was late for a meeting and, as always, bridged the distance between them with his checkbook. "Go on a shopping spree," he'd said. "Buy some new clothes. Anything you like. Charge it to me. Charlene will go with you."

Charlene was less than enthusiastic at the prospect and made this clear to Star in no uncertain terms. "So what do we buy you?" she asked. "There's no maternity store on Rodeo Drive."

Star had laughed. She was used to cracks about her overample size. It didn't matter, she said, she didn't really want any new clothes. She looked terrible, whatever she wore, so why bother?

At this Charlene got really furious.

"Listen," she said, "it's nothing to brag about. If you ask me, you should be ashamed, going around looking like a pregnant hippo. Do you have any idea how lucky you are? How many kids do you suppose have doting daddies to pick up the tab? Most of us have to work our asses off to get anything in life. You want to join the human race? Throw away the candy box and act your age."

Looking back it seemed to Star that she'd just been waiting for someone to prod her into action. Someone who wouldn't say "You're fine as you are" or "It suits you to be cuddly." Why she had not been able to take the initiative on her own she neither understood nor stopped to consider. She was content to be taken over by the forceful Charlene and do as she was told. She dieted rigorously and exercised until she dropped. The results were spectacular. In just a few weeks the ex-pudge was replaced by a slim, bronzed goddess. A top-flight hairstylist reshaped the ponytail into a skillfully highlighted cascade, and Hermès, Bonwit Teller, and half a dozen elegant boutiques renewed her wardrobe. She even managed to cope with contact lenses. Everyone said she looked fantastic. Especially her father. "Now we know just where you're going," he said. "To hell with A levels. With those looks, who needs them? You, my darling, are going to be an actress."

For once Star was adamant. She shook her head and said "No" very firmly indeed.

"Why not?"

"I don't want to, that's all."

"You're crazy. There's a part in this series I'm setting up, be perfect . . ."

"No. Forget it."

"So, what will you do?"

From force of habit Star fell back into the old method of self-defense—put yourself down before others do it for you. "I've not quite decided," she said, mock serious. "Either a brain surgeon or maybe an astronaut."

Vernon laughed. Then, putting his arm round her and giving her a hug, he said, "You *should* act. You know you can. But if it doesn't turn you on then I suppose you'd best marry and have a lot of kids."

Before Star could comment the telephone rang and Vernon, seemingly forgetting her and her plans, was immediately immersed in the really important matter of up-front finance for his new TV project.

That evening she met Gary.

Six foot two, with corn-colored hair and blue eyes direct and honest as daisies, plus a build like an Olympic athlete, Star felt sure he must be a successful young actor. In fact he was a successful young lawyer. At twenty-six Gary Kennard was already established in his family law firm. He was quiet, serious, and treated Star with respect, unlike most of the other men she had encountered since her metamorphosis, who pounced almost before they learned her name. Although she enjoyed the novel experience of receiving male flattery, she had little idea how to handle it. This new exterior was all very fine, but somehow the person inside hadn't caught up with it. The Hollywood beauty and the shapeless English schoolgirl were not yet comfortable companions. So she was grateful for Gary's pleasant if unstimulating company. Modest and unassuming as he might be, he still knew exactly where he was going and what he wanted from life. And he knew immediately after he saw her that he wanted Star. On their second date he asked her to marry him.

Convinced he must be joking, Star joked back, "But I can't cook!"

Gary didn't laugh. "You won't have to. I wouldn't want my wife to cook."

Still Star laughed it off and still Gary persisted. He introduced her to his family and friends, all of whom made her welcome and accepted her as "Gary's girl." As the weeks passed she became increasingly fond of him, enjoying his attentiveness, his consideration for her feelings, his respect and obviously sincere affection. If he wasn't all that exciting, well, that wasn't everything. She thought of all the show-business marriages she'd known that had started out on cloud nine and ended up in muddy disillusionment—including her parents'. Lots of women found fulfillment in marriage and children, so why not her? The next time Gary asked her she surprised them both by saying "Yes."

As Gary drove her home that night in his sleek blue Maserati she felt a deep sense of contentment. At last she belonged somewhere, with someone who loved her and accepted her uncritically. She wanted to make it the perfect and complete relationship she was sure it could be. To show him that she too was sincere and serious. That she did love him.

"Gary," she said softly, "I'd like us to go back to your apartment."

He slowed the car and gave her a quick, intense look.

"If it's what you really want," he said.

"It is, Gary. It is what I want."

But it wasn't, was it?

She put the aquamarine ring back in its velvet box and closed the lid. She felt confused and bewildered. And, it was no use pretending, horribly disappointed. Gary had been kind and tender but his lovemaking had meant nothing to her. She did so hope that she had succeeded in fooling him that it had been great for her. She would have hated to hurt his male pride. But was this *it*? Was this what all the fuss was about? Perhaps next time . . . ? But did she want there to be a next time? If she was going to marry him there would have to be lots of times. Forever. For the rest of her life. If she really loved him, surely everything would be all right. And she did love him, didn't she? She wouldn't have gone to bed with him otherwise. She felt totally lost. What should she do? If only she had someone to talk to. Someone who cared. Someone like . . . Jessie.

Of course! Why hadn't she thought of her sooner? Jessie, the one constant factor in her life, who always had known what was best for her. Jessie, with her dyed petunia-pink hair and her vividly rouged cheeks: ex-chorus girl, ex-dresser, and for the past seventeen years housekeeper cum companion cum nanny. In fact the center and support of the Merrick household, and Star's own special guide and comforter. When her parents had no time for her, Jessie always had plenty. When Vernon took off with a girl half his age, Jessie had seen Laura through the crisis. Dear Jessie, always there when you needed her. Wise, patient, wonderful, Jessie was the answer.

Star reached for the telephone, then hesitated. This was not a subject for a telephone conversation. No, if she was going to talk it over with Jessie then it must be face to face. She pulled down a suitcase and, opening the closet door, grabbed clothes at random and started to pack.

Charlene and Vernon were still asleep when she left. A short note explained her sudden departure.

She rang Gary from the airport. He was surprised but made no attempt to dissuade her. "I understand," he said. "You want to talk things over with your mom, right?"

Talk to her mother? What an odd idea. Laura was the last person Star had ever been able to confide in. But she wasn't going to admit that to Gary, so she said, "That's right," and then thought, Oh God, I'm lying to him already. How awful.

"You just take your time," Gary said. "We've got years ahead together."

* * *

The taxi lurched to a halt outside number forty-eight Belgravia Place.

"Here you are, gorgeous."

Star paid the driver, refusing his offer to carry her bags into the house. He had tried to chat her up all the way from Heathrow and she was glad to be rid of him.

"Independent, eh? Okay then, darling. Mind 'ow you go." And with an appreciative wink he drove off.

The late September sun filtered through the soft green of the lime trees that were a feature of this elegant London square and helped to make it such a pleasant place to live. Star looked up at the imposing Georgian house, now converted into superluxury apartments, and could see the roof garden with its ornamental shrubs and flowers that belonged to her mother's luxurious penthouse. To her surprise she felt quite glad to be on home ground with the reassuring knowledge that in a few moments she and Jessie would be flinging arms round necks and hugging close in the way they had always greeted each other. She grinned to herself in anticipation and, picking up her bags, hurried up the steps to the imposing porticoed entrance.

A sleek tabby cat sat on the top step, warming itself in the sunshine. Star recognized an old chum, Tiger, who belonged to Thomson the porter. She greeted the animal with a bright, "Hi there, Tiger." The cat ignored her.

"What's the matter? Don't you remember me?"

She held out a hand. The cat got up and darted down the steps toward its home in the basement.

Star felt an irrational stab of rejection, then immediately reproached herself. For Pete's sake! How chippy could you be? It was only a cat. Still, she entered the house feeling vaguely put out by Tiger's reaction.

Thomson's familiar figure—neat blue uniform, sandy

hair carefully brushed, mustache close cropped—was immediately recognizable in his usual place behind the reception desk. As Star entered he looked up inquiringly.

"Can I help you, miss?"

Star smiled. "Hello, Thomson."

The porter looked at her blankly.

"It's me . . . Star Merrick."

Thomson blinked. "Well, I never . . . I'm sorry, miss, I just didn't recognize you."

"That's all right," Star said lightly. "I've been away. In California."

"Ahh . . . that's it then, I expect." Thomson infused this remark with an implied significance that somehow escaped Star. He hurried out from behind the desk. "Let me take your bags for you, miss."

"I can manage, thanks."

The porter touched the lift button and the gate slid open. As she entered the lift he stood staring at her. "If I may say so, miss, California seems to have done you a world of good."

"Thanks, Thomson. I certainly feel great."

She pressed the penthouse button and, as the lift started to ascend, repeated the word great rather loudly, for no reason she could imagine except perhaps to cover the fact that suddenly she felt decidedly nervous.

Of what? Just why should butterflies be flapping around inside her?

In a word: Laura.

Really, it was embarrassing. A reasonably intelligent adult female was scared of the way her mother would react to the fact that her little girl had finally, and very belatedly, grown up. Though perhaps she should have worn something a bit more subdued for their reunion? Candy-pink culottes and wild-orange blouson with gold stiletto-heeled shoes and accessories might be consid-

ered low-key in L.A., but in Belgravia . . . ? Laura did
like to promote that discreet, ladylike, National Theatre
actress image—even though she'd never played there.
Actually, her own taste in clothes could be pretty flamboyant at times. So stop agitating, Star told herself. You
are an independent woman, engaged to be married.
Practically. But that could come later.

The lift reached the landing. As Star stepped out she
glanced at her watch—five-thirty—perhaps Laura
would still be at the studio and there would be time to
change into jeans or something before she had to face
her. Even more important, there would be time to talk
to Jessie.

She delved into her tote bag for her key and then
changed her mind, ringing the doorbell instead. She'd
give Jessie a surprise. She struck a jokey pseudoglamor-
ous attitude with arms outstretched and mouth open
wide in a mock model-girl smile.

The door opened. Star froze in her would-be comic
pose. Instead of Jessie, who always answered the front
door herself, a small oriental-looking young woman
wearing a spotless white overall gazed at her with expressionless, immobile features.

"Please?" the girl asked politely.

Embarrassed, Star lowered her arms and closed her
mouth. Where was Jessie? And who was this Chinese,
Korean, or whatever stranger? Star frowned. Had she
gone crazy and come to the wrong apartment? Had
Laura, on some whim, moved house without letting her
know? She looked past the inscrutable oriental girl into
the entrance hall. There she saw the gleaming chande-
lier, the gold damask-covered walls, the oversize portrait of Laura gazing out from its carved gilt frame. No,
this was home all right. Star picked up her bags and
stepped inside.

"Please one moment," the white-uniformed girl protested mildly.

Star plunked down her bags. "Where's Jessie?" she asked.

"Here is living Miss Laura Denning."

"I know that, but where's Jessie?"

With no change of expression the girl signaled for Star to follow her and with swift silent steps darted off across the wide expanse of deep pile wheat-colored carpet toward the sitting room.

"Listen, I live here. I'm . . ." Star called after her, but the slight figure had already disappeared through the pillared archway that led to the main part of the flat.

Feeling puzzled and rather anxious, Star followed her. Maybe Jessie was away on holiday. Or was something wrong? Perhaps she was ill.

The spacious sitting room was just as she remembered it: luxurious and impersonal. Swathed silk honey-toned curtains at the long windows with subtly darker shades of velvet for the overstuffed sofas and armchairs. Elaborate flower arrangements adorned marble-topped coffee tables, and on the damask-covered walls a number of mirrors were each placed to reflect yet another portrait of Laura, giving the impression of a multitude of Lauras filling the room. Leading onto the terrace were sliding glass doors that, when open, could make the terrace an extension of the sitting room. It was a wonderful setting for the parties that Laura delighted in giving. The young oriental girl stood waiting by the open terrace door. Now Star understood. Of course, Jessie was out there doing her "gardening." Fussing over the precious geraniums and lobelia that were her pride and joy.

"Please, lady," the girl announced, and with a quick

bow of her head, turned and left. Smiling in anticipation, Star stepped out onto the terrace.

The great earthenware Provençal pots and white-painted tubs spilling out their profusion of pink and white petunias and geraniums were there, but no familiar figure in a floppy straw hat and gardening gloves was tending them. Quite bewildered, Star turned to go back inside, but was stopped by the sound of a deep male voice. "We didn't order you today," it said tersely.

Star spun round.

He lay stretched out on a lounger, half hidden by a wrought iron garden table. A man of about thirty, he was wearing shorts and a T-shirt, revealing tanned, muscular limbs. A book lay open across his lap. He gave every appearance of being quite at home but distinctly annoyed. A lock of dark hair flopped over his forehead, raven black eyebrows were drawn together in a frown, the wide sensitive mouth set in a straight line.

"Why can't that blasted agency ever get it right?" he said, pushing his sunglasses up into his hair. Star looked into wide-set smoky-gray eyes and felt the totally stable terrace shift under her feet.

Jet lag, she told herself, and knew that it wasn't.

"I . . . er . . ." she stammered.

He wasn't listening. "As you're here I suppose I can find something for you to do—copy typing—and there's always fan mail to answer."

He stood up, an easy, muscular movement. Star felt her throat tighten and a strange, unknown heat seemed to be generated somewhere deep inside her. As he stood looking at her she saw that he was not a tall man, perhaps five foot ten, but he exuded an overwhelming feeling of strength, of barely controlled power. Her high stiletto heels brought Star almost up to his height, and their eyes leveled. Close up, she saw green flecks in the smudged gray, the fringe of thick black lashes. She also saw something remote, watchful, veiled.

"Have you been here before?" he asked.

"Oh, yes. In fact . . ."

"Then you know your way to the office."

Dismissing her, he turned his attention to a pile of papers on the garden table. With his disconcerting gaze off her, Star managed to gather her scattered senses.

"I'm not a secretary," she said. "I live here."

He turned slowly and looked at her, puzzled.

"I'm Star," she said, and realized that her voice sounded too loud and forceful. She lowered it a tone and added, "Laura Denning's daughter."

He looked at her intently for a long moment and then, with a slow and pseudosorrowful shake of his head, he said, "I suppose I have to believe you, but . . . oh, dear." And he shook his head again.

Star felt attraction turn to resentment, and quickly to anger. Who the hell was this guy anyway? Lounging around on her mother's terrace—on *her* terrace, come to that—acting as though he owned the place. But still he disturbed her, stopped her from thinking straight, from finding a suitably sharp retort to put him down. All she could manage was, "I just got in from Los Angeles."

He made no comment, just continued to stare at her with the same cool appraisal. "I wish I'd met the other one," he said ambiguously.

"Other what?" Star asked.

"The other Star Merrick. I've seen photographs. The girl with the high intelligent brow and smoothed-back hair. With eyes gazing through those granny glasses, that were eager and interested. I was looking forward to meeting her."

"Who are you?" Star asked, furious that this stranger should presume to comment on her appearance.

He ignored the question. "I suppose some Hollywood would-be Pygmalion, confronted by your individuality, couldn't stand it and felt compelled to try and change you."

Star bridled. "If you're really interested, it wasn't a man who helped me get myself together, it was a woman. In fact, my father's girlfriend, Charlene."

For some reason he seemed to find this funny.

He chuckled, a superior, maddening kind of sound that made Star even more furious. With an effort she controlled her feelings and in icy tones asked, "I suppose you think it incredible that a woman could be influenced by anyone other than a male?"

"Of course not. It's just that name—Charlene." He chuckled again in a patronizing way. "Quite unbelievable. Truly appalling. However, she seems to have had a profound influence on you."

Star was on the verge of resorting to physical violence. With an effort she retained her cool. "Just who are you exactly?" she repeated. "And what are you doing here?"

He drew himself up, stood tall; leg, stomach, and thigh muscles tensed. The head was inclined sharply in a mock formal bow.

"Max," he introduced himself, "Maximilian Macdonald."

"If we're on the subject of names, I'd say that was something of a mouthful."

"Ah, but a name with roots. Mother, Austrian, hence Maximilian, and father Scot, so Macdonald. It's a real name, not a confection like . . ."

"Star?"

"I've always thought it a most appropriate name for the daughter of an actress. No doubt one you plan to live up to."

Star refused to discuss herself any further with this arrogant stranger.

"Where's Jessie?" she asked, not only to change the subject but because she really wanted to know.

Max looked blank. "Who?"

"Jessie. She lives here."

"You mean the lady with the bright red hair and the rouge?"

Jessie's dyed hair and old-fashioned makeup might have been the cause of some affectionate amusement within the family, but Star deeply resented ridicule from this intruder.

"Jessie is part of the family," she flashed. "We couldn't manage without her."

"Well, I'm afraid you'll have to," he replied. "She's gone."

"Gone?" Star, shocked by this information, could hardly take it in. "She can't have. You must be mistaken."

"No, I'm not."

"But why? Was something wrong?"

Max shrugged disinterestedly.

"Where has she gone to?" Star persisted.

"No idea. Ask your mother."

"I don't understand."

"Probably felt it was time to retire."

Star shook her head. Retire? Jessie wouldn't even contemplate the idea, or certainly not without telling her first. Had she and Laura quarreled after all these years? It wouldn't be the first time, but whatever the reason she must have been dreadfully upset just to pack up and leave. Something was wrong, Star sensed it. And somehow it had to do with this man, now leaning with his back against the parapet, eyeing her in that cool, analytical way she found so disturbing.

The deep masculine voice interrupted her thoughts.

"Don't look so sad. These things happen. Nothing lasts forever."

Star looked closely at him, but the enigmatic expression on the dark, handsome face betrayed nothing. Their eyes met. Held. She was aware of a deep animal attraction, but also a gut reaction of distrust. She had an overwhelming urge to get away, out of his company. She wanted to be alone to think.

He anticipated her. "Aren't you going to say hello to Laura?"

"Of course. As soon as she gets back from the studio."

"She's back. Finished early."

"Where is she, then?"

"In the Jacuzzi. Unwinding."

"I won't disturb her yet. She doesn't know about me coming home."

"I know she doesn't."

You know too darn much, Star thought. "Are you something to do with *Harringtons*?" she asked.

"Good heavens, no."

His dismissive tone infuriated her, but before she could reply they were interrupted.

"Max!" The familiar voice sang out from somewhere inside the apartment, deep, slightly husky, once described by a drama critic as being like "honeyed yogurt," unmistakably Laura.

Max sauntered over to the open glass door. "Yes?" he called in the direction of Laura's bedroom.

"I'm dying of thirst, darling," she called back. "Bring me a drinkie."

Star registered the "darling." Not that the endearment had any particular significance in itself. Laura called everyone "darling."

"Coming up," Max replied. And without a backward glance at Star went through into the sitting room. He crossed to the drinks cupboard and got out glasses. He opened the concealed fridge and withdrew a bottle of champagne. Star knew that her mother seldom touched spirits but enjoyed wine. A glass of champagne at the end of a working day was something of a ritual. One with which Max was obviously familiar.

Skillfully he eased the cork out of the bottle of Dom Perignon. There was no loud explosion, no gush of effervescent bubbly, just a discreet "plop" and the pale golden liquid fizzing gently as he filled two glasses. He picked them up and carried them over to Star, who had followed him into the sitting room and was hovering, undecided whether to go and face her mother or to retire to her room and change her clothes. She cursed herself for this irrational feeling of apprehension, like a schoolgirl who's been up to no good and has to report to the headmistress.

Max held out the two glasses. "Why don't you take it in to her?" he asked, his voice unexpectedly gentle as though he sensed her anxiety. "I know what I said about the change in your appearance and it did come as a bit of a surprise, but to be honest you look pretty good."

Star looked at him, suspecting that he was making fun of her again. But the gray eyes, though cool, were not mocking. She took the flutes from him and as she did so their hands touched. It was as if a high voltage shock ran up her arm and through her body, and she spilled some of the wine. But if he experienced a similar sensation he gave no sign of it.

"Does she always have this effect on you?" he asked, seeming genuinely interested.

"What effect?" Star snapped, instantly defensive. "The glasses are too full, that's all."

An amused smile flickered on his lips at this hastily invented excuse.

"Talking of glasses," he said in a conversational tone, "how do you manage without yours?" And he mimed a pair of spectacles.

"Contact lenses, of course. Any other questions?"

"Maaax!" Laura caroled from the bedroom. "Hurry up."

He was still looking at Star.

"Possibly," he replied, "but they'll keep."

With as much poise as she could muster while balancing two brimming glasses, Star walked toward her mother's bedroom. Here the situation was further complicated by having both hands full in front of a closed door.

Before she could decide on a course of action Max was at her side. With a mock bow he opened the door for her.

It was only later that it struck Star that he hadn't knocked.

Laura was seated at her dressing table. Her thick auburn hair was piled up on her head, still damp from the Jacuzzi. She wore nothing but a thick fluffy bath towel wrapped sarongwise around her body, revealing magnificent shoulders, almost too broad but still soft and sensually feminine. She was concentrating with that objective intensity Star knew so well on her reflection in the mirror. No ordinary dressing table mirror—but then no ordinary dressing table, more a laboratory. There were dozens of bottles of lotion and jars of cream, each with their designated function of lubricating, moisturizing, and generally enhancing this dedicated beauty. The mirror was as functional as any to be found in a television makeup department or theatrical dressing room. None of your discreet Victorian tip-ups or traditional three-sided affairs. No, this mirror meant business: starkly practical, uncompromising, surrounded by brilliant 100-watt bulbs. If you looked good in that you were doing all right. Laura was nothing if not professional when it came to her appearance.

As Star entered her mother didn't turn round, but continued to concentrate on her reflection in the mirror.

"What kept you? My tongue's hanging out," she said, the down-to-earth words in sharp contrast to the glamorous aura she exuded even in this off-guard moment.

Star looked at her mother, as always, with wonder. Deep inside she would have liked to run to her and fling her arms around her but she knew better than that. For all her extroverted, outgoing personality, Laura was not a woman who enjoyed physical contact, at least not in Star's experience. Echoes of "Careful, baby, my hair . . . my makeup," made her suppress the impulse. Instead she crossed slowly to the dressing table and put down a glass without speaking. Laura was massaging thick nourishing cream into her neck with long expert strokes. Without stopping, she said, "Thank you, darling. You're an angel."

Still Star didn't speak, but stood watching her mother's reflection in the mirror. How beautiful she still was. How old was she now? Star wasn't quite sure, nobody was, possibly not even Laura, who had readjusted her birthdate for so many years that she had managed to forget the original. But she was certainly past fifty although the general impression was of a woman at least fifteen years younger. Both motherhood and success had come to Laura quite late—in her thirties. If her role as real life mother had had to make way for the fictitious role she played on the TV screen, Star had never resented it—at least not consciously.

Laura wiped her hands on a tissue and picked up the glass. Only then, as she raised it in a toast and was about to drink, did she remove her gaze from her own image and glance up into the mirror to see Star's reflection looking down at her. Laura blinked in surprise, not only at seeing a female instead of the expected Max, but a strange female at that. She stared with no sign of recognition.

"Hullo, Laura," Star said quietly.

Laura put down her champagne glass and spun round on the stool.

"Star? Is it really you?"

"Yes, it's me. How are you?"

Laura ignored the question and continued to gape at her daughter in amazement. "But . . ." she spluttered. "What's happened to you? I honestly didn't recognize you. What the hell have you done to yourself?"

"I . . . er . . ." Star started, but got no further.

"And why aren't you wearing your glasses?"

"Contact lenses . . . they're . . ."

"You know I don't approve of contact lenses. Get a bit of grit or something in your eye, and it could be really dangerous. And you've lost so much weight."

"Twenty-seven pounds," Star said with some pride.

"I just hope you've not been on some crazy crash diet. Young girls can get anorexic just like that, and then you've got real trouble."

"No. I just gave up sweets and stuff, and ate lots of salads and . . ."

Laura wasn't listening. "Go and stand over there so I can get a proper look at you."

Obediently Star stepped a few paces back, and in order to cover an overwhelming feeling of insecurity struck the same comic model-girl pose with which she had planned to greet Jessie.

"Cut the clowning," Laura said impatiently. "Stand up straight." She spoke as though Star were still age ten and being fitted for her school uniform.

Laura screwed up her eyes critically, then after a moment said, "Hmm . . . turn round." Dutifully Star turned. "Back again to me."

After due consideration Laura finally gave her verdict: "Figure—good. Take ten. But don't lose any more. It doesn't suit you to be scraggy. Hair—too freaked out, not your style. I give it five. Clothes minus nothing! Sorry, darling, but they're terrible. All right for some Hollywood hustler, but not for my girl. Still, we can soon fix that. We'll go shopping together. I know what suits you. Anyway, it's wonderful to see you, Starlet." Finally Laura proffered her cheek for Star to kiss, then lifted her champagne glass: "Welcome home."

Star raised her glass and they both drank. Immediately Laura turned away. She picked up a nail file and diligently went to work on her nails. "Why didn't you let me know you were coming? Nothing wrong, I hope. And how is my dear ex? Still chasing every young thing in sight?"

Star sat on the edge of the king-size, satin-covered bed. She knew from experience that Laura seldom required answers to questions unless they concerned her personally, so instead she asked one of her own. The one she really did want the answer to. "Laura, where's Jessie?"

Her mother interrupted her manicure momentarily, nail file held suspended in midair, then with an air of assumed vagueness, asked, "Jessie?" as though hearing the name for the first time in her life.

"Yes," Star persisted, "Jessie. Where is she?"

Laura didn't answer at once but with great concentration pressed down her cuticles with an orange stick. Finally she sighed and said: "The fact is, darling, I had to let her go."

"But why? I don't understand."

"She became impossible, that's why."

"Jessie did? How? In what way?"

"You know how devoted I've always been to her, but

I must have someone totally dependable. She just got past it."

Star frowned. She still didn't understand. "But what happened exactly? I really do want to know, Laura. Jessie means a lot to me."

"Well, to be honest, she started getting a bit funny. Thought people were against her."

"What people?"

"I suppose . . . Max, really. You know how possessive she always was with me, and when Max started . . . helping me, she got all uptight about it. I just couldn't have it, darling. I'm under too many pressures as it is, God knows, without temperaments in the home."

"Where is she now?"

"No idea. I got home from the studio one day and she'd gone. Left no address. Nothing."

"Not even a note for me?"

"No."

"How long has she been gone?"

Laura threw the orange stick down impatiently and took a swig of her champagne. "Could we stop this interrogation, darling, d'you mind? You told me yourself that you'd grown up, so surely you don't still need a nanny. And I have to say that the house does run much more smoothly now. Suki—this Korean girl—is quite wonderful, except she can't answer the telephone. But then, Max sees to all that."

As if on cue the telephone started to ring. Laura made no attempt to pick up the receiver and after a moment the ringing stopped. She gave a little smile of satisfaction. "You don't know what a blessing it is to have someone I can really rely on. You'll like Max. He's a sweetie."

Star thought "sweet" a most inappropriate description for Max, but something made her keep the observation to herself. She couldn't yet make out their relationship but, like Jessie, somehow didn't care for it. Nor did she feel satisfied with Laura's explanation of Jessie's departure but knew better than to press the point against her mother's will. She didn't want to risk tantrums so soon after her return. Deliberately she changed the subject to the one Laura never tired of discussing.

"How are things at 'the store'?" she asked.

Star had been only two years of age when Laura had landed the part of Kim Carson, the beautiful, brave daughter of the late Sir Charles Carson from whom she inherited Harringtons, the famous London department store, running it with skill and flair despite endless adversity in both her professional and personal life.

For years it had seemed to Star that her mother went off to work not at the television studio but at the great store. Often it seemed that she had two mothers, Laura and Kim, and much of the time Kim held the greater reality for her. Well, she saw more of her than she did of Laura, even if only on the TV screen. And Kim was such a wonderful person. Perhaps a bit ruthless at times, but vulnerable and sensitive underneath. As she grew older Star got to know the entire cast of *Harringtons*. They became a sort of extended family. They, too, all had dual identities. For those who worked on it, *Harringtons* was not just a television series—it was a way of life.

"I hope you videoed all the episodes I missed," Star continued.

But to her surprise Laura didn't dive into details of the current story line nor did she impart the latest studio gossip. Instead she gave a noncommittal shrug.

"Wouldn't say you've missed much, actually. The scripts have been getting progressively more putrid and we have falling ratings to prove it. I do my best, but you know what bloody Sylvester's like—pumpkin-head know-all."

Sylvester Chance was the producer of *Harringtons,* and depending on the state of their relationship at any given time Laura deemed him either genius or cretin.

Before Star could comment, the door was pushed open, and Max stood in the doorway surveying both mother and daughter appraisingly. He held a glass of champagne in one hand and the bottle in the other. His presence seemed to fill the room. Star averted her eyes, but Laura looked up at him and smiled warmly.

"That was Harry on the phone," he said. "I arranged for him to come here at seven-thirty."

"Fine," Laura said. "He can take us all out for a slap-up dinner. Heaven knows he makes enough out of all the commission I pay him."

Max sauntered over to Laura's dressing table and topped up her glass. "I suppose even agents have to live," he said.

Laura took a sip of the wine and then returned her attention to her reflection in the mirror. Either by oversight or design she omitted introducing Max to Star.

Max held the bottle up in silent question to Star, who shook her head, declining. He then put the bottle down and settled himself onto a pink velvet armchair, swinging one muscular leg carelessly over the arm. Star frowned. She resented this display of familiarity and resented even more the way in which her mother not only accepted but seemed to enjoy it. She didn't like it. Not one little bit did she like it.

Laura's voice interrupted her troubled thoughts. "Well, Maxi," she said brightly, "what do you think of my punky daughter?"

Max sipped his champagne, but did not reply.

Star found the silence unendurable, and glancing up found the smoky eyes fixed on her in cool appraisal over the top of his champagne glass. To her deep chagrin her cheeks flashed scarlet. Max lowered his glass, amusement twitching the corners of his sensual, curved mouth. Finally he spoke.

"I think," he said with ironic deliberation, "that she is almost as lovely as her mother."

2

Balloons!

Star looked round her bedroom in disgust. Balloons everywhere: on the walls, at the windows, on the bed. She had forgotten, or perhaps deliberately put out of her mind, the wallpaper and matching curtains and bedcover that Laura had chosen to redecorate the room during her last term at school. As a child Star had been fascinated by hot-air balloons—still was, come to that— but as decor for an adult female? Why not Snoopy or characters from Disneyland? She remembered now that she'd thought it pretty ridiculous when she'd first seen it, so why hadn't she objected then? Why was she so timid whenever it came to expressing her opinions to her mother? And why hadn't she been consulted about the decor of her own room? But then she could hardly remember being consulted on anything that concerned her.

And now that she'd at last done something on her own . . . She caught sight of her reflection in the long wall mirror. Perhaps Laura was right. Perhaps her taste in clothes wasn't that great, although, as she now recalled, even this hadn't actually been *her* taste. Not really. It had been a combination of Charlene and a fast-talking, high-powered sales assistant who had persuaded her that the outfit was absolutely "her." Didn't that go for everything about her new personality? Had any of it really been her doing? Who exactly was she? "I wish I'd met the other one." Max's words taunted her. How dare he? Who the hell was he to criticize.

Conflicting emotions welled up inside her, anger competing with something much more disturbing: a mixture of excitement and dislike, or, to be more accurate, distrust. What exactly was he supposed to be doing here? Clearly Laura thought the sun shone out of his ears. Was he her secretary or was it a more intimate relationship? Or both? Whatever it was, Star found herself despising him. What kind of man becomes a hanger-on cum lapdog to an actress twenty years his senior? Certainly not one who merits respect.

She thought of Gary and how different he was. Perhaps she should get on the next plane and go straight back to L.A. and be grateful to accept his offer. But she had a strong hunch that she ought to stay put and protect Laura from this intruder who seemed to have insinuated himself into her affections. And she had to find Jessie. Not just to ask advice, but to make sure that she was all right. How extraordinary that the old lady should have gone without leaving her a note or message of some kind. Perhaps . . . Star went to her desk, opened up the top and started to look through the assorted letters and cards that she had hung on to over the years; just possibly Jessie might have hidden a letter for her to find. But there was nothing. A search through the drawers of her dressing table proved equally unrewarding. There really didn't seem to be any other feasible hiding place. Star had to accept that Jessie must have gone on impulse and that was it. Though she knew she wasn't going to let the matter rest there.

Her thoughts were interrupted by the sound of the house phone bleeping: Laura had had it installed some years ago so that she could easily converse with Star or anyone else whose room was up on the top floor. Star lifted the receiver.

"Starlet darling, listen." Laura's voice had the gentle persuasive tone she adopted when she was determined to get her own way. "I know you're a big girl now and all that, but darling, just what are you planning to wear tonight? I don't mean to interfere or anything but Harry will probably take us somewhere pretty posh, and, well . . ."

"Don't worry, I won't let you down." Star immediately regretted making this sharp retort. It sounded petulant and childish just when she was trying to establish her newfound maturity. "What I mean is," she continued hastily, "I do understand. Everybody knows who you are and you want your daughter to look . . ." She searched for the appropriate word and came up with "respectable," which seemed pretty lame.

Laura laughed, a low melodious sound.

"I hope I'm not that dreary, darling. Of course I want you to feel your best—we all want that. Perhaps that blue dress . . . the one with the big white collar. You always looked so sweet in that."

Star couldn't at first remember and then couldn't believe that Laura was seriously suggesting she wear a dress that had been too young for her a year ago.

"I'm afraid it would be about ten times too big for me now," she said, trying to be tactful. "Leave it to me. I promise not to wear leather and studs."

Laura said of course and Star mustn't mind her being a fussing mum, she only wanted Star to look her best. "And you really are looking nice, dear," she conceded, and then added almost too casually, "You heard what Max said—and believe me, he doesn't just tell you what you want to hear."

Star thought that was probably exactly what he did do—at least to Laura, if not to her.

"He's a super person, Star," Laura continued with almost schoolgirl enthusiasm. "I honestly don't know how I ever managed without him. You've no idea what a help he is to me."

"Oh?" Star asked, unable to keep a note of skepticism out of her voice. "In what way?"

"Oh, organizing the office work and . . ." She hesitated. "Actually, I'm writing my autobiography and he's sort of working on it with me."

"I see." Star had the distinct impression that this last was an improvisation, but Laura pressed on.

"He's absolutely wonderful about filing and sorting out material and that kind of thing. He's frightfully clever. Really brilliant. And such fun. . . . Now, I can't chat anymore, darling," she said, as though it were Star doing the talking and not she. "See you later. . . . And, Star, I'm not telling anyone about the book, so nothing to Harry. You know what an old gossip he is. Ciao, baby."

Thoughtfully Star replaced the receiver. Laura was showing all the symptoms of a woman in love. Pity she couldn't have chosen someone worthy of her affections. Well, it was her business and no one else's. Not even mine, Star thought with irony, remembering her earlier protective urges. She sprang briskly to her feet. Better get the show on the road, as Jessie used to say when she needed to get her charge moving. All very well to tell Laura somewhat airily that she'd wear something suitable when she hadn't even unpacked. But where was her luggage?

She looked round and saw the deflated zipperbags stacked neatly in a corner of the room. Someone had unpacked for her. Must have been the new Korean girl. She opened her wardrobe and, sure enough, her clothes were hanging in a neat file. What luxury, and how Jessie would disapprove, she thought with a smile. Jessie, with years of touring behind her, determined that Star would become an actress, had always insisted that she look after her own things.

"No one's going to run after you picking up your clothes in digs in Scunthorpe," she'd say. "So better get used to it."

It hadn't been bad training. Star had got used to it. Now everything had been done for her, silently and efficiently, and she wasn't at all sure she liked it. She surveyed her newly acquired wardrobe with increasing anxiety. She tore down one dress after another, holding them up against herself critically, trying to assess the effect in the glass. This one too low cut. That one too short and tight. Red—too bright. Black—too sexy.

Eventually, feeling rather desperate and with the bed piled high with discards, Star tore off the culottes and blouson, kicked off the gold heels, and went into her ensuite bathroom. She turned the shower on full and stepped under it. The water pelted down on her, drenching her firm suntanned body. Star soaped herself vigorously and scrubbed shampoo into her strong, luxuriant hair. She reveled in the almost violent sensation of this cleansing as if it could wash away all her problems. When the dial was turned to cold, her body responded joyfully to the stinging onslaught. She got out of the shower glowing, invigorated, feeling able to face the evening ahead.

Wrapped in a soft oversize bath towel, Star padded

out of the bathroom, leaving a trail of wet footprints in the thick carpet. As she trained the hair dryer onto her soaking hair she happened to glance at the open wardrobe. There on a hanger was one remaining dress. Of course, that was it: creamy white with a demure high neck and long sleeves. What could be more suitable? Star grinned mischievously to herself, looking suddenly like a naughty child. The front might be modest, but the back view was something else again, cut so low that it could hardly claim to cover more than the bare essentials. Well, she could sling a wrap over it—and if they were all going to be sitting at a table that back wouldn't show, would it? Not even Laura could object. And Max? Well, who cared what he thought? The brush caught painfully in her tangled hair, bringing tears to her eyes.

"Blast!" she said. "And blast Max."

The almond-green Rolls Royce made its way sedately along Piccadilly and skillfully maneuvered Hyde Park Corner, defying other, lesser vehicles that might attempt to cut in or challenge its right of way. As it turned into Knightsbridge the driver removed the automatic lighter from the dashboard and tried to relight his cigar, which had infuriatingly died. Harry Conrad enjoyed nothing more than a good cigar but for some reason he had never been able to fathom, he always had the greatest difficulty in keeping them alight. He pulled hard on the Havana but it stubbornly refused to ignite except for a small segment of leaf that detached itself and fell, burning, onto the lapel of his dark blue Savile Row suit.

Angrily, Harry beat out the offending cinder and stuck the lighter back into its container on the dashboard. He gave the sigh of a man inexplicably wronged, and only just in time realized that he should have indicated a left turn into Sloane Street. A van driver hooted. Harry would dearly have liked to signal the traditional response but Rolls owners should be above such behavior, shouldn't they? He resisted the temptation and continued his dignified way.

He chewed irritably on the dead cigar. He was not looking forward to the evening ahead. Usually he relished the company of his favorite (and very lucrative) client, but tonight was going to be tricky. Harry had been hearing stories through the grapevine, a particularly reliable branch of the grapevine what's more, that all was not well for Laura at "the store." Ratings were down, and when that happened the front office started looking for a scapegoat. Usually it was a star. In this case, Laura. He'd have to tread carefully. Mustn't alarm her. Knowing Laura, if she had any inkling of what was going on she'd be quite capable of storming into the office of God Almighty, Sir Leonard Latham, and having it out with him. Which could prove fatal. The great Sir Len, head of City Television and self-styled patriarch to all who worked for him, would not be receptive to an actress who no longer pulled the viewers—whatever the reason.

On the other hand, of course, if she did pack it in . . .

Harry had been trying to persuade Laura to marry him ever since Vernon had taken off with that blonde. But no, he pushed the thought aside. He had a deep sense of duty toward his clients, and their professional interests came first. "The store," and her position as one of the first ladies of television, was Laura's life and he was prepared to fight for her.

Laura was the greatest. He'd known it the first time she'd walked into his office wearing a cheap, unbecoming dress, still unaware of her powers either as a woman or as an actress. She'd toured the country in third-rate

productions, played repertory, pantomime, summer sea-
sons, but just couldn't break into the West End or television. She sat in his outer office, badgering his secretar-
ies, until finally he'd agreed to see her. He'd never
regretted it. He got her a small part doubling as an
understudy in a West End comedy. The leading lady
had fallen down the staircase or whatever and Laura,
word perfect, had jumped in and made an overnight
success. After that it had been pretty much of a fait
accompli. A couple more West End shows and then
television. She photographed like an angel, projecting a
unique combination of sexiness and naïveté that added
up to magic. A few plays and then *Harringtons,* the best
soap on the box. It had taken off immediately and had
stayed in orbit ever since.

Until now.

The public could be fickle. Today, with such a vast
range of programs to choose from, not to mention
video, was it really possible that Laura was beginning to
lose her appeal? It was very worrying. The story was
being put around that she was becoming increasingly
difficult at the studios. Perhaps this new boyfriend-sec-
retary was having a bad influence on her. Harry chewed
on his cigar with increased fervor. He just hoped he'd be
able to talk to her alone without that guy sitting on the
sidelines, always watching and listening, taking it all in
and saying nothing. Something about him made Harry
feel uneasy. Let's face it, he didn't really like him. He
was honest enough to recognize that some of the antipa-
thy was based on jealousy. Still, Harry's personal feelings didn't really matter. What mattered was Laura and
Harringtons.

He steered the Rolls into Belgravia Place and drew
up outside number forty-eight. Then walked briskly toward the building, pausing only to throw away the bedraggled remains of his cigar.

* * *

Star stared critically at her reflection in the long wall mirror as though it were some stranger looking back at her. Certainly nobody could accuse her of looking way out or punk. The soft silk jersey of the dress rippled over her body, subtly indicating the line of her small, high breasts and the slim curve of her hips. The high neck line showed off her long neck to advantage; the sleeves buttoned tightly round her wrists emphasized her slender, delicately shaped hands with nails varnished a pale shade of frosted pink. She had slightly modified the cascade hairstyle and her hair fell in loose waves with a few strands curling artlessly over forehead and ears. The general effect was understated, almost conventional—so long as she didn't turn round. And even though the back view might be a bit startling, it was in no way indecent, particularly if she found a wrap, an article of clothing that she hardly ever wore. She hated furs of any description, could never understand women wanting to wear the skins of dead animals, but somewhere there was a shawl she'd once bought at a charity shop.

She rummaged in the back of the wardrobe and let out a small cry of triumph. The shawl was hand-embroidered natural silk, almost exactly the same tone of creamy white as her dress. Star slung it around her shoulders and examined her back view. She made a small grimace—it wasn't what she would have worn by choice but it would have to do. Apart from a pair of small gold earrings and a thin gold bracelet, she wore no jewelry at all. Slingback sandals and matching off-white clutch handbag completed the outfit.

Yet, as so often happened lately when Star was dressed and ready to go out, she felt unsure, dissatisfied, wanted to tear everything off and start again. It had been so simple in the days when she'd pulled a bag over her head and dragged her hair back in that ponytail. Perhaps she should put on that dreary blue dress with the white collar? At least Laura would be pacified. She glanced at her watch—no time to change. Anyway, she was being ridiculous. It was up to her what she wore and she supposed she looked passable. She fiddled yet again with her hair and fervently wished that she didn't have to go out. The prospect of an evening spent in Max's company made her feel tense and apprehensive. She couldn't remember ever having taken such a dislike to anyone. She remembered Jessie. Show on the road, she thought, and without another glance at her reflection turned and marched out of the room.

She walked quickly along the passage toward the wrought iron spiral staircase that led down to the main part of the apartment. She was halfway down when she heard Laura's voice, not loud or shrill but with the hard edge she used when she was really angry. "Not to put too fine a point on it, darling," she was saying, "she's a bitch."

Star heard Harry's mumbled reply but couldn't make out what he said. She didn't want to eavesdrop, but could easily guess that the subject under discussion was *Harringtons*.

She decided to continue down the stairs. After all, she'd been party to these kind of inquests for most of her life: probably someone had said something about someone to someone else, which would all get sorted out eventually. You couldn't have a group of people working together for fifteen-odd years without some in-fighting. It could just be the periodic soul searching about ratings, with blame being apportioned and sleepless nights all round until the show climbed up the charts again and everyone was happy. Star had learned not to take all these overheated crises too seriously.

As she crossed the hall to the sitting room she heard

Laura's voice again. "Listen, Harry, I am not imagining the cuts in my screen time. This week I have two lousy scenes, lasting precisely four and a half minutes. And do you know what has been written in for dear Diane? She is in every scene except one, which takes place in the men's room—otherwise you bet your ass she'd be in that too."

Star hovered in the doorway, uncertain whether to go in or not. Harry slumped in an overstuffed sofa, his legs crossed. He looked worried and was staring down at one of his highly polished handmade shoes as though he could find the solution to Laura's problem reflected there.

Laura was pacing, a bad sign in Star's experience; her mother must be really upset. She looked wonderful, however: green had always been her color, matching her eyes and bringing out the rich red of her auburn hair. The dress was almost severe in cut, its wide shoulders accentuating Laura's still slender waist, skirt swirling to reveal the shapely legs of which she was so justly proud. The neck plunged, outlining full, round breasts. Her only jewelry was the emerald pendant that Star remembered Vernon giving her when *Harringtons* reached its tenth anniversary. Star took in at a glance that Harry was finding the conversation hard going and might welcome a diversion.

"Hello, Uncle Harry," she said with a smile, and walked quickly toward him, arms outstretched.

Harry got slowly to his feet. He showed no surprise at her changed appearance, just held out his arms and said, "Star, baby. Great to see you." He hugged her and kissed her cheek, then, still holding her shoulders, looked at her steadily, his normally lugubrious expression replaced by one of obvious pleasure. "Just about what I reckoned," he said. "You look terrific and it's not surprising. With such a mother, how could it be otherwise? I knew that pudgy little duckling was hiding some terrific swan. The only surprise is that someone in Tinsel Town didn't snap you up."

Star didn't tell him how near to the truth he was. She didn't say anything. She was increasingly aware of some pretty chilly vibes emanating from Laura and knew she'd better quickly divert Harry's attention away from herself and back onto her mother. In any event, she didn't act fast enough. She got no further than "Thank you, Uncle Harry, I—" before Laura interrupted.

"Starlet," she said, with barely contained irritation, "Harry and I are having a very important discussion. Get yourself a drink or something."

"Sure," Star said, unworried by this dismissal. Ever since she could remember she'd known and accepted that work problems had priority over everything else.

While Laura continued to regale Harry with the injustices that City TV was inflicting on her, Star crossed to the drinks table. The room was now softly lit for evening by a succession of strategically positioned lamps whose tinted shades threw pools of discreet and subtly flattering light. Only Laura's highly romanticized portrait was brightly lit by a skillfully concealed spotlight.

Star lifted the champagne bottle out of the ice bucket and was about to fill her glass when she stopped, bottle poised in midair, aware of a disconcerting sensation of being watched. She glanced up and found she was looking into those appraising gray eyes that had so disturbed her earlier on. Half hidden in a shadowy corner of the room, Max leaned back in a large white leather armchair, champagne glass in hand, regarding her with mild interest. He rose easily and, for such a muscular man, with surprising grace from the depths of the chair and came to join her.

"Allow me," he said quietly.

He took the champagne bottle from her and filled her glass, lifting his own in a silent toast. As they drank their eyes met and once again Star experienced a physical reaction that made her skin tingle and the small blond hairs on the backs of her arms react as if they had a life of their own. She shivered.

"Cold?" he asked.

"No," Star whispered.

"I could close the window," he offered.

Star shook her head. If only he would go away. Back to his chair. Anywhere out of her sight. She was overwhelmingly aware of his proximity. Now formally dressed, he seemed even more attractive than before. She began to understand Laura's feelings and felt an urgent need to get out of the room, out of the flat, anywhere . . . away from a situation that might prove to be unmanageable. On impulse and without a word, she left Max and went to stand by the open glass door, which led out onto the terrace. She looked out into the dusk of the warm September evening, at the lights coming on over the city, and felt relieved that Max made no attempt to follow her. Yet a moment later she felt an unreasonable stab of disappointment when she turned to find herself no longer the object of his attention. Instead he seemed completely absorbed by the heated discussion still going on between Laura and her agent.

Star allowed herself a good look at this stranger who had somehow insinuated himself into her mother's life. Not handsome in the conventional sense but quite fearsomely attractive, he had something oddly secretive about him—apparently so detached and yet deeply attentive as if trying to commit the whole scene to memory. Like some kind of spy. Star couldn't help smiling at the idea: perhaps a secret agent from a rival television company, or even the BBC?

As if sensing her attention Max looked round at her,

and an expression of puzzled curiosity flashed into his eyes. For once he seemed at a disadvantage, as if her secret smile made him vaguely uneasy. Star felt absurdly gratified at even the slightest hint of discomfiture on his part, but almost immediately he turned his attention back to Laura, whose voice was becoming quieter but harder.

"The trouble is my bloody contract," she was saying.

"Oh, come on, sweetheart," Harry protested. "Your present contract is the most valuable ever agreed on by any British television company for any actor playing in a serial."

"Basically, Harry, it's worthless."

"What are you talking about?" The folds of Harry's bloodhound face quivered with indignation. "It's a great contract. I drew it up myself."

"Well, the next one *I'll* draw up. And I shall make sure there is a clause inserted that should be there already: complete script approval."

"Impossible. It's the one thing Lennie won't wear. At least not for series artistes."

"Then I shall tell him what to do with his contract," said Laura with a chillingly sweet smile. "And if he can imagine *Harringtons* without me, without Kim Carson, I doubt if the Great British Public can."

Harry didn't reply, but his face seemed to crumple and Star saw that something was worrying him. Something he hadn't so far mentioned.

"Don't even consider doing anything so foolish, Laura," he pleaded. "Please."

Laura held up an imperious hand.

"Listen," she said, "for weeks now I've had so little to do I might as well have stayed home and phoned my scenes in."

"Okay," Harry said. "You've made your point."

Laura blinked large, troubled eyes, green as the emer-

ald at her neck, veiled by just a hint of tears. Suddenly
she changed tack and was the helpless orphan of the
storm. "I need protecting, Harry," she whispered.

He, as always, fell for it. "I'll get on to Sylvester
tomorrow . . ." he stated.

"No use, I told you. He's having a fling with Diane
and is scared gutless his wife will find out. You'll have
to talk to Lennie. You know he always listens to you."

Harry took a long swig of his Perrier water, playing
for time. The last thing he wanted was trouble with
Len. Of course he wanted what was best for Laura, but
to do as she asked could only have the reverse effect at
the moment. He helped himself to one potato chip and
crunched it thoughtfully.

"You will do this for me, won't you?" Laura asked,
almost pleading. "Of course if you won't, I'll just have
to tell him myself."

"No," Harry said quickly. "No need. As a matter of
fact I'm lunching with Len tomorrow."

"Great! You can sort it all out then. Tell him exactly
what I'm going through."

Laura continued to itemize the points that Harry
should make in his meeting with Sir Len. Star glanced
at Max to see how he was reacting to this scene. He
seemed fascinated, totally absorbed, like someone
watching a suspense movie. She wondered again why he
seemed so interested. Was it just idle curiosity or was he
more involved with Laura than she had imagined?

Harry was saved from having to commit himself further to Laura's demands by the appearance of Suki. She
was carrying an enormous bouquet of long-stemmed red
roses.

Laura's peevish expression was transformed to one of
delight. Rather endearingly she still loved receiving
flowers, despite all the bunches and baskets of "floral
tributes" she'd had over the years.

But Suki made no move toward her. "No please," she said. "Not for Madame. For Miss." And padded silently over to Star, proffering the huge bouquet.

Laura expressed Star's thoughts for her. "Are you sure, Suki?" she asked tersely.

Suki nodded and repeated, "For Miss Star." She handed the flowers over and suddenly that awkward schoolgirl was back, taking over from the cool, poised young woman, as Star clutched at the bouquet while trying unsuccessfully not to spill her champagne. She was aware of four pairs of eyes fixed on her. She felt clumsy and embarrassed and for some obscure reason guilty, as though she had no right to be receiving flowers instead of Laura. It was Max who came to her rescue by relieving her of her champagne glass.

"I . . . er . . . I'll go and put them in water," she stammered.

"Please, I make beautiful for you," Suki said, and Star gratefully relinquished them.

"Don't you want to keep the card?" The question came from Max. "At least," he added with a superior smile, "you should know which of your admirers is this extravagant."

Star had no need to look at the card. Still, she opened the tiny envelope and read: "Miss you. Love you. Gary." His quiet strength seemed to reach out and embrace her. Perhaps she should go back. . . . Then she looked up at Max, into those enigmatic smoky-gray eyes, and knew that she wanted to stay.

Laura's voice, overbright, almost strident, broke the silence. "I'm starving," she said. "Let's go and eat."

Both Max and Harry sprang to do her bidding.

Star slipped Gary's card into her handbag and followed after.

* * *

Star had never been to Renata's before and wondered why on earth Laura had chosen it.

Crowded, noisy, with an inferior band and food unremarkable except for its prices, it seemed to have little going for it apart from the inexplicable and undeniable fact that it was the "in" place to go—and, even more important, to be seen.

Renata herself was much in evidence: fifty, fat, hair dyed banana yellow, dressed in an absurdly inadequate yellow mini dress that revealed surprisingly spindly black stockinged legs, she reminded Star of a tightly corseted canary. She had small, black bootbutton eyes forever darting, watching to see who was with whom, and how and why, and what in any given situation could be turned to her own advantage.

She greeted her guests as though they were long-lost relatives, provided they were either rich and/or famous. Both Laura and Harry met these requirements and Renata gave them the full treatment as they entered.

"You look fabulous, darling," she gushed to Laura. "Just wonderful. Younger and more beautiful all the time." The words were addressed to Laura but the beady eyes were on Star, coldly assessing her with all the critical detachment of a peasant buying a chicken in a market. "And this"—she waved a stubby, crimson-tipped hand in Star's direction—"is your little sister, perhaps?"

Laura laughed, recognizing the flattery but nevertheless enjoying it. "No, Renata, this is Star, my daughter."

And then Renata made all the right noises about it not being possible, how Laura was far too young to have a grown-up daughter, and how incredibly lovely Star was—just like her mother.

Star could hardly believe the way Laura lapped it all

up. She'd been listening to this kind of rubbish for so long, and Star had imagined her to be immune to it, but seeing the smile of gratification on her mother's face she realized with something of a shock that this really was meat and drink to her.

They were ushered to their table by an obsequious maître d', but progress was slow.

At almost every table they passed, some friend or acquaintance of Laura's stopped them to exchange effusive greetings, to kiss, to chat—or rather to shout above the noise. And each one asked or demanded to be introduced to Star. As they continued their protracted procession it became obvious that the real focus of attention was not Laura, an all too familiar face, but Star.

By the time they finally reached their table, the maître d' was showing signs of impatience and Laura's smile had become somewhat fixed. She glanced quickly at the table, checking that it was acceptably positioned in the right part of the room, where the privileged few usually sat.

"Now then," she said with deceptive sweetness, "Star darling, you sit here." She pointed to a chair where her daughter would have her back to the room and the dance floor. Star willingly took the seat. Laura didn't seem to realize how happy she was to be in a position where she was unlikely to attract any more attention.

"Harry . . . Max." Laura waved her hand and the two men sat on either side of her. The waiter handed each of them an oversize menu and Star gratefully took refuge behind hers.

But no sooner had they ordered (Star, still diet conscious, went for melon and grilled sole) than the table hopping started in earnest; it seemed as though everyone in the place suddenly laid claim to Laura's friendship although, quite transparently, this was just a ruse to meet Star.

Actors, directors, photographers, all manner of well dressed, well-heeled men found an excuse to come to the table. If they were strangers they asked for Laura's autograph. Laura could not but become aware of what was happening, and as yet another intruder hailed her with "Laura! Long time no see," snapped "Not long enough" and, turning to Max, continued, "I'd like to dance." It sounded like a command.

Star had been too embarrassed to look at him but now noticed the smile of amusement on his face as he rose to take Laura on to the mini dance floor. Instantly, she felt a rush of resentment and anger: what a really nasty piece of work he must be actually to enjoy Laura's obvious displeasure and her own discomfort. She tore a chunk of bread roll and started to munch fiercely, diet or no diet.

"Want to dance, Star?" Harry asked without much enthusiasm. She shook her head. "Too crowded."

They sat without speaking for a moment, then on an impulse Star said, "Uncle Harry, is something wrong . . . I mean with Laura and 'the store'?"

Harry didn't answer at once. "Nothing that can't be put right," he said evasively.

"Meaning you're not going to tell me."

"Meaning there's nothing that isn't the usual kind of shemozel that sorts itself out in time."

Before Star could press Harry any further on the subject she became aware of someone standing by the table, staring down at her. The first impression was of the sheer force of personality embodied in a tall, big-boned, masculine-looking woman of about thirty-five. It was the eyes that gave the strong-featured face some claim to beauty: wide set and velvety brown, the color of bitter chocolate, with the line of the lid slightly sloping downward, giving a veiled, almost sleepy, look. But the intelligence reflected there, the expression of intense interest, denied this. Dense black hair was cropped into a mass of crisp curls. Star could not have imagined anyone else who could have got away with the gold jumpsuit she was wearing, or the heavy, barbaric-looking ornaments that dangled from neck and ears.

After a long moment in which she continued to gaze down at Star she whispered something that sounded like "Boli Kala!" then followed it up with "Fa-a-antastic." Without a glance at him she said, "Okay, Harry, so introduce me." She spoke with a strong foreign accent.

With just a hint of hesitation, Harry said, "Oh, hello, Dee. This is Star Merrick, Laura Denning's daughter. Star . . . Dee Costatinos."

Star recognized the name at once. Dee Costatinos was one of the most brilliant and successful photographers in Europe, or anywhere else, come to that. She continued to stare at Star for another moment then turned her attention to Harry.

"You handling her?" she asked.

Harry shook his head. "Not so far."

"I'm not an actress," Star explained hastily.

Dee shrugged. "Not yet. But like it or not you are a model. Made for. I know. Fa-a-antastic."

"I'm not a model either," Star protested, "and I don't want to be. Nothing like that."

"You should change your mind. You make top. Come see me. Call me. I'm in the book." And without a backward glance the photographer swept on her flamboyant way.

Star blinked, momentarily speechless. Eventually her only comment was, "Crazy!"

Harry looked thoughtful. "Could be worth thinking about, baby," he said. "She is a bit . . . odd . . . if you know what I mean, but nothing you couldn't handle, I'm sure. If she takes you up you're made, at least in the modeling world. We could see where we go from there."

"Once and for all—I want no part of show business. I've seen too much of it, thanks."

Star went back to munching her bread roll and realized that she was feeling very hungry. Probably they wouldn't get any food until Max and Laura returned to the table. She hoped they wouldn't be long. She looked round at the dance floor and saw the two of them not exactly dancing, just moving in time to the music, apparently deep in conversation. As she turned back to the table she saw that Harry was watching them too.

"Who exactly is he, Uncle Harry?" she blurted out.

Harry tugged at his mustache, a trick he had when he felt nervous or uneasy. "Some kind of secretary, Laura says. From what I've seen so far I'd say more like a . . ." He searched for a polite word, reluctant to use the one he obviously thought applied.

Star couldn't come up with an appropriate word either. "You mean a bit of an opportunist?" she suggested at last.

"Could be. I can't pretend to like him. And it's not just love scorned talking. Plays everything too close to the chest for my taste. Know what I mean?"

Star nodded and at that moment Laura and Max returned to the table. "That band," Laura's voice had a slightly querulous note, "couldn't collect a hatful of buttons playing for a theater queue. I must tell Renata. No food yet? Honestly, the service in this dump . . ."

At that moment the smoked salmon mousse that she had ordered was placed in front of her. The others were served, the wine poured, and all four started to eat.

"Not bad," Laura conceded.

Star found her melon rather turniplike but didn't mention the fact.

"What was that weirdo photographer talking to you

about?" Laura asked between mouthfuls of mousse. Star hesitated. In view of Laura's belligerent mood, and considering the amount of attention she had already received since they'd arrived, she deemed it wise to find an evasive answer. Unfortunately she couldn't think of one. She glanced at Harry for help but he was concentrating on chasing a shrimp round his glass dish and made no effort to come to her aid.

To her surprise it was Max who spoke. He picked up his wine glass and addressed his observations to it although, clearly, they were intended for her. "Wants to photograph you, I imagine? You're an obvious candidate for her kind of high fashion stuff. Not quite your scene, though, is it?"

"I wasn't aware that I'd asked for your opinion, Max," Laura said tartly. "I asked Star a question and I'd prefer that she answer for herself."

Max sipped his wine and with great precision placed his knife and fork on his plate to show he'd finished eating. Inconsequentially Star noticed that the smoked trout did look pretty dry and that he had left most of it.

"Well?" Laura asked impatiently.

Star scraped the last resistant shred of melon from its skin. "Actually," she said, "Max is right. She seems to have the idea that I could be a model."

"What did you say?"

"Star's not interested in show business." Harry spoke up at last. "You know that, Laura."

"Can't you two let the girl speak for herself? Maybe she fancies herself as a model."

Star looked across the table at her mother. Laura's wide green eyes were fixed on her, somehow defying her to want anything that could in any way compete with her own jealously protected position.

"I'd be hopeless. Turn a camera on me and I'd run screaming," she joked.

Laura laughed. She seemed pleased with this reply. Star felt herself relax. Laura's wrath had been turned aside.

"Nonsense, Star." Harry dabbed at his mustache with his table napkin. "You *are* an actress. Whether you'll ever use the talent I don't know, but it's in you. Part of you." He turned to Max.

"Know how she got her name?"

Laura groaned. "Harry, must we?"

To Star's surprise Harry ignored her and continued. "I gave it to her. She was a kid, aged six or seven, and one of the *Harringtons* writers had the bright idea of writing her into a script. You never saw anything like it. She just lit up that screen. Took over. Stole every scene she was in. I christened her 'Star' and it stuck."

"Harry," Star remonstrated. She wished he wouldn't tell the story. It was an event in her life she preferred to forget. "Every kid is a scene stealer—that's why actors hate working with them."

"Did you appear in any more episodes?" Max asked her, apparently with real interest.

"No, she certainly did not," Laura said before Star had a chance to reply. Max laughed. Laura assumed her Mother Courage look and said, "I was not going to have my little girl turned into one of those stage brats. I was determined she was going to be a plain, ordinary kid and enjoy her childhood."

Star was tempted to comment but decided it was neither the time nor the place. But, she wondered ruefully, when would it have been? She realized that Max was still looking at her.

"So, what is your given name?" he asked.

Again, before Star could answer, Laura spoke. This time her tone was mellow with sentiment. "Angelina," she said, separating the syllables, giving each one full loving value. Star squirmed in her seat and took a large swallow of wine. Laura continued, "I know I sound corny but I don't care. I held this perfect little creature in my arms and said, 'She's not a baby, she's an angel. My little angel. Angelina.' She was gorgeous."

Harry nodded. Then undiplomatically added, "Now, all these years later, she's even more gorgeous."

Star laughed to cover acute embarrassment. Her mother frowned. Conversation lagged. Laura drummed long coral-varnished nails on the stiff damask table-cloth. "The service in this joint is not to be believed."

Almost immediately the remains of their first course were whipped away and the four of them sat in uneasy silence, sipping wine and picking at bread rolls. Star glanced round at her three companions: Harry, anxious; Laura, sulky and bored; only Max seemed for some inexplicable reason of his own to be enjoying the situation. His eyes, bright and interested, were like a zoo visitor's observing the animals. It was he who picked up the conversation. He turned to Star and said, "Well, how about a dance, 'Little Angel'?"

"Don't call her that," Laura snapped.

"Why not?" Max asked with an air of assumed innocence.

"I'd really rather you didn't," Star said, coldly polite, furious at his impertinence.

Quite unfazed he got up and stood looking down at her, waiting. Star hesitated. It seemed absurd to refuse, to fuss about her stupid name. But she didn't want Laura any more upset than she was already. And there was the matter of her low-cut dress. So far she'd managed to keep the back concealed. Laura would probably explode when she saw it. Harry tried to come to the rescue. "Good idea," he said brightly. "Laura, may I have the pleasure?"

Laura shook her head, her expression petulant. "It's

all right, Harry. You don't have to take pity on the poor old wallflower."

Star felt angry at this childish reaction, and hurt for Harry that Laura should snub him. Deliberately she slipped the shawl from her shoulders and stood up. She smiled at Max and with long easy strides walked onto the dance floor. So she had a dress with a low, low back. If Mummy didn't like it—too bad. Max followed her. The music changed from a heavy rock beat to a slow, smooth tempo. They stood facing each other for a moment, then Max took hold of her—one hand holding hers, the other light against her naked back. She was deeply aware of his proximity and an involuntary shiver ran through her at his touch.

Their two bodies merged in perfect unison as they swayed in time to the music. His hold on her tightened imperceptibly and the closeness of his hard masculinity sparked a flame of desire in Star of such intensity that she felt quite breathless. She had to exert all her self-control not to slide her left hand from his shoulder to explore the back of his suntanned neck. To stroke the dark, well groomed hair. She realized, with something of a shock, that she wanted to know and experience every part of that muscular body, which for the duration of the dance held her, guided her, dominated her. When the music stopped he still held her close for a few seconds as if unwilling to release her. When he did she felt quite shattered, unable to move.

His voice brought her back to earth. "We'd better go back to the table—I think there could be some little problem."

Laura's face had the pained, martyred look that Star knew meant that she wasn't getting her own way and so felt dreadfully misused. "I've asked Harry to take me home," she said as Star and Max sat down at the table. "I've got the most ghastly headache and I have to work in the morning." The inference being that nobody else on the face of this planet ever worked as she did. "You should get an early night too, Star. After all, you did fly the Atlantic today."

"I wasn't actually doing the flying," Star said, trying to keep the tone light and somehow retrieve the evening. Laura shrugged. "Stay on if you want to. I don't want to spoil anyone's fun," she added with a meaningful look at Max, who did not respond. Star hastened to reassure her mother. Of course she was quite right, she mustn't stay in this noisy atmosphere if she wasn't feeling well. In fact it did strike her that Laura suddenly looked drawn and tired.

"Fine. Okay," she said. "Let's go home then, shall we, Mother?"

Between clenched teeth, Laura hissed, "Don't call me that."

Harry drove them home in the Rolls, an unlit Havana clenched between his teeth. Concerned and worried about Laura, he looked even more like a dyspeptic bloodhound than usual. Nobody spoke. When they arrived at Belgravia Place, Laura pecked Harry on the cheek. "I forgot my keys, Max. I hope you've got yours," she said.

Max didn't reply. He thanked Harry courteously for his hospitality and waited until Star too had wished him good night. Then, in an offhand, leisurely manner he joined Laura, who was waiting with every sign of impatience at the front door. He fished in a pocket and produced a set of keys, selected one, and unlocked the door. Laura and Star went inside. "Good night," he said, and made as if to close the door after them.

Laura's hand flew out to hold the door open. "I want to talk to you," she said.

Star saw Max's expression freeze. His eyes turned

pewter gray with anger. "I thought you had a head-ache," he said.

"Max, please," Laura pleaded.

Star found the situation unendurable. "Well, good night," she said decisively and went into the house. She pressed the button to summon the lift and before it arrived was joined by Laura—and Max. As the lift traveled up to the top floor Star stared down at the floor, horribly aware of tensions and unspoken reproaches. With enormous relief she finally climbed the spiral staircase to the safety of her bedroom. She flicked on the light and was greeted by the sight of Gary's red roses, artistically arranged by Suki. Perhaps Charlene had been right when she told her to grab the chance to marry such a thoughtful, generous person. She could be back with him tomorrow. So what was stopping her? She preferred not to think about that. She was too tired, too disturbed. She must get to bed.

While she was brushing her teeth she heard voices raised in anger: Laura and Max apparently quarreling. She couldn't hear what they were saying and was glad of it. She turned off the tap and went quickly back to her bedroom. Then, abruptly, the sound of the voices ceased. She climbed into bed and found she was straining her ears to listen. Nothing. Silence. A reconciliation? An imagined scene between Max and her mother sprang into her mind. She screwed up her eyes in an effort to obliterate the image, turned off the bedside lamp, and dived under the balloon-patterned duvet.

But the feather eiderdown could not smother the sudden sharp sound of the front door slamming. Star sat up in bed, staring into the darkness. Max must have left. Her immediate reaction was one of relief. He was not after all with Laura. But did that mean he'd walked out? Gone for good? That she wouldn't see him again? To her dismay she realized that she found the prospect alarming. She sank back onto the pillows, almost in a state of shock. She'd come home in order to sort out her problems, only to be confronted by a fresh source of confusion. Could it really be that she had these wild feelings for a man her own mother seemed to be in love with? Then it was for the best if he had gone. At least this way an intolerable situation could be avoided and she and Laura could maintain their uneasy peace.

Determinedly she pulled the duvet over her head and closed her eyes. I will not think about him—I will not.

But for the second night in succession Star hardly slept. It was nearly dawn when exhaustion finally overwhelmed her and she fell into a deep, dreamless sleep.

3

"Good morning, Miss Star."

The way Suki pronounced it sounded like "Mister." Star smiled, still half asleep, as with quick neat movements the Korean girl placed the breakfast tray on the bedside table and crossed to the window to draw back the curtains. One glance told Star that yesterday's perfect blue skies had given way to menacing gray clouds. Squalls of rain gusted against the window panes.

"I sorry for raining."

Suki spoke as though she were personally responsible for the change in the weather. She reached out a small, delicately shaped hand toward Gary's roses. "Here sunshine." She smiled and moved silently toward the door. "I hope you find breakfast all okay."

Star glanced down at the impeccably arranged tray: fruit juice, bran cereal, yogurt, and black coffee. How on earth had Suki known? She wondered, and then remembered that this was what Laura always had too.

"Thanks, Suki," she said. "Fine. But you needn't have bothered to bring my breakfast. I can fix my own."

Suki looked puzzled. "I bring later if you prefer."

"No. No. It's just that I . . ." She saw Suki's expression of incomprehension and decided that she just wasn't up to explaining Jessie's golden rule, "If you're in one piece and on your feet—you're 'on.' " In other words do things for yourself and no excuses. But this wasn't the moment for expounding show-biz lore. There were too many problems to be faced.

"Has my mother gone to the studio yet?" she asked as Suki turned to leave.

"Oh, yes. Long time. Now is ten o'clock."

"Heavens! Did I sleep that late? That's terrible."

"Madame say best you sleep. You very tired."

Star smiled. For all her self-centeredness Laura could be really considerate sometimes—she couldn't have slept any too well herself after that row with Max, and yet she still had to be at the studio bright and early, looking great in front of the cameras. Star felt a wave of anger and resentment against Max. She did so hope he'd gone for good.

She picked up the napkin from the tray and unfolded it. "And Mr. Max?" she asked casually. "Is he here?"

"No. He not here," Suki said, and left the room, closing the door noiselessly behind her.

Gary's roses had opened, revealing petals of soft magenta velvet. Star looked at them as she sipped the sharp, freshly squeezed grapefruit juice and reflected on the sad fact that, beautiful as they were, they gave her no more pleasure than that gorgeous ring had done. Dear Gary. Kind, loving Gary—what on earth was she going to do about him? Could she, in all honesty, consider marrying a man when someone else was capable of arousing in her the feelings and sensations she had experienced in Max's arms? Feelings that had been so lamentably lacking from her lovemaking with Gary. Even if she never saw Max again—and she certainly hoped that she wouldn't—the fact remained that she had found him wildly attractive. Perhaps she should forget the two of them. Get a job. Live a little. Be free.

But the very idea swamped her with feelings of insecurity. All very well to talk of getting a job, but what? No one could call her highly qualified. The sort of jobs she could get wouldn't pay the rent of a broom closet in London. Perhaps that photographer had meant it about modeling? Star immediately rejected the idea; she'd be useless, die of embarrassment posing in front of a camera. No, modeling was definitely out. She sighed. Why was she so bloody inadequate?

She swallowed down the rest of the bitter black coffee and felt horribly alone. If only Jessie were there. Then she remembered Laura's comment that she really shouldn't need a nanny at her age. But she didn't want Jessie as a nanny, she needed her as a friend to talk to. She was also concerned about the old lady's welfare. It just had to be possible to find her.

As she stood under the hot shower, she had a brainstorm: Jessie had a sister somewhere. But what was her name? Gertrude, she remembered that much, but Gertrude what? Not Raye like Jessie—Raye was only a stage name anyway. Star turned off the shower and started to dry herself with a towel thick and soft as lamb's wool. Still the name escaped her. She remembered that Jessie always laughed because she said it was so unsuitable since her sister was big and bony and the name sounded round and comfortable . . . was that it? Comfy? Not quite. Cheery? No . . . Cozy. That was it, Gertie Cozy. How could she ever forget a name like that? Perhaps she was in the phone book. One thing was certain—there couldn't be another. There would only be one Gertie Cozy.

The rain was still bucketing down. Obviously none of her California clothes were suitable for this all too English weather. She'd have to buy new cold weather gear, but meanwhile adapt some of her old things.

She snatched down a pair of jeans and an oversize sweater. The jeans were at least five inches too large around the waist and the legs folded like a concertina. She laughed out loud at her reflection in the mirror. Elephant legs, she thought, but had no option other than to gather the waist with a belt and leave the legs to flap. She pulled the sweater over her head. It hung like a tent around her, but Star shrugged. Who was going to see her, after all?

She ran a comb through her still damp hair then tied it back loosely with a scarf. A pair of sneakers completed the outfit. She put on her glasses instead of fiddling with her contact lenses and took a last brief glance in the mirror. She grinned at her reflection. Dee Costatinos should see her now!

Star went to what used to be Vernon's study in search of Gertie's telephone number. She selected the A-to-D directory and sat down at the vast leather-topped desk. As she was flicking through the pages she noticed a folded piece of paper propped up against the typewriter. The single word "Max" was written on it in Laura's flamboyant scrawl. Star stared at the note and felt an overwhelming urge to open and read it. The temptation was all the greater as the note was not sealed. Nothing would have been easier than to read and then replace it.

Almost immediately she felt ashamed of the impulse but still could not restrain the curiosity that consumed her. Perhaps she had completely misinterpreted what she had overheard last night. It had sounded like a quarrel, but was it? And even if it was, it didn't mean they hadn't made up. For all she knew Max had not left the house on his own. They might have gone together, perhaps for a walk or a drive. Whatever it was, Laura must be expecting him back or she wouldn't have left the note for him. And, Star reminded herself sternly, it had nothing to do with her. If they were having an affair it was their business and they must work out their own problems.

Frowning severely, she opened the telephone directory and looked under C for anyone called Cozy. There were Cozy Cafes and Cozy Cars but no Gertrude Cozy. She must have the spelling wrong. She tried Cozey and Cozie before discovering Cozzey. Quite a number of them. As she ran her finger down the list she heard footsteps in the passage outside. She looked up just as Max came into the room.

He was wearing a waterproof trenchcoat that seemed to accentuate his masculinity, and Star realized that his effect on her was not one iota less disturbing than it had been at their first encounter.

For a brief moment he stood in the doorway and they looked at each other without speaking. Slowly he walked toward her and said, "Good morning," somehow managing to invest even this simple greeting with an air of irony.

"Hi," Star replied, and with a determined show of indifference went back to studying the names. She was only too conscious of him as he stood looking over her shoulder at the open directory.

"Decided to take her up on her offer, have you?" he said. It was more of a statement than a question.

"Sorry?" Star asked, without looking up.

"Dee Costatinos, photographer extraordinaire." Max jabbed a finger at the directory and Star saw the single entry "Costatinos," a couple of columns from where she had been searching.

"Oh," she said, "I didn't notice. It's not where I was looking."

Max gave a maddeningly superior smile.

"Okay. No need to cover up. I'm sure you'll be a highly successful model. If that's what you want."

A wave of anger swept over Star. "How dare you assume that I'm lying? Apart from anything else, what makes you vain enough to think I'd bother to lie to you?"

Max raised an eyebrow. "I see you have your mother's temperament. And I thought you subdued—almost intimidated. I'm glad I was mistaken."

He perched himself on the corner of the desk and regarded her with an air of detached interest. Angry spots of red leapt into Star's cheeks. She wanted nothing more than to get up and walk from the room, away from those mocking gray eyes. With all the dignity she could muster, she said quietly, "You really are pretty insufferable, aren't you?"

To add to her chagrin Max threw back his head and laughed. "I didn't think it showed."

Biting hard on her lower lip Star resumed her study of the list of names in the telephone directory. "As you seem so interested," she said with determined composure, "I am not looking for Dee Costatinos's telephone number because I couldn't care less about it. Or her. I'm trying to find the number of Jessie's sister. I thought perhaps Jessie might have gone to stay with her."

Max turned away, obviously uninterested, and picked up the note that Laura had left for him on the table. He opened it and started to read. Surreptitiously Star watched his face but his expression did not change. He finished reading and threw the note in the wastebasket with every indication of indifference. "Any luck?" he asked.

"Hmm?"

"The sister."

"Oh . . . no. Her first name is Gertrude but there's no initial G here."

He frowned and suddenly seemed to take her quest seriously. "I take it your mother doesn't know either?"

"Seems not."

"Would there be anyone at the television studios who might have some idea where she's got to?"

Star hadn't considered this possibility but now she remembered Madge. "Could be," she said slowly. "Madge Graham . . . She's an elderly actress who sometimes plays one of the shop assistants in Harringtons. She used to work with Jessie years ago when they were both chorus girls. I don't know that they're still close friends exactly, but she might just know."

"Well, I'm driving out to the studios," Max said casually. "Why not come with me and talk to her?"

Star hesitated. Judging from her behavior last night, Laura might not be too pleased if her daughter made an unscheduled appearance at the studios, especially during a recording.

Max looked at her with a penetrating gaze. He seemed to know what she was thinking. "Or are you afraid that Mummy might disapprove."

"Of course not." Star's reply was rather too quick to be convincing. "I've always gone to the studios whenever I wanted to."

"Then let's go," he said.

"Now?"

"As soon as you like."

"I'll . . . have to change."

Star closed the telephone directory and stood up. Max took in the baggy jeans and floppy sweater. "Why?" he grinned. "You look great."

Star made a grimace, dismissing what she took to be a bad joke, and made for the door. Max stood in her way. "I mean it," he said. "You look how I imagine you did before you went to Hollywood. And the windows really suit you." He adjusted the large horn-rimmed glasses on her small straight nose. "They make you look like a sexy owl. Very wise."

Star laughed, suddenly self-conscious. "Me, wise? No way. Where most people have brains, I have wood shavings."

Max looked at her thoughtfully. "I don't believe a word of it." He glanced at his watch. "Well, go and change if you must."

Star had often repeated the time-worn wail of most women that she "hadn't a thing to wear," but now it was pretty near the truth. She rummaged through her old wardrobe and finally came up with one of the many shapeless, loose-cut dresses in which she'd been so glad to hide her overample form in the past. It was an attractive coral shade with a small stand-up collar, but it hung on her like a king-size duvet cover. She frowned at the reflection of her billowing form in the glass then pulled an extra wide, black patent belt off one of her new outfits and with it managed to gather in the excess folds to display her neat, slim waist. A pair of high heeled black boots and an oversize shoulder bag that Vernon had given her last birthday matched up well with a black raincoat cut to swing from the shoulder, which she'd worn in her last year at school. Now, with the collar turned up, it looked most effective. She decided to leave her hair tied back—better not to try to look too glamorous—and was about to put in her contact lenses when she remembered Max's crack about the "sexy owl." Smiling to herself she adjusted her glamorous new glasses, purchased to supplement her contacts, telling herself that she couldn't care less what Max did or did not like about her. A brand new powder-blue

Hermès scarf and she was ready. She left the room with a quite inexplicable feeling of excited anticipation.

And without so much as a backward glance at Gary's roses.

Max drove the Porsche fast, with great skill and precision. His moves were decisive; no waffle, no hesitation as he darted through the traffic of the Cromwell Road and into the congestion of the Warwick Road Extension, like a minnow circumnavigating a shoal of whales. He seemed to become one with the car. They had something in common, Star thought, a sleek elegance combined with a potentially dangerous degree of power. The rain was beginning to ease off and as the car joined the M40 a ray of sunlight shafted dramatically down from behind a cloud.

Max glanced up at the sky. "Touch of the William Blake's," he observed.

Star did not reply at once. She remembered the biblical pictures that she had studied without great interest at school. And Miss Mills, the art teacher, declaiming, "Blake, gels, an Important English Artist." Looking up at the sky, Star understood for the first time what Blake was about. "It does make you feel a bit small and unimportant," she said, almost to herself.

Max did not react but continued to concentrate on his driving, now letting the car have its head. Star looked at the speedometer. "I don't want to backseat drive or anything," she said, "but we seem to be doing ninety."

He didn't reply and made no attempt to reduce speed. Strangely, Star felt complete confidence in him. He was so totally in control, all she had to do was sit back and leave everything to him. He never took his eyes off the road and seemed almost unaware of her presence. She stole a look at him and wondered yet again exactly who he was and why he was involved with her mother. She longed to question him but was equally resolved not to display even the slightest interest.

Something didn't add up. The expensive clothes and luxury car didn't fit in with her idea of a secretary. Perhaps they were presents he had received from other "employers"? And where had he stayed last night? Obviously somewhere he could change his clothes. Perhaps he had a flat of his own somewhere? Or another "friend"? She felt impatient with herself for making these wild surmises. Why should she bother with him when clearly he had no interest in her?

She looked out of the window at the unedifying sight of suburban houses and factories that lined the motorway and tried to distract her thought from the man so unnervingly close to her in the driving seat.

They sped on in silence and Star became conscious of a relaxed kind of companionship between them in the confines of the car, despite Max's obvious preoccupation with his driving and with his own unfathomable thoughts. When he suddenly spoke she was quite startled.

"Have you always called her Laura?" he asked abruptly.

So that's who he'd been thinking about.

"Yes," Star replied. "At least as long as I can remember."

"Never 'Mother' or 'Mum'?"

"No. Neither she nor Vernon—my father, you know —cared for that Mummy and Daddy stuff."

Max made no further comment and continued to drive in silence. Star waited for him to say something and finally could contain her curiosity no longer. "Why do you ask?"

"Just wondered," he said noncommittally.

"You must have had a reason."

He didn't reply at once, and then, as though working out a puzzle that had been bothering him, he said, "There's a paradox in a woman who wants her daughter to remain a child and yet apparently always demanded that the child address her as an equal, not as a parent."

Star was quite stunned that anyone who knew so little of her relationship with her mother should make such a penetrating observation, and yet her immediate reaction was to reject what she felt was an intrusion. If she and Laura had their problems it was nobody's business.

"I see nothing odd in calling my parents by their names, and you're quite wrong about Laura trying to keep me a child. I enjoyed school and was perfectly happy to stay the extra year. Some people just develop later than others, that's all."

Max made no attempt to continue the conversation as he swung the Porsche off the motorway onto the road that led to Firbank, the once sleepy Buckinghamshire village that was now a commuter outpost for well-heeled executives.

They drove along pleasant tree-lined avenues until they came to the wide gates of Firbank Studios. A uniformed gatekeeper asked them to identify themselves, and once satisfied he lifted the barrier and they drove through.

In the heyday of the British film industry, Firbank Studios had belonged to one of the major film companies, and though it had long since been taken over by City Television it still retained some of the old glamour. The beautifully tended gardens with their sweep of fir trees and the imposing Georgian manor house, which had been in existence long before either films or television were dreamed of, seemed more suited to a country club than a TV studio. The house was now used for offices and nobody had time to stroll in the grounds, but it was company policy to keep up the old traditions—at least on the surface. The actual studio building with its no-nonsense, functional lines was something of a let-down after the pseudogracious living aspect of the rest.

Max parked the car in the large, crowded car park. He locked the car doors and they walked in silence toward the studio entrance. Star found their lack of communication embarrassing and pointless. They'd not quarreled, and as they were in each other's company they might as well be civil. Still it was difficult to know what to say and she could only think to ask, "Have you been here before?" Instantly she realized that he must have been or else how had he know his way so easily?

"Yes, a couple of times," he said, and his tone implied that he considered this of no great interest and was not going to make it a subject for small talk.

"I just wondered," Star persisted. "It can be pretty confusing if you don't know your way around."

Max gave her a sideways glance. "I suppose you were first brought here in your baby carriage."

"Not quite, but I was very young."

"The scene of your first acting triumph."

Star laughed even though she detected a note of sarcasm in his voice. "First—and last," she said firmly.

They climbed the wide stone steps to the entrance and the glass doors slid open automatically as they approached.

"Always makes me feel like Moses dividing the Red Sea," Max observed as they went inside. They crossed the spacious reception area with its low-slung leather sofas, glass-topped tables, and enough potted plants to fill a large conservatory, and stopped at the imposing-looking reception desk behind which sat three well-groomed young women who all looked as though they should be in front of the cameras themselves. They were also apparently much too involved with their own concerns to pay any attention to visitors. Star was quite used to this ritual and prepared to wait when she realized that Max, after taking in the three preoccupied ladies, had walked away toward the lifts and main staircase. One of the receptionists looked up. "Excuse me," she called after him in a peremptory tone.

"Pleasure," Max threw over his shoulder, and continued on his way.

"Have you an appointment?"

Before Max could reply, Star said, "Hello, Sandra."

The receptionist blinked at her in nonrecognition.

"We've come to see my mother," Star continued.

"Star," the girl squeaked in surprise. "Didn't recognize you. You look terrific. What happened? Where've you been . . . ?"

The receptionist was clearly dying for a gossip, but Star saw that Max was waiting for her with every sign of exasperated impatience and quickly extricated herself.

As they made their way through the maze of corridors that led to the studios and dressing rooms, Star wondered just why she had reacted as though he were someone she must please and humor. She had to hurry to keep up with his purposeful stride and felt a growing sense of anger and humiliation that he was able to provoke her into behaving like a timid, obedient child.

She had meant to ask Sandra whether Madge Graham was on today's call sheet. After all, that was why she had come. Not to spend the day trotting round after Max, whose only interest was in seeing Laura—which he seemed in a great hurry to do. When they reached her dressing room Max stopped. Obviously he knew where to find her. But, Star observed, this time he did not barge straight in as he had done at home. He knocked, and then he waited.

There was nothing particularly glamorous about Laura's dressing room. In fact, it was not, strictly speaking, hers. She shared it with several other actresses who occupied it on the days when *Harringtons* was not being taped. As soon as she vacated it an assistant floor manager slipped her name out of the name-frame and substituted that of the next day's occupant. But for the last sixteen years, on one day of the week this room had been Laura's private, personal domain. No one ever dreamed of intruding without invitation, or else needed a very sound reason for invading that closely guarded privacy.

At this moment Laura was waiting tensely for just such an invasion, and when she heard the knock on the door called "Come" in her most autocratic tone of voice.

Star immediately recognized that belligerent note in Laura's voice and knew that it meant trouble for somebody. When Max opened the door she hung back a little, being none too sure of her welcome. She could see her mother, wearing a pale yellow terry-cloth robe, made up and coiffed, ready for the cameras, standing by the dressing table spooning up yogurt out of a carton. To Star's surprise Laura did not seem all that pleased to see Max. "Oh, it's you," she said, and continued to scrape out the remains of the yogurt, licking it off the spoon with catlike darts of her tongue.

"If it's inconvenient . . ." Max said, and Star heard that same cool irony in his voice that he had used on her earlier.

Laura threw away the empty yogurt carton and ran her fingers under the tap at the wash basin. "I was expecting that prize creep, Sylvester. I've been trying to find him all morning, but surprise, surprise, he's nowhere to be found. Bloody taping we're doing and our dear producer is not in the studio. Nor is he in his office. Nor is he at home. Vanished! And I know why. Only too well do I know!" She picked up a script from the dressing table and waved it menacingly above her head. "This load of . . ." Just then she noticed Star standing in the doorway.

"Hullo, Starlet," she said, with even less enthusiasm than she had shown toward Max. "Well, don't stand hovering in the doorway, child. Come in, as you're here." Star did as she was bid, making a mental note to get out again as soon as possible.

Laura flung the offending script down on the table with a gesture of deep disgust.

"Nor is our brilliant script editor available, and as for that wimp of a so-called director, he's still trying to work out one end of the camera from the other."

"Why don't you ring Uncle Harry?" Star suggested.

"He's supposed to be having lunch with Sir Lennie-boy to sort out the little matter of my disappearance from this saga. I bet right now he's slurping up the filet mignon and selling Lennie every other actress on his books. Somewhere over coffee and brandy he'll remember to mention my name, and Lennie will make his 'I love that girl, I really do. One of the family, they're all my family' speech, and Harry will wipe away a tear and say how devoted I am to Lennie, too, and look on him as a father figure . . . dum, dum, dum. Then they'll both go back to their respective offices thinking they've had a highly productive lunch. Meanwhile I'm still feeding my two and a half lines to Miss blind-ambition Bennet from some place well off camera! I tell you, they make me puke. They *all* make me puke." She tore a tissue out of its box and angrily blotted her mouth. Then sat down at the dressing table and started to repair her makeup.

"Why do you go on with it?" Max asked with genuine interest.

"Good question." Laura shrugged. "It's all I know how to do, I suppose. And the money's good."

Star wanted to add that *Harringtons* and the character of Kim was Laura's whole life but knew this was not the time to mention it so remained silent. As, for a moment, did the other two. Finally Laura said, addressing Max's reflection in the mirror, "I'm glad you decided to come. I could do with a friendly face around here."

Star felt momentarily hurt at being so obviously excluded from this remark but then she saw how uncharacteristically stressed and unhappy Laura was under the angry bravado. Immediately she said, "It'll be all right, Laura. It always is."

Laura continued to fiddle with her makeup. "If you say so, Star," she said without looking up, her tone cuttingly sarcastic.

Max contributed nothing. As always he seemed to be an outside observer whose interest was purely objective.

"Today," Laura said, speaking hardly above a whisper while brushing mascara onto already heavily made-up eyelashes, "I did something I've never done before in my entire life—I walked off the set."

Star gasped. Not possible. Not Laura, the totally dedicated professional who scorned the idea of throwing tantrums or making scenes. At least not when she was working! Something must be seriously wrong. She didn't know what to say and didn't want to put her big foot in it again. Before she could formulate a suitable sentence Max spoke—just one word: "Why?"

Star half expected one of Laura's succinct, highly colored comebacks. Instead she seemed to think carefully before replying.

"For years," she said, "this has been the best series of its kind on the box. Now it's being run into the ground by a bunch of opinionated, incompetent fools. Something has to be done to make them sit up before it's too late. Nobody else is going to. I tried doing it the nice way—but that's a waste of time in this business. Unless you spit fire, nobody respects you." She looked up at Max, her green eyes fiercely bright. "I hate actors who come on heavy, and I'll be led anywhere, but I will not be shoved. Certainly not by this bunch of bullshitters."

Max nodded as though he was making a mental note of all that Laura had said, and Star almost had the impression her mother was dictating instead of talking to him. Before he could speak there was a knock at the door.

"See who that is, will you, Starlet?" Laura said casually.

Star opened the door to a man who made up for his lack of stature by an overabundance of hair. Carrot red, it frizzed over his head and bristled in an unkempt beard on his face. On each side of the mushroom-cap nose gleamed eyes as brown and round as toffee apples. He smiled almost constantly, showing large, overcrowded teeth. He was dressed in the latest trendy gear, which was at least twenty years too young for his middle-aged figure.

"Hullo, Sylvester." Star smiled politely and held the door open for him.

Sylvester scrutinized her with that God-of-all-creation expression he reserved for nubile, ambitious young actresses when he was trying to convince them that he was more interested in their talent than their bodies, which was most certainly never the case. He circled her, looking her over reverently as though she were the only woman on earth. "It's not," he said in apparently awed amazement, "it can't be . . . little Star?"

She peered at him with comic intensity over the top of her enormous spectacles. "The same," she said.

"Oh, no. Not the same. Not one teensy bit the same. Dearest girl, you look truly beautiful. Quite gorgeous. We must write you into 'the store' at once."

"Try writing *me* in first, would you?" Laura snapped.

Sylvester gave a nervous trill of a laugh. "Darling Laura, you kill me!"

"Don't put ideas in my head. Where the hell have you been all day?"

"Angel, I couldn't be more sorry, but I've been closeted with Sir Lennie until five minutes ago."

"Canceled his lunch date with my agent, did he?"

Sylvester knew when he was beaten and temporarily sought refuge with Star. "What about this little girl of yours, then?" He slipped his arm round Star's waist in a most unfatherly fashion. "She has your magic, Laura darling. I can see it."

Before Laura had time to explode, Star slipped out of the encircling arm and quickly opened the door. "I'll go and say hello to some of the others. See you."

As she closed the door behind her she caught Max looking at her as though he had found the whole scene highly entertaining, but he made no attempt to follow her. Well, he'd come to be with Laura, hadn't he? Through the door she could hear her mother's voice pitched low, ominously low, protesting not only at the cuts in her part but the favoring of Diane in camera shots. "When I do say my couple of paltry little feed lines, *she* is in reaction shot. Listen, don't explain. I'm not interested in your personal life. Just rewrite and replot the scenes."

Star didn't stay to hear any more and walked quickly away down the corridor. She felt that Max should have left with her. Oh, not because she gave a damn where he was or who he was with, but these *Harringtons* fights were like family quarrels and not for strangers. She considered the word "stranger" and decided it just summed him up. He was a cuckoo in the nest, albeit a disturbingly attractive one. Well, he wasn't her problem. She had other things to think about, like talking to Madge and maybe finding Jessie.

She glanced at her watch: one-fifteen. If Madge were here today Star knew just where to find her. The shortest route to the bar and restaurant from the dressing room and makeup area was across Studio One, where *Harringtons* was being taped. Star knew that it would be all right to cut through there now as the actors and crew would have broken for lunch.

She pushed open the heavy iron door to the studio. The smell of plywood and size assaulted her nostrils. If she smelled that smell blindfolded she would know in an instant where she was. Without lights, with no actors to give them life, the familiar *Harringtons* sets—the departments, the boardroom, the staff lounge—looked what they were: a mixture of canvas, wood, and paint, plus all the furnishings, set dressings, and props.

Star walked slowly to the center of the studio and looked around her. For the last sixteen years—the major part of Star's life—Laura/Kim had sat at the head of that long boardroom table. Had gone to sort out problems in this or that department. Had returned exhausted at night to her own flat. . . . Star stopped and looked around. No set of Kim's flat. So much of the drama took place there that she felt puzzled and somehow uneasy to find the set missing. As she wandered through the studio she saw what was obviously a new "home" set. A trendy, expensive-looking living room quite unlike Kim's elegantly simple apartment. She stood staring at the strange set with its white leather sofas and red venetian blinds and wondered what was happening to this other life of Laura's. Her thoughts were interrupted by the sound of footsteps approaching.

"They've all gone to lunch."

The voice belonged to a tall wiry man with frosty-white hair that contrasted strangely with black beetling eyebrows. He wore immaculate brown coveralls and Star recognized him at once. Bill had been in charge of props for *Harringtons* right from the beginning and took his job very seriously. Anything from a cup to a coat hanger was his responsibility. It was no surprise to Star to see him in the studio during the lunch break, as he never went to the canteen but ate sandwiches in the prop room, his holy of holies. At this moment he was carrying a piece of abstract sculpture, all angles and spikes. He held it out for Star's inspection.

"What d'you think of this, then?" he asked with obvious disapproval.

Star examined the shapeless object. "Not much," she said.

"It's for the new one—her flat. Seems she likes this sort of thing."

"You mean Diane . . . that is, Tracey?" Star quickly added the name of the character Diane played.

"The new buyer, that's her. He's after her now, that Granger fellow. Him what Kim's had all the trouble with. Don't know what she ever saw in him. Stinking rich, mind. But not everything, is it?"

Star frowned. The fact that the character of Sir Rupert Granger, the tycoon who had been having an on-off love affair with Kim for the past two years, was now to be switched to being Tracey's admirer seemed to endorse Laura's complaints that her part was being reduced in favor of her rival's.

Bill continued his way over to the new sitting room set. Star followed him and watched as he put the sculpture down on a low, glass-topped table. "It's all wrong, you know," he observed.

Star wasn't sure whether he referred to the sculpture,

the latest development in the fictitious lives of the characters at the store, or the real-life problems.

"What is, Bill?" she prompted him.

"We hear things. More than them what's in it sometimes. Ask me, your mum done quite right walking off this morning. She's been running the store all these years and she's done all right. Had her ups and downs but she's the boss." He looked at Star intently. "You tell her that, young Star."

She could have hugged him for recognizing her without commenting on her changed appearance. She smiled. "Okay, Bill. I'll tell her."

"She's not to be pushed off her perch by any jumped up, flighty bit of a buyer," he added vehemently.

Star was not in the least put out by this somewhat schizophrenic way of thinking. Most people who worked for any length of time on the series seemed to get the wires of reality and fantasy crossed. Star recognized the old man's concern for Laura and it made her take the situation more seriously than anything that any of the rest of the cast or production team might have said. Bill went back to his work, checking and rechecking the props, and Star crossed the studio, stepping over the thick electric cables that snaked across the floor and past the cameras standing like robots waiting for someone to throw the switch and set that ruthless, all-seeing eye into action. She pushed open the iron door on the opposite side and left the controlled confusion of the studio behind her.

The restaurant was packed. Actors in makeup, some wearing period costume, shared tables with directors, writers, and cameramen. The *Harringtons* table was in the huge window overlooking spacious lawns and flower beds. Quite a number of the actors had finished their meals and had left to go to makeup or back to their dressing rooms to brush up on their lines. Some still sat chatting over coffee. Star was delighted to see that one of these was Madge Graham.

Madge was in her sixties, a large woman with tightly curled gray hair and bright blue eyes. She affected a vague, somewhat scatty attitude, but was actually quite a tough old bird. She needed to be to have survived as a working actress for so long. She looked up blankly as Star spoke her name. "I'm so sorry," she twittered. "I'm sure I do know you, but my memory, darling. Forget my own name soon."

"It's Star, Madge. Laura's daughter."

"Star, darling! I'm so sorry, but I just didn't recognize you."

This is beginning to get monotonous, Star thought, but she smiled and sat down next to the old actress, who blinked at her with exaggerated wonder. She turned to her neighbors, a group of actors who were deep in conversation.

"Just look who's here, turned into a raving beauty."

The others stared at Star, who smiled self-consciously. The same reaction. The same expressions of disbelief, of admiration for her changed appearance. She found herself the center of interest of people who in the past had always treated her with friendly tolerance. With all the chat, the questions about California and how she had achieved the miraculous transformation, Star did not have a chance to ask Madge about Jessie. Someone suddenly looked at a watch and said they should have been in wardrobe five minutes ago and left. Others soon followed and Madge said that it had been wonderful seeing Star but she ought to get "back to the factory" too. Star held out a hand to stop her. "Please, Madge," she pleaded. "Just another minute. There's something I'd like to ask you. It's rather important."

"I don't know what I could tell you, darling. You know me. Never know what's going on."

Star forced herself to control a smile—Madge was known as the company gossip. "It's nothing to do with 'the store,' " she reassured her. "It's sort of personal."

"Oh?" Madge blinked at her, now obviously intrigued. Star began to regret that she had mentioned the matter at all and hesitated before deciding that even if Madge did make something of it, she had to try any possible way to find Jessie.

"You probably know that Jessie doesn't work for Laura anymore."

"Well, I didn't know for certain. Though it did strike me that I hadn't seen her around for some time."

"The thing is . . . er . . . she left while I was away and Laura has mislaid her forwarding address. I'd love to see her, and knowing that you and she were friendly in the old days, I thought perhaps you might know."

"Sorry, love. As I said I've not seen her for ages."

"She has a sister."

"Gertie?"

"That's right. Do you by any chance know where she lives?"

"I did have an address once upon a time. When she was still in the business. Did an act with a frightful man called Fred something . . . The Magnificent Frederico and Gloria—that was Gertie. Terrible act it was. Magic and conjuring. He was a beast. Don't know what happened to him. I think Gertie gave him the boot."

"But what about her?" Star interrupted, stemming the reminiscent flow before it became a flood. "Do you think you could find her address? I'd be so grateful."

"Be in an old address book if I can find it. I'll ring you tonight. You be at home, will you?"

"Yes, I'll be at home but . . ."

"Oh? The way you look now, love, shouldn't think you'd ever need to spend an evening at home."

"Actually, Madge," Star said, "it might be easier if I rang you."

Madge raised an eyebrow. "Oh, yes?"

"Yes," Star hurried on, not wanting to explain that Laura would not welcome the idea of her tracking down Jessie. "Could I have your number?"

"All right, dear. But don't ring tonight. With your mother's little flare-up this morning, I'll probably have to work late. But any time tomorrow."

Star scribbled down the number on the back of her used airline ticket, which was the only paper she could find in her bag. "I'd be so grateful, Madge."

The old actress gathered her bags, scripts, and the inevitable knitting she did endlessly and gave Star another searching look.

"What does your mother think of the way you look?"

Star shrugged. "Quite pleased, I think."

"Hmm . . . well, that's good." Madge stood up. "She'll have to watch out for that new boyfriend of hers. . . . Well, he *is* nearer your age than hers." And after placing this poison dart she swept out of the restaurant, leaving Star sitting alone among the debris at the long dining table. She felt thoroughly disturbed by Madge's parting crack, which, of course, had been the "dear old thing's" intention in making it.

Star ordered a salad and a black coffee. She glanced at her watch. The taping wouldn't start for another fifteen minutes. She was undecided whether or not to stay and watch it. In talking to Madge she had achieved what she came for, and with the strained atmosphere around the studio she wasn't too sure that Laura would want her there. She'd have to find some way of getting back to London. Heaven knew where Max was or whether he would be staying on or not.

Max . . . Madge's bitchy remark made Star wonder whether everyone looked on him as Laura's boyfriend.

Somehow Star still rejected the idea. She hated the thought of her mother having an affair with a man years younger than herself. Not Laura and a toy boy. It seemed so undignified.

Immediately she reproached herself for being prudish and prejudiced. She stabbed at the lettuce on her plate with her fork and felt disproportionately angry. This whole thing was Max's fault. No, that was plain ridiculous. Laura's problems with "the store" had nothing to do with him. And yet when Star had left for L.A. everything had seemed fine: her mother still the undisputed star of the show; Jessie happily running the home as always. And no Max. It might just be coincidence, but one way or another he did seem to be bad news. Especially, she thought ruefully, for me.

The camera lens zoomed crazily round the studio, taking in in rapid succession the set, actors, makeup girls, grips, scenemen, and all the other personnel who go to make up a television crew. Finally it settled on the almost perfect face of Diane Bennet.

From her seat in the darkened viewing room Star had a chance to study her mother's rival. The large screen that showed the studio, and in time the rehearsal, and finally the shots selected by the director from the control box, now revealed this young actress in merciless close-up. Merciless, because she was unaware that the camera was focusing on her and had not arranged her features to best advantage the way actresses do instinctively in performance. Nevertheless Star had to concede that Diane Bennet had a lot going for her. With natural gold-blond hair and wide violet-blue eyes, she had a fresh, girl-next-door quality, but with no element of saccharine sugariness. On the contrary she seemed to have an inner energy and vitality that she kept only just under control, bubbling away under the surface. She lacked Laura's poise and glamour but was totally today's woman. Star watched her on the screen as she chatted unconcernedly with a fellow actor; and then, as she responded to the cameraman's request for her to look into the camera, Star saw how she came on strong. There was a hard, determined set to that sexy mouth. Laura certainly had her work cut out here. This was a combatant who would fight to win and who wouldn't care what methods she used to do so.

Up on the screen the camera swung away from Diane and Star saw the floor manager call for quiet. Then he listened intently through his "cans," the earphones clamped on each side of his head, to last minute instructions being issued by the director from the control box, which was situated like some vast fish tank at the rear of the cinemalike viewing area where Star was sitting.

The floor manager relayed the instructions to the actors, called for quiet again, raised his arm and gave the signal for "action."

"Cue Diane."

The scene was played in the boardroom of Harringtons, between two characters: Tracey (Diane) and Sir Rupert. They got through their dialogue without a hitch. The door opened and Kim (Laura) stood in the doorway. Yet again Star was struck by the sheer strength of her mother's personality. As soon as she came on screen she demanded total attention. She should be called Star—not me, her daughter reflected. This is something you can't learn. You either have it or you haven't. Laura has it.

Laura/Kim looked in shocked amazement at the two others.

To Star's surprise the camera did not linger on her but cut back to Diane. Laura spoke her lines from off-screen: "Oh. I thought everyone had gone."

The camera zoomed in close on Diane.

By the subtlest change of expression in her eyes Diane showed the reaction of her character to this intrusion: a mixture of guilt and defiance. Star conceded that not only did she look good, the girl could also act.

"We were just going over the budget of the rebuilding project." Diane almost threw the line away, so making it all the more effective. She had technique too.

The camera picked up Laura and followed her as she crossed to the other two and stood between them. She gave the little tilt to her chin that was a well-known mannerism of Kim's when she was in a difficult situation and was so familiar to the millions of fans who followed her through all her travails. So, here she was with yet another problem to face. How would she deal with this one?

How indeed? Star thought as she watched her mother skillfully walk in and take the scene over from the younger woman; how she held back for a moment and then turned away from Diane toward Sir Rupert, thus excluding her. When Laura spoke she pitched her voice low.

"I thought that was all settled. I thought we—"

The scene was interrupted by the floor manager, who came on camera and stood for a moment listening with great concentration to instructions coming over the earphones from the control box. "Right," he said. "Right. I'll tell her." Then to Laura, "Laura, love, don't cross over to the others. Stay by the doorway and speak your dialogue from there. Right?"

"No. Not right." Laura's voice was deadly calm. Her face expressionless. "Perhaps you could find out just who will be shot during all this?" The question apparently directed toward the floor manager was in fact for the benefit of the director, Matt, and even more for Sylvester.

Star turned in her seat and looked toward the control

box. She could see but not hear Matt and Sylvester obviously arguing, mouthing angrily at each other. Then Sylvester got up and stormed out of the box.

On the screen the floor manager could be seen relaying a message to Laura. Star thought she could detect a touch of nervousness in his manner. "Right . . . er, Laura . . . seems the camera will be on Diane just then. . . . Actually Sylvester's coming down to talk to you."

Laura's expression did not change. "If he has anything to say to me I'll be in my dressing room." And for the second time that day she walked off the set.

"Good for you, girl."

The voice came from someone sitting in the row behind Star. In the dim light of the viewing room she recognized one of *Harringtons* regular scriptwriters, Donald something, who she knew had worked on the show for years. He obviously had no idea who she was. He leaned forward and rested his arms on the back of the seat in front of him.

"I've been instructed to write her down," he said in conspiratorial tones. "Personally I think the whole thing stinks. She's a bloody good actress and she's given years of her life to this grotty setup. Now she's getting a bit long in the tooth, they want to get rid of her."

Star felt shocked by what he said but gave no sign of it. She didn't want to reveal her identity in case the writer clammed up.

"Really? You're sure?" she asked with no great show of interest.

"Absolutely. Sylvester's got the burning hots for Diane. He's determined she's going to be top banana. Well, I can tell you, he's wrong both artistically and commercially. That tough little number may get the fellows switching on to watch her, but I've been at this game long enough to know that a successful soap depends on female audience loyalty. And that's not so easy to arouse."

"Too right." Star looked back at the screen. The camera was still on Diane. Now completely relaxed she was looking at her watch and then making a little grimace as if to say, "Why should I have to wait around like this?"

"Look at the cocky little bitch," the writer continued. "She knows she's got it made. Poor old Laura."

Star felt a surge of intense anger and resentment on her mother's behalf. Laura, who had always said she'd sooner be hated than pitied. And as for the old . . .

"She's not finished yet," Star snapped. "No way."

Her tone obviously took the writer by surprise. He said he hoped she was right, of course, just that in this bloody business . . .

Star didn't wait to hear any more. She wanted only to go to her mother, to tell her not to take any rubbish from any of them. To try to support her the way her father used to in the past when production problems blew up. Though of course in those days, whatever rows or disagreements, no one ever questioned Laura's unassailable position.

Star stopped outside Laura's dressing room door, raised her hand to knock, and then hesitated. Perhaps she should just walk right in?

"I wouldn't if I were you."

Star froze, her clenched fist poised in the air. The voice was unmistakable. Turning, she saw Max shrugging on his trenchcoat.

"What business is it of yours if I want to talk to my mother?"

He ignored her question and said, "I believe it's raining again. I'll give you a lift if you like."

"I wouldn't like, thanks all the same." And again she raised her hand to knock on the door.

"Leave it," he said quietly. "Believe me."

"When I want your advice, I'll ask for it." And without knocking, she opened the door and went inside.

Laura and Sylvester were glaring at each other like two dogs about to fight over a bone. Laura hardly glanced at Star as she entered the room.

"Not now, Star." She spoke in the same sharp tone that she had used when Star was five and interrupted her when she was learning her lines. Star should have read the signs, but she felt Laura must know what she'd just heard in the viewing room. Must be warned. "Laura, I . . ."

"You heard me," Laura insisted. "Get lost."

Star retreated and closed the door behind her. Without looking around she was sure that Max's mocking eyes would be trained on her—gloating. She tensed herself against the sardonic comment. The mini triumph. Instead, in the most matter-of-fact tone, he said, "Right then. Let's go."

As they drove out of the studio grounds and through the neat suburban turnings, there was no attempt at conversation. Star felt disturbed by what was happening to Laura, but at the same time was conscious of a deeply unsettling awareness of the man beside her, driving the car with such skill and precision: the clear-cut profile, the gray eyes under the black brows, the strong sensitive hands on the wheel, and the faintest whiff of aftershave mingled with some musky masculine scent of his own. Star looked away and stared fixedly out of the window at the monotonously well-maintained houses and gardens.

They reached the point where the minor road joined the motorway. Max slowed the car, made sure that the way was clear, then took a right turn and accelerated away from London.

"Hey," Star protested, "you're going the wrong way. You should have taken a left turn."

"Not for where we're going."

"Where *are* we going?"

"To my cottage. I have to pick up some mail and one or two other things."

"Oh?" Star tried hard to sound cool. "And just where is this cottage of yours?"

"Near a village called Barhampstead. About thirty miles from here."

Star was inwardly seething. He had tricked her. She didn't like this man and she didn't trust him.

"Why didn't you say you were making this detour? I'd have found my own way home."

Max chuckled and gave her a sideways glance.

"Don't worry," he said. "I'm not taking you there to seduce you."

4

The cottage was at the end of a lane so roughly made up as to be hardly more than a cart track. Even the Porsche registered some bumps as Max maneuvered it carefully, trying to avoid the worst of the potholes now filled with water after the morning's downpour.

"At least it's stopped raining," he observed. They were the first words he had spoken since his flip assurance about his honorable intentions when they set off. Star had not uttered a word throughout the journey and didn't speak now.

"In really wet weather you need a paddle to get up here," Max continued. There was no hint that he was making conversation for its own sake nor seemingly any awareness that he might have angered or offended her—it was merely an observation. There was a bend in the lane and Max said, "I landed in the ditch here last winter. Up to my waist in mud. Then discovered I'd lost my key and had to break in through a back window. All part of the joys of country living."

Star still didn't answer, partly because she couldn't think of anything appropriate to say, but mostly because she wasn't really listening, she was too busy looking.

Max stopped the car outside the garden gate and without a word Star got out and stood gazing at the cottage. She experienced that fleeting sensation of déjà vu, the inexplicable impression of recognizing a place that is certainly unknown to you.

It was half-timbered, with soft rosy brickwork and mullioned windows reflecting the pale September sun, which had just now broken out from behind the clouds. A wild flush of dark crimson roses rambled up and over the gable of the front porch. Max walked past her, showing no interest in her reaction to the house, and opened the gate. He stopped as something lying behind the garden hedge drew his attention. "What the hell . . . ?" He bent and picked up what Star saw was a real estate agent's "For Sale" sign. Max scowled, his mouth tight with annoyance. "Fat lot of good that's going to do lying down there. Not that it does much good anyway. Nobody ever comes up here except the farm workers and a few cows, and they're not in the market for 'tasteful conversions.' "

Star stared at the board. "You're not . . . you can't be going to sell it?"

"I sincerely hope you're wrong."

"But you can't! I mean, how could you bear to?"

Max shrugged and threw the sign back down on the ground. He ignored her question and walked up the narrow brick and stone path to the front door. Star followed him, taking in as she went that the garden looked neglected and overgrown, which somehow added to the magic of the place. And the sweet scent that filled the air . . . Herbs? Tobacco plants? Roses? Whatever it was made her feel quite lightheaded.

Max opened the front door and went into the cottage ahead of her. There were some envelopes lying on the mat and he bent and picked them up. He rifled through them. Only one seemed to catch his attention. Star noticed it had a foreign-looking stamp and was addressed in overlarge, looped handwriting.

"You'll have to entertain yourself for a while," he said. "I have to sort some mail and make a couple of phone calls. Just wander round . . . whatever you like." He was already on his way to an adjoining room. "Make yourself some coffee. The kitchen's through there." He indicated vaguely in the direction of a door on the far side of the living room. "There should be some instant somewhere but there won't be any milk," he called over his shoulder and disappeared from sight.

Star was too interested in looking round the room to react to his lack of manners. The exterior of the cottage had led her to expect the traditional kind of dark, cozy living room. Instead it was light and spacious. There was no entrance hall, and more than one interior wall must have been removed to make the large living area. Initially the eye focused on the view of gently undulating farmland that could be seen through the floor-to-ceiling glass doors, which made up the whole of the back wall. Rather like those in Laura's flat, Star reflected. Did this denote some character trait in common? A train of thought that would get her nowhere, she decided.

She ventured further into the room and saw that extra lighting had been skillfully achieved by removing part of the first floor and adding what looked like a minstrel's gallery with the stairs leading up to it. The furnishings were pleasingly simple with one or two good antique pieces, but the main feature of the room was the old, original, inglenook fireplace so wide that Star could stand inside it and look straight up the chimney and see the sky. The whitewashed walls and the polished oak-plank floor reflected the autumn sunlight slanting through the windows, adding to the bright and airy atmosphere. Much care and thought must have gone into refurbishing the place without in any way destroying its character, and yet there was some element missing. Somehow it felt unlived in, sort of unloved. The thought filled her with a strange melancholy; it seemed such a terrible waste.

Then resolutely she shook the feeling off. If Max chose not to live in the house it was no concern of hers. Still—she was intrigued to see the rest of it.

The kitchen was uncompromisingly modern and functional, expensively equipped with every known electrical gadget. To her surprise Star noticed a shelf of cook books. Max, a cook? It didn't seem quite in character, but lots of men cook very well—so why not? There was nothing to indicate where she might find the coffee, so she opened cupboard doors at random. China, glass, cooking utensils . . . all neatly stacked and practically new. Yet another cupboard proved to contain staples: flour, sugar, tea, and finally coffee, ranged in matching glass jars. How odd that Max should be such a meticulous housekeeper. She stretched out a hand to lift down the coffee jar when she noticed a piece of paper secured to the inside of the cupboard door.

"Max," it read. "Replace coffee and sugar. Freezer running low. Sorry." The handwriting was large and looped and vaguely familiar. Star stared at it for a moment, frowning, and then remembered the letter on the doormat. The same hand. A woman's hand. A woman who had lived in this house? Or perhaps still lived in it? Suddenly she went right off the idea of coffee and only wanted to get out and into the fresh air.

The back door was locked so she had to return via the living room to the front of the house. The air was keen and fresh on her cheeks and she set off at a brisk pace to explore the back garden. As she rounded the house she stopped and stood for a moment, quite enchanted by what she saw. The lawn swept down from the house toward a winding stream whose progress was marked by a line of weeping willows. Beyond it sheep grazed unconcernedly in fields of lush grass. It was hard to believe that such a peaceful, pastoral scene could be so near to motorways, to city noise and pollution. She noticed that like the front garden this too needed attention: the lawn was unmowed, flower beds thick with weeds, and what should have been a herbaceous border looked bedraggled and beaten. The odd clump of michaelmas daisies and a few drooping tiger lilies did nothing to dispel the impression of neglect. But somewhere a thrush was singing joyously, and a squirrel scampered across the lawn and up a beech tree. Delighted, Star stood quite still, watching the little animal's acrobatics high up in the branches. So engrossed was she that she didn't notice the sound of quick, firm footsteps approaching.

"Madam!"

The woman's voice was bright and eager. Then again, "Madam!" The word was repeated before Star realized that it was addressed to her. She turned and saw a stout, middle-aged woman wearing baggy slacks and a duffel coat hurrying toward her. Star looked at her blankly.

"Yes?" she asked politely. "Can I help you?"

The woman stopped in her tracks. She seemed quite shocked to see Star.

"Oh . . ." she said. "I'm sorry, miss. I thought . . . that is, I thought you was . . . seeing the car and then seeing you, well, for a moment I thought you was some-

one else. Just from the back . . . look that alike . . .
I do beg your pardon, I'm sure."

Star smiled. "That's quite all right." She was dying to
ask who it was she resembled but didn't want to add to
the stranger's obvious embarrassment.

"Turned into a nice afternoon," the woman observed,
trying to cover her awkwardness. "After that rainy old
mornin'."

"Yes," Star agreed. "Very nice."

"Oh, I'm Mrs. Crompton—I live up the farm. I come
in and see to the house for Mr. Maxwell."

"I see. Well, he's indoors. Making some telephone
calls, I think."

"Then I'll go and see if there's anything he wants.
Bring him up-to-date sort of thing."

"Good idea."

"Sorry to have disturbed you."

"You didn't. Really."

"Right, then . . . er . . . nice to have met you."

Mrs. Crompton turned and marched off toward the
house, her heavy shoes making sharp clacking sounds
on the brick path. Star watched her as she let herself in
and closed the heavy front door behind her.

Madam? she thought, puzzled. Who in hell was
Madam? Presumably the lady of the large looped handwriting who left notes about coffee and deep freezes for
Max. And why had this Mrs. Crompton referred to
Max as Mr. Maxwell? Perhaps Max was short for Maxwell. But he'd said his name was Maximilian. Just who
exactly was he? And was he married? If so, where was
his wife? And what about Laura? What kind of a game
was he playing with Laura, who was having to deal with
enough flack at the moment without being double-
crossed by some two-timing little . . .

Star checked the anger that was rapidly building up
inside her. It was not just on Laura's behalf that she felt

indignant. She deeply resented the fact that this man, whom she didn't even like, could arouse so much conflict within her. As if to shake thoughts of him out of her mind she continued on her way toward the stream. Her high-heeled boots made progress difficult on the rough unmowed lawn and her ankle turned painfully. Star swore softly to herself. Balancing precariously on one foot at a time, she pulled the boots off and then, with an exhilarating feeling of freedom, ran in her stocking feet down to the stream.

Max stood looking through the window of his study, watching as Star galloped across the lawn. She's still a child, he thought, beautiful, but just a child.

"I'm sorry about it. I do hope I didn't upset the young lady."

Mrs. Crompton had been babbling on for some minutes about her case of mistaken identity. Max hardly listened. He made no comment, but that in no way inhibited the outpouring.

"From the back she just seemed the dead spit. It was seeing the car did it, that's what made me think . . . well, I just took it for granted, them being that alike. . . ."

Max smiled to himself, a crooked smile with more than a touch of bitterness in it. He could hardly imagine two people less alike. He had to stop the woman—this was the last subject he wished to discuss, and certainly not with Mrs. Crompton.

"I quite understand," he said in a brusque tone that put an end to the matter. "Please don't worry about it. I see the garden's looking a bit sorry for itself."

"Well, Fred was planning to come up this weekend and give that a good go. It's been difficult for him to find the time, what with harvesting and that."

"Well, as soon as he can. A well-cared-for garden will

help to sell the place. I need to get on with it. Another month and I'll have it on my hands until next spring."

"Not changed your mind, then?"

"No, Mrs. Crompton, I've not changed my mind."

She blinked sorrowfully at him. "That do seem a crying shame. After all the work that you and madam—"

"Can't be helped. The sooner it goes the better."

Mrs. Crompton shook her head and sighed deeply. "Well, if you're sure there's nothing I can do . . ."

"Not a thing, thank you, Mrs. Crompton."

"I'll be getting along then. They'll all be wanting their teas. And I am sorry about that little misunderstanding. I reckon perhaps I was hoping it *was* madam." She glanced at Max but he was again staring out of the window. Best drop the subject. "Well—nice to see you, Mr. Maxwell, and mind how you go."

"You too, Mrs. Crompton. And thanks for looking after everything."

"That's all right. Just so long as you're satisfied."

She hovered for a moment as if she were going to add something then changed her mind and clattered out of the room.

Max heard the front door slam and then the silence. The almost uncanny stillness seemed to envelop him. He gave an involuntary shiver. He wanted to get out of the place as quickly as possible. He glared at the telephone as if the machine were deliberately delaying him.

"Come on, Jon," he muttered impatiently. "Move your ass and call me back."

Next to the telephone lay the letter, where he'd thrown it down unread. He ought to chuck it in the wastepaper basket or burn it. Odd how Mrs Crompton referred to her as "Madam." Always had. He and Helen used to laugh about it together. Was it possible that they had ever laughed together? That he had ever felt anything toward her but this bitter anger and resentment?

He snatched up the letter. There were pages of it, covered in that familiar, overlarge childish scrawl. It was impossible not to see what she had written. "It's not working out . . . all a terrible mistake . . . Tony doesn't understand me. . . ."

Max smiled wryly, feeling almost sympathetic toward the unknown Tony, who was now trying to cope with Helen and her moods in some remote village in Spain. He screwed the letter up and was about to get rid of it when he read the words: "I love you and only you . . . please try to forgive me if you can." He hesitated and then slowly smoothed out the pages. Instead of throwing it away, he stuffed the letter in his desk drawer. He wouldn't reply, probably wouldn't even read it. But still he couldn't bring himself to do what any reasonably sane person would and tear it to shreds. Someday, somehow, he'd get Helen out of his system—although unfortunately that time was not yet. Enchanting, elusive Helen had really demolished him.

And now he was dealing with another complicated lady. But this was different. Despite her self-absorbed egotism he respected Laura. Admired her beauty. Enjoyed her company. Thank God he was in no way emotionally involved and that was how he intended to keep things. And not just regarding Laura. Love, he thought, is for children and idiots. And stared moodily out of the window.

He didn't notice Star at once, she was standing so still down by the stream. She was bending over and looking intently at something in the grass. Max frowned, puzzled. She seemed to be talking. He smiled. So, he wasn't the only one who talked to himself. He opened the door of the French window and stepped out onto the terrace to get a better view of her.

Star was, in fact, in conversation with a toad. A very leathery, warty specimen who, aware of her strange presence, sat transfixed with terror, only a throbbing pulse giving a sign of life.

"I won't hurt you," she said reassuringly. "I'm only sorry I can't kiss you and turn you into a prince. I could do with a nice, straightforward, considerate, handsome prince right now. I know, I know, I have one already—in California. Why don't I just get on the next plane and go back to him . . . ?"

She felt rather than saw Max watching and immediately stopped talking to the toad. She straightened up and glanced casually back toward the house and there he was, standing on the terrace. She immediately looked back at the ground but the toad, released from her hypnotic scrutiny, was lumbering off into the undergrowth. Star felt self-conscious and rather foolish, as though she had been caught in some ridiculously childish behavior —which, on reflection, she supposed talking to toads could reasonably be construed as. She stood tall, determined to stay cool and unfazed by the watchful figure on the terrace. She looked out over the fields, up at the wide, argent sky, and strolled with every appearance of composure by the side of the stream. If he wanted her, if he was ready to leave and return to London, let him call and tell her so. She did feel her efforts to appear self-possessed were somewhat marred by the boot she held in either hand; also that the soft earth by the stream was squelching muddily through her stocking-covered toes.

Max thought, she's not at all like Helen. Old Crompton's a fool.

And then as Star turned and strolled away from him there was a similarity that made his throat constrict for a moment: the tall, slender grace like a sapling willow tree. But no sooner had the image flashed through his mind than he rejected it. Star turned back toward him and, as if sensing that something was amiss, stood very still, looking at him across the expanse of unkempt gar-

den. An early evening breeze lifted strands of her gold-
streaked hair and billowed out the black raincoat so
that it seemed to make a frame for her. She continued to
gaze at him steadily out of the sea-bright eyes that even
her oversize spectacles could not dim. And Max continued to stare at her. Not Helen. Oh, no. When Max
spoke he called another name: "Abigail!" He said it
aloud, forcefully, and Star, hearing it, thought she must
be mistaken. Why on earth would he call her Abigail?
Sounded like a cat.

I can't just stand here up to my ankles in mud indefi-
nitely, she thought, and started to climb slowly back up
the incline of the lawn toward the house.

The going was rough and she felt awkward and
clumsy, horribly conscious of his eyes on her, and vividly reminded of a certain sports day at school that for
once both Laura and Vernon had decided to attend.
That obstacle race, where she'd so disgraced herself—
and them—by trailing in last, miles behind anyone else.
The cries from her schoolmates on the sidelines: "Come
on, Podge. . . . Keep going, Podge." And one bright
spark exhorting her to "Try running, Podge. You've got
the field to yourself." She wouldn't have minded if only
Laura hadn't been there, looking sensational in a wide
picture hat and long white gloves. She hadn't even
minded being called Podge. She was used to that and
knew that it was almost a term of affection, certainly
not really intended as an insult. But Laura and Vernon
didn't know. Laura had been asked to present the prizes
and had been so amusing and bright as she made a joke
of presenting her own daughter with the booby prize.
But Star had known just how furious she felt about her
ungainly, hopelessly inadequate child, although neither
she nor Vernon ever referred to it, which only made it
worse, like a shameful secret. They just made arrangements with the school for Star to be kept on a strict diet,

which after two weeks of dedicated cheating was forgotten by her and everyone else.

Max watched her progress across the lawn with a growing feeling of suppressed excitement. It was as if a figure from a dream were suddenly materializing. A thin drift of mist brought by the sun after the rain wafted across the lawn, adding to the sense of unreality. Perfect. She's perfect, he thought. Then Star stumbled and let out a small cry of pain and Max went to her, putting his arms around her and helping her to her feet. Just for a fleeting moment they stood close on the damp lawn with the mist drifting round them, like lovers alone in a magic land, she passively protected, he strongly supporting. The feel of him, his scent, the warmth that emanated from the hard masculine body, made her feel momentarily faint.

Then he broke the spell.

"What's the idea, walking around in bare feet?" he asked crossly, as if she were a naughty child.

"These boots are horrible." She held them up as though one look at them would explain all.

"Then why wear them?"

"They're all right in town. But here . . . well, it is pretty rough going, isn't it?"

"You'd better go and dry your feet. Wash them, too, by the look of them."

He turned away from her and strode back toward the terrace. Star stumbled after. He led the way into the house through the study. En route she had a quick impression of booklined walls and leather armchairs, and of a rather shabby-looking oak desk with a typewriter on it. She trotted after him, her feet making muddy imprints on the rug, and just as they reached the foot of the stairs the telephone rang. Max stopped.

"Ah, that's my call." Once again as he went to the study he issued orders over his shoulder: "Top of the stairs on the right is the bathroom. There's a cupboard with towels. The bedroom's straight ahead if you want it." Star heard him lift the receiver in the study. "Hi, Jon. How are you, you old bastard?"

She continued up the stairs.

The bathroom was decorated in various shades of pink. Large, pale pink cabbage roses twined and twisted their way up the wallpaper while the floor was covered in a thick pile carpet of deepest cyclamen. The fittings were not of that blancmange hue so favored by sanitary fitters but of the tone Star fancied was called "flesh." All a bit too feminine by half, she thought. She found a cupboard, which was indeed a linen cupboard piled high with thick, fluffy, pink and white towels. She selected one, then peeled off her tights, and turning on the bath tap washed her muddy feet under the running water. The water was cold, but it still managed to get her feet acceptably clean. She sat on a stool (pink and white candy stripes) and dried her feet carefully. She now had to face the problem of getting her boots on over her bare feet. Talcum powder would do it.

On a shelf by the bath stood a Victorian-type dish patterned with rosebuds and full of assorted tablets of soap (pink). Next to it was an oversize container of rose geranium talcum powder. There was also a dead African violet in a shiny pink ceramic pot. Star sprinkled the talcum generously over her feet and then into her boots. They slipped on quite easily in a cloud of rose geranium. She washed her hands in cold water, dried them, then folded the towel and hung it neatly over the unheated towel rail. Rolling up her damp tights, she put them in her pocket.

She went out onto the landing from where she could hear Max's voice, still engaged in his telephone conversation. To her surprise he was discussing something with which she was only too familiar from years of listening to endless business discussions of her father's: references to production costs and then something about a tight shooting schedule. From what Laura had said, Star had supposed he might possibly be some kind of a writer but here he was, sounding like an L.A. film producer setting up a deal. She realized that she was eavesdropping, which was something her public school education had trained her to look on as sneaky in the extreme. He'd said the bedroom was straight ahead. Not that she really needed the bedroom, she could comb her hair quite well in the bathroom, but curiosity got the better of her and even admitting that nosiness was not much more acceptable than eavesdropping, she opened the door and went inside.

If the theme of the bathroom had been roses, the bedroom was ruled by the lilac blossom. Great swaths of them ran repeatedly up and down the wallpaper. Matching material had been used for the curtains and on the king-size bed. The paintwork was picked out in lavender and the carpet a deep purple. Where possible anything that could be frilled was frilled. Star frowned. This surely couldn't be Max's taste, this almost offensively overwhelming femininity? No, this was just too itty-bitty for words. This must be the work of the "madam" the cleaning lady had mistaken her for, and Star felt a quite unreasonable wave of resentment that she should in any way resemble her—whoever she was.

And now, sitting at the unknown's dressing table, combing her hair, she reflected on the total unpredictability of men and of Max in particular. Who was this flowery woman and where was she? She again wondered if Laura knew of all this and felt newly protective toward her mother. If she was really . . . Here Star hesitated, not even wanting to form the thought coherently, but it could be that Laura was really in love with Max and that he was just using her. Perhaps to do with this film project she'd just heard him discussing on the phone? She wondered if she should mention any of it to Laura and at once knew that she wouldn't. Knew that her mother would deem it an unforgivable intrusion on that part of her life that had nothing to do with anyone else, especially not her daughter. Star heard the telephone bell ping as though the receiver had just been replaced and Max had finished his conversation. She checked her reflection in the mirror then left the lilac bower and went back downstairs to the study.

Max was seated at the desk, absorbed in writing something on a note pad. He did not look up as she entered or show any sign of being aware of her presence. Star sat down in one of the leather chairs and looked round the room. She liked what she saw. A real room this one. Functional. Intended as a place in which to read or write, and used for just that.

"Like a drink?" This question interrupted her thoughts. She considered and then said, "Shouldn't we be getting back to London?"

"I'm in no hurry. But of course if you have a date or something . . ."

"No. No date."

"So let's have a drink. Unless you think Mummy might be cross if you're not back home waiting for her."

The taunt could not fail but get a rise out of Star. However, she was beginning to get used to these sudden unbidden swipes of his, and frowning with assumed concentration, she said, "Actually, considering the sort of day she seemed to be having at the studio and all that shit she had thrown at her, quite possibly she might be pleased to have someone sympathetic to come home to. So on second thought, no, I won't have a drink with you."

She got up out of the leather chair and with a defiant set of her chin looked this exasperating, far-too-attractive man full in the face, feeling rather pleased with her riposte.

He looked at her intently for a moment, his eyes slightly narrowed in concentration. "Do you know anything about witchcraft?" he asked, apparently in all seriousness. Star was momentarily thrown.

"Witchcraft?" she asked, then added flippantly, "Not quite my scene actually."

"To be more precise—witches, rather than witchcraft."

"Old hags who fly on broomsticks?"

"That is the accepted, traditional image of them, yes."

"Can't say I've even thought about them," she said, still keeping her tone light. "I know people used to burn them, which wasn't awfully nice."

Max didn't smile.

"Men have always tended to destroy that which they don't understand," he said. "And they have not understood and therefore have always been frightened of women. Particularly intelligent or unusually gifted women."

Star grinned. "Speaking as a member of the male sex, would you say that you understand women?"

Max ignored the question. Crossing to a table that was piled high with books, he selected one and held it out to her.

"I'd like you to read this," he said.

Star took the book and read the title: *Satan's Daughter.* She frowned.

"If it's one of those Halloween-type horror books— no thanks. They bore me."

She turned the book over as she held it out to return it to him, then quickly retrieved it. There was a photograph on the back cover. The face was only too familiar. In fact, it also faced her. Max. She blinked at it in surprise. Then she looked again, with real interest, at the front cover and realized why she had not immediately made the association. *Satan's Daughter,* it read, by Donald Maxwell. She said the name aloud. "Donald Maxwell—that's you?"

"Yes. That's the name I write under. As you so shrewdly observed, 'Maximilian Macdonald' does have a certain incongruity to it. Suggests an Austro-Hungarian hamburger rather than an author."

Star laughed and then said, "But . . . aren't you rather . . . sort of . . . well known?"

Max smiled. "Am I?" he asked infuriatingly.

"Well, I've heard of you."

"Then I suppose I must be." He smiled and Star laughed again. "I'd like you to read it," he continued in a peremptory tone.

"Then of course I shall," Star replied with only the slightest hint of sarcasm, which did not escape him.

"I don't think you'll be bored. There aren't too many long words."

"I can always look them up in the dictionary if I find them beyond me." She smiled and turned the book over to examine the photograph and blurb on the back cover. Why, she wondered, did he want her to read this particular book? It seemed totally out of character for him to care whether or not she read anything of his. He'd not even mentioned that he was, in fact, this Donald Maxwell, who, as the blurb informed her, was the author of many best-selling novels, including . . .

"Don't bother with that." Max took the book from her and turned it right side up again. "It's more fictional than the contents."

"Aren't you a best-selling novelist, then?"

"A few have done pretty well. But it's all in the past, anyway."

"You mean you don't write anymore?"

He didn't answer immediately, flicking through the pages of the book and seeming suddenly remote and distant. He handed the book back to her. "Not at the moment," he said, dismissing the subject.

Star was about to ask about Laura and her proposed autobiography. Did she know his true identity, and what part was he playing in that? But as though determined to put an end to a conversation he wished he hadn't started, he said, "Let's have that drink. Come on," and walked away and out of the room, leaving Star to follow, clutching onto his book.

Logs were laid ready in the great inglenook fireplace. Max put a match to the kindling wood, which caught and blazed with blue and yellow energy, giving out more light than heat until the logs too began to smolder and flame and warm the hearth. He produced a bottle of red wine from the kitchen. "A nice friendly little Beaune," he said, with a touch of self mockery at the pretentious turn of phrase. Star, who knew even less about wine than she did about life, said that would be lovely. Which it was. Max found a packet of cheese biscuits that were only slightly stale and a tin of peanuts that weren't stale at all, and they sat side by side in companionable silence on the oversize sofa, sipping and munching and staring at the flames leaping up the chimney, just as though they had been sitting and sipping and munching together for years.

Night had still not quite taken over outside and Max made no attempt to light a lamp. Only the flames from the fire lit the room, reflecting gently in highly polished mahogany and in brightly burnished brass and copper, giving the impression that the room had a life of its own, of being warm and sheltering. Star could not remember any moment of greater contentment in her entire life and again had the sensation she'd had when she first arrived, of returning to a place where she belonged.

It was then that she broke the silence—and the magic. "Why are you leaving this place? How can you bear to?"

Max's expression changed. The jawline tightened and his mouth formed into a thin, hard line. "You ask too many questions," he said, and picking up the wine bottle from the coffee table, he topped up his glass and drank.

"I . . . I'm sorry," Star said, and meant it. She was sorry to have intruded into something that obviously was a very sensitive area for him. And sorry to have spoiled the atmosphere when for once they seemed to be at ease and happy with each other. She reproached herself for being clumsy and tactless. However much her outer appearance may have changed she still had two great big left feet, didn't she? He was right—it was none of her business why he wanted to give up the house and it didn't take much imagination to know that he wouldn't be doing it easily.

"I am sorry," she repeated. "Really." She spoke with such quiet sincerity that he turned his head sharply and gave her a long, quizzical look.

"You haven't lived long enough to know that things seldom pan out the way you hope they will." He seemed about to elaborate but instead continued to gaze at her, the firelight catching flashes of green and yellow in the pewter-gray eyes, fringed by the black, black lashes. The tension seemed to leave his face and the wide, sensual mouth softened, the corners turned gently upward. Star felt that same uncontrollable lurching sensation that she had experienced the first time she'd laid eyes on him. She wanted nothing more than to feel those lips on her own. To touch and caress. To have him hold her close, close. But he made no move, just continued to stare at her as though he were trying to commit her every feature to memory.

Then he spoke, quite softly and gently. "Could you take the windows off for a moment?" he said.

So! Men do make passes at girls who wear glasses, only they like to have them removed first. Star took off the oversize specs and waited. Still he made no move, but now Star had no idea what he was thinking or what expression he might have on his face because it—and everything else—became a blur, as though some monster paintbrush had given a vast water stroke to the whole scene. But as her visual perception diminished, her other senses became more acute. She heard quite clearly the one word he whispered: "Perfect." He breathed it rather than spoke. And then as he leaned slowly toward her she could smell that exciting mixture of spicy aftershave and masculinity.

She tried to control the strength of her response to his proximity, but as he slowly ran the back of his fingers along the contours of her cheek she again felt that sensation like an electric current running through her. She half expected bits of her to light up. Her lips moistened and parted a little despite her attempt to seem cool, and inside her boots her toes curled and uncurled in an uncontrollable reflex action. The action stirred up the layer of rose geranium talcum powder that was lining the inner sole of the boot. The scent of it wafted upward and enveloped them with its sickly sweet smell. Max stopped stroking her cheek abruptly. His nose twitched and he sat bolt upright—stiff and tense.

"That scent? Where's it come from?"

"Actually . . . my boots, I think."

"Boots?"

"It's difficult to get boots on over bare feet. I couldn't put my muddy tights back on so I used some talcum powder that was in the bathroom. Used rather a lot, I'm afraid."

"Rose geranium."

"I think so. Yes."

There was a slight pause in which Max drained his glass.

"Right," he said. "We'd better get moving."

And the moment was gone. The delicate communion irretrievably shattered. Star could only guess at the reason. Slowly she replaced her glasses and watched as with swift, decisive movements Max dampened down the fire.

That, she thought, was a near thing. And didn't know whether to be glad or sorry.

5

Harry Conrad sat at his double executive desk, chewing on the unlit Havana cigar that Sir Len had given him after their lunch. Harry was not happy. The lunch had been like so many others shared with Sir Len—unappetizing, unrewarding, and full of devious double talk.

Harry could remember Lennie when he was a fifthrate variety agent, and even further back when he had a juggling act with that French girl . . . what was her name now? Red hair and big boobs. Harry sighed. These days names eluded him, he must be getting old. Certainly had not been on form today. He'd let Len have it all his own way. Hadn't been able to pin him down on one single point regarding Laura. What the hell was he going to tell her?

The light on the intercom flashed. Harry flicked the switch. "Yes, Alice?"

"Still no reply from Miss Denning, Mr. Harry,"

Alice's voice quacked through the machine. "Just the answering machine. Should I leave a message for her to call you?"

Harry hesitated. The situation was very tricky and needed to be handled with tact. No way must Laura feel it was a crisis.

"No thanks, Alice," he said finally. "I'll contact Miss Denning later from home. And, Alice, you can go now. Sorry to have kept you so late."

Alice said, "Thank you, Mr. Conrad, and see you tomorrow," exactly as she'd been saying it for the past thirty years and, as in the past thirty years, Harry said, "You too, Alice," and off she went to a home life of which Harry knew nothing and had no wish to know. She was good-natured and efficient and lived for her job as Harry's personal secretary, which suited him fine.

He continued to sit at his desk, his troubled thoughts centered on Laura. One fact was now only too clear to him: Laura's days at *Harringtons* were numbered, and no ifs or buts. Lennie hadn't said it in so many words, but he didn't need to. Harry knew the signs and they were all there. What a great artist Laura was and how much he, Len, appreciated all she'd given to "the store" over the years. And then, as he'd picked over his low-cal cottage cheese salad, he'd frowned, apparently deep in thought, and proceeded to trot out what was obviously a well-rehearsed speech.

"Of course I should hate to lose Laura, but an actress of her stature shouldn't have a one-part career. It's time for her to develop her talents in other directions. Take on new challenges. Perhaps"—he stabbed a piece of pineapple triumphantly as a supposedly fresh idea struck him—"perhaps return to the theater? Let her public see her in person. She owes it to them, Harry. We must never forget those people out there—without them we're nothing. Mr. and Mrs. Joe Public, God bless them."

Now Harry was really worried. When had Lennie ever given a tuppeny toss about the public except as figures on a viewing chart?

Over sugarless black coffee Len guided the conversation round to anecdotes about his brilliant grandchildren and the house he was building in Surrey so that he could have all of them to stay for holidays. Which led directly, without pause or hesitation, to the importance of the family and high moral standards in this decadent and Godless age. Then on to his other family at City. People like Laura whom he looked on as a daughter . . . and on and on, juggling words the way he used to juggle balls. Which, Harry reflected, was just about what it boiled down to. Laura was for the chop but Lennie wasn't going to admit it. He knew she was capable of walking out before he was ready for her to go, and no way was he going to have that happen. People at City TV were hired and fired when Sir Len said so and not before.

Harry heard the outer door of the office close as Alice left. He felt an unaccustomed wave of helplessness sweep over him. In the business he was considered to be a pretty shrewd operator but here he was with his top client about to be thrown aside like last week's copy of *Variety*. Of course Laura wouldn't be stuck for a job. Sure he could get her a theatrical tour. Some good solid revival: an Agatha Christie or perhaps a period piece. Laura would look great in costume. Pack them in, she would. But even as he listed the possibilities to himself he could hear Laura's dismissive comment: "You only tour when nobody wants you on telly."

Harry struck a match and tried to relight his cigar. He sucked and puffed and choked but at last he got it to light. He was not a drinking man, usually stuck to Perrier water, but now he went to the drinks cabinet, poured himself a large Scotch, and knocked it back. He shuddered. He really hated the taste. He took a long pull on his cigar. It had gone out.

"I suppose this kind of in-fighting is pretty routine in television?"

Max's voice startled her. They had been driving in silence for nearly half an hour. In fact, he'd hardly addressed a word to her since the incident—or near incident—on the sofa at the cottage, after which Star had heard him banging round the house, presumably collecting up clothes and then papers from the study while she washed their glasses under the cold tap at the kitchen sink and left them to dry on the draining board. Since they had set out he seemed completely absorbed in driving and she had the impression that he had forgotten her presence. A kind of angry bewilderment suffused her whole being. She stared determinedly away from him through the car window into the darkness, half hypnotized by the lights of the cars streaking by in the opposite direction along the motorway. One thing at least was quite clear to her: This man sitting next to her in the driving seat, at present exceeding the speed limit by some twenty miles an hour, was a prime-time, copper-bottomed bastard. Making out with a woman (she now did not doubt that he must be involved with Laura) and quite happy to start something with the daughter, while still so tied to his unknown "madam" that he couldn't stand the smell of her talcum powder without practically throwing a fit. She couldn't wait to get away from him, and stay away.

"Sorry?" she asked, as if coming back from a million miles away but actually to play for time before forcing herself to talk to him with at least some degree of civility.

"All this conflict about who is in what scene and which camera angles . . . this goes on all the time?" he asked.

There was something patronizing in his tone, as if he were discussing kiddies' fights in a play group, which infuriated Star.

"Not all the time—no." She spoke with the studied patience of someone trying to impart information to a fool. "Certainly not. In fact, I think you'd find more cooperation and mutual support in any company of actors than you would in most other groups of working people."

She was aware of sounding more than a little pompous but she believed what she said to be true. She returned her gaze to the darkened window and Max fell silent again. But not for long.

"How come you don't want to enter the profession, in that case?"

"For one very good reason," she snapped. "I can't act."

"Have you ever tried?"

"I don't want to."

They drove in silence again for a few moments. Then Max asked, "So, what are your plans?"

To her surprise he sounded genuinely interested. She also knew that she had no idea what to answer. Plans? She only wished she knew. But no way was she going to admit that to him.

"Not sure. Haven't quite made up my mind." Jesus! How lame can you sound? She turned away again, hoping to put a stop to the conversation. But Max persisted.

"What were your interests at school?" he asked.

"Mostly eating and dodging gym."

"Surely more than that," he said.

"Not much."

"Have you considered going to university?"

"You're joking! I told you—between the ears I have this great vacuum."

"I wonder why you feel you have to put yourself down all the time."

"Just don't have any illusions about myself, that's all."

"So, in your considered opinion you qualify for just about nothing?"

Star hesitated and then she said almost defiantly, "I shall probably marry and have lots of children."

Max did not respond and she felt compelled to pursue the subject.

"I know it's not fashionable to say so, but I think marriage and bringing up kids could be terrific, absorbing, and . . . highly rewarding."

He seemed to consider this for a moment, and then much to her surprise said, "Yes, I imagine it could be. In fact I think it could be great so long as the urge springs from a real conviction and isn't just a cop-out."

Touché!

When Star did not reply, Max continued, "But you're far too young to be considering this as a serious possibility."

Star still said nothing, and then reproached herself for her duplicity. What about Gary? She was supposed to be engaged, wasn't she? She cursed herself for being a woolly mass of confusion. Bloody hopeless. All she wanted was to get rid of this man who so provoked her and disturbed her and . . . yes, aroused her, but she felt she had to say something.

"Not yet, no," she stuttered. "I . . . I'm really not quite sure what I want."

"I know the feeling," he said quietly. Almost sympathetically. Just as Star was warming to him for his understanding, he added with an ironical edge, "Of course, you could always take up Dee Costatinos's offer. You certainly have the looks for it."

He somehow managed to turn a compliment into an insult and Star bit her lip to stop herself from rising to the bait. Through the window she could make out the bleak shabbiness of the Cromwell Road and felt a surge of relief. Thank God they were back in London. Nearly home. Although even this was no guarantee of making her escape. He would probably come up to the flat to see Laura. After all, it was supposed to be his job, wasn't it?

Belgravia Place was packed with cars parked nose to tail, filling every available inch of space. Max edged the Porsche carefully through the narrow lane left for maneuvering. Obviously he wouldn't be able to park anywhere there. Outside number forty-eight he drew up alongside a discreetly luxurious Mercedes and double-parked.

"You won't be able to stay here," Star said. "There's no double-parking allowed in the square."

"I know."

"Then . . . ?"

"I'm not parking here."

"Perhaps in the mews?"

"Stop worrying. I'm not parking because I'm not stopping."

To her surprise Star found that instead of relief she felt disappointment. It must have shown. Max grinned. "I thought you'd be glad to get rid of me."

Star shrugged. "I don't care what you do. I just thought perhaps that Laura . . . that you . . ." She found she couldn't go on and gave up.

"As you said earlier, she'll be feeling pretty exhausted after throwing all those wobblers today. She'll want an early night," he said.

"Yes, I expect she will."

Star knew she should open the door and go, and yet somehow she felt unable to move. In the constricted space inside the car, lit only by the diffused light of a streetlamp, the feeling of physical attraction toward this man was overpowering. She looked up at him and found the gray eyes regarding her, not mocking or teasing but with an expression of puzzled interest.

"I meant it about the modeling," he said. "It might help to build your self-image, which for some unfathomable reason seems to be pretty negative."

"Just not used to looking . . . oh, I dunno . . ."

"I think perhaps 'beautiful' is the word you're after?"

"I thought you deplored my transformation."

"I must admit I've grown to appreciate it. But there's much more inside that's just waiting to be brought out. Plus a special kind of animal magnetism."

"No, you've got it wrong. I'm not any of those things. There's nothing special about me."

"It doesn't seem special to you because it comes naturally."

"If you say so."

"I do."

"Okay," Star said, feeling awkward and absurdly embarrassed.

"I'll let you go then," he said, dismissing her.

He leaned across to open the car door and his hand came in contact with hers. He raised it to his lips and kissed her fingertips. His touch seemed to knock the breath out of her body. The nerves at the back of her neck tensed and a hot ball of fire sprang to life somewhere in the area of her solar plexus. Then, on impulse, the action preceding the thought, she kissed him full on the lips. Almost immediately, as reason overcame desire, she pulled away. Guilty thoughts of Laura, of Gary, of the unknown "madam," flooded in to reproach her, and in an effort to abrogate the act she said with exaggerated brightness, " 'Night, then. Thanks for the ride." He must not be allowed to think that the kiss meant anything. After all, show-business people kissed each other all the time, didn't they?

Before Max could speak she was tumbling out of the car and starting to edge past the Mercedes to the sidewalk.

"Hey! Not so fast," he called after her. "Come back."

Her cheeks flushed, her heart did a minimarathon around her chest. She stopped and looked back at him, hesitated for the barest moment, then went into reverse to rejoin him in the car. She knew it was crazy, but if he wanted her then she had no will to refuse him.

She was about to climb back into the car when she realized that he was not holding the door open for her to get in but in order to give her something. The book. She had forgotten his book. Slowly she took it from him.

"Read it!" he ordered. Then slammed the car door. Before Star could catch her breath, the Porsche roared off and out of the square.

"Madam Dennin' ask for you very much."

"Oh. Thank you, Suki."

"She very tired. She go to bed. I take her what she want on tray."

Star nodded. She knew the form. Laura believed in conserving her energy and spent evenings when she wasn't working or socializing tucked up in bed, learning lines or watching television.

"More flowers come for you, Miss." Suki smiled widely, showing rather large, uneven teeth. "I put in you room."

Star frowned. Gary! What a bitch she was. Suki misinterpreted the frown as an expression of disapproval. "You not want me put in you room?"

"No, that's fine. Thank you, Suki. I'll go and say hello to my mother."

At that moment just about the last thing she wanted was to face Laura. But old habits die hard, and without stopping to take off her raincoat, still clutching Max's book, she went to her mother's room.

Laura was in bed, sitting propped up against a pile of lace-trimmed pillows. Across her lap was a wickerwork bed table and tray. She pushed the food around, eating without relish. Her attention was focused on the television set situated at the bottom of the bed, at this moment showing *Dynasty*, with Joan Collins in full emotive force.

Star said "Hi!" with the same kind of artificial brightness that she'd just recently manufactured for Max. Laura barely glanced up.

"Hello," she said curtly.

Warning bells rang inside Star's head. This wasn't going to be easy. Things must have gone really badly at the studio. She thought how drained and tired Laura looked. Suddenly almost old.

"I tell you, Collins got it right," Laura proclaimed, her eyes still glued to the television screen. "In America they appreciate mature women. If she'd stayed here she'd be lucky to get on an interview program by this time."

Star perched on the end of the bed as she had so many times before. What could have happened to make Laura sound so bitter? Had she been told she was being written out? Or did she just guess it? She felt a wave of sympathy for her mother and would have liked to have said something reassuring, but that might just be the worst thing possible. Better keep it light. "Tough day?" she asked, as though it were a routine question.

"Pretty bloody," Laura said.

The episode of *Dynasty* finished and the end-captions

began to roll. Laura touched the remote-control switch and the picture faded.

"But I won this battle," she said, picking up the conversation with a satisfied air. "And I'll win any others that may be coming."

"Sure you will."

"I sent that sniveling little sod Sylvester off with his tail between his legs—which, incidentally, is where he should keep it—to write me up in the next episode and write his little tart down."

"Good," Star said, trying to sound as though she really believed this would happen, which she didn't. "Have you . . . that is . . . have you spoken to Harry—since his lunch with Sir Len?"

"He says there's no real cause for alarm. Of course I know exactly what Len's game is—my option's coming up and he thinks if he can demolish my self-confidence he'll get me on his terms. Well, I can tell you . . ."

And she launched into a diatribe against Len and British television in general and how tough she was going to be in the future, how things would be done her way with complete script approval and Diane written right out. Sylvester must be replaced. He was the pits as a producer anyway, should never have been put on the show in the first place . . . and on . . . and on . . . and on.

Star listened with growing dismay, remembering what she had heard from the scriptwriter and old Bill, the prop man. She thought of Madge's snide hints and Diane's cockiness, and it dawned on her that everyone seemed to know the seriousness of the situation except Laura. Perhaps Star ought to tell her what she'd heard? But if Harry had deemed it wise not to, then what was the point? She looked at her mother's angrily distorted expression, at the deep shadows under her eyes, and decided that Harry was probably right. Why upset her until it was a fact? Certainly not tonight. She wouldn't be able to take it. Probably wouldn't even believe it.

Laura laid down her fork and shoved the bed table from her with an irritable gesture. "Take this mess away, would you, Starlet? I don't think scrambled eggs can be part of Korean cuisine."

Star was about to say, "Not like Jessie's," but quickly changed her mind and didn't say that either. She lifted the bed table off the bed. "I'll take it to the kitchen," she said, anxious to make her getaway.

"No. Don't go yet. Anyway, let Suki take it. God knows I pay her enough. And she can't even answer the phone."

Star put the bed table on the floor.

"Oh, by the way," Laura continued, "there's a message for you on the machine. From someone called Gary in L.A. I listened to some of it, I'm afraid. He sounds very smitten."

"He is, I think. Quite."

"Well, who is he?"

Star smiled, then shrugged. A reaction that went back to earliest childhood when faced with Laura's interrogation.

Her mother said, "You don't have to tell me if you don't want to." And Star knew that she didn't want to, although she didn't quite know why. Probably because she was so totally confused about her feelings for him.

"I keep forgetting you're not a little girl anymore. The way you look now, of course you have boyfriends. And," she added with the merest hint of self-pity, "I know it's nothing to do with me."

Star was saved from having to answer or comment by a sneeze.

"Bless you," Laura said automatically.

Star sneezed again.

"Got a cold?" Laura asked anxiously. "A cold would be all I need."

Star thought of the wet grass squelching through her toes down by the stream at Max's cottage, and said, "No, I don't think so."

"Let's have a drink. Not champagne tonight—vodka, neat, on the rocks."

"Right."

Star went off to the sitting room to get the drinks while Laura babbled on. "This is usually Max's job," she said. "Don't know where the hell he's got to. I tried ringing him but there's no reply. Suppose I was a bit rough on him at the studio but I had to deal with the situation my way and I couldn't do it with outsiders around. I'll have to make it up to him. Apologize. He's very simpatico."

Star did not even notice that Laura didn't consider apologizing for any hurtful behavior toward her. She was quite used to being summarily dismissed when not wanted at "the store."

She poured the drinks and carried them back to the bedroom. Noticing that Laura had suddenly gone very silent, she wondered why until she saw that her mother had her glasses on and was studying Max's book, which Star had left on the bed. She stopped abruptly and some vodka spilled onto the thick white carpet. Silently she called herself every insulting name she could think of for bringing the book into Laura's bedroom. How could anybody be that stupid?

"Where did you get this from?" Laura asked.

"Your vodka." Star held out the glass, playing for time. She could have lied, said she'd bought it in a bookshop. But she knew that Max would not go along with that. He did things his way, and if he wanted to give her the book he'd give her one without asking anyone else's permission.

"Max gave it to me."

Laura sipped her drink.

"He said he'd like me to read it," Star continued.

"Left it here for you, you mean?"

"No."

Star took a deep breath. She had nothing to hide, had she? Done nothing wrong. "He took me to his cottage and . . ."

"Did he now?" An icy tone crept into Laura's voice.

"Yes. Well, he was giving me a lift home from the studio and . . ."

"You went on a little tour?"

"He had a few things to collect. Mail and stuff."

"Took from midday until now? Must have had a lot to collect."

"Phone calls. He's selling the place."

"You seem to know a lot about it. But then you had quite a long time there in which to find out, didn't you?"

"Look, don't go making something out of this."

"I'm not making anything out of it that doesn't appear to be there already."

"He spent most of the time shut up alone in his study."

"I see."

Star sneezed again. Sniffed.

"Oh, for God's sake blow your nose, girl."

Star fished in her pocket, pulled out a tissue, and to her horror produced with it her soggy tights. She had forgotten about them and now they seemed to acquire a life of their own, leaping from her hand onto the bed. For a moment both Star and Laura could only stare down at the offending garment snaked across the silk duvet. Neither spoke. Then Laura said in an artificially controlled voice, "No wonder you've caught a cold. I think you'd better go off to bed. Good night, Star."

"Listen. You don't understand—"

"Please. I'm tired. There's nothing to discuss, is there?"

"I got my feet wet, that's all. So I took my tights off and—"

"In an age when most girls lose their virginity before they get their O levels, I can hardly expect an eighteen-year-old who's just spent three months in L.A. not to have sex." Laura's cool was deserting her, her voice becoming shrill. "However, when it's your own daughter, it is a bit of a shock when she comes home like some little slut with her knickers in her pocket."

"That's a disgusting thing to say, and it's not true! You've got it all wrong."

"Jesus! You only met him yesterday."

"Right. So can't you see that what you're thinking is ridiculous? There's been nothing . . . I don't even like him, let alone fancy him. And he certainly doesn't fancy me. So forget it."

Laura seemed somewhat mollified. "Don't misunderstand me, Star. Max means nothing to me either. Absolutely nothing."

She's protesting too much, Star thought. She's in love with him all right.

"It's you I'm thinking of," Laura continued. "I wouldn't want you to get hurt."

"Thanks." Star tried but couldn't quite keep the irony out of her voice.

"And you know how bitchy people are. Nobody knows that Max and I have been working together, so we're seen around as a pair. If you—"

"Look, I won't even talk to him if it upsets you so much."

"Star, I'm doing my best to be reasonable."

"By accusing me of behaving like a slut? Someone

who cares so little for you that she deliberately sets out to make you look a fool?"

"This is just the perfect end to an all-time sod of a day, isn't it? Here." Laura picked up Star's tights between thumb and finger as if they were contaminated and held them out to her. Star snatched them from her. Anything either of them might say now could only make things worse, so she turned and ran from the room.

It was not until much later that she realized she had forgotten to take Max's book.

"To say that I miss you is just about the understatement of the century. I realize that anyone can listen to this message but I love you, Star, and I don't give a damn who knows it. Call me collect as soon as you can."

Here Gary's message ended and Star switched off the tape. She sat motionless at her father's desk. The room was in darkness, apart from the circle of light thrown onto the leather-topped desk by the reading lamp, like a spotlight on an empty stage. The silence was so intense that it was hard to believe that this was the center of the city.

She felt terribly alone. The scene with Laura had distressed her more than she had shown. She still found her mother's anger unbearable—something she would go to any lengths to avoid, just as she had when she was a child. Gary's words of love seemed like a warm bath of reassurance. She had forgotten how good it felt to lean on him, to feel sure of his integrity, of his quiet strength. And yet when she closed her eyes it was not Gary's open, handsome face that she saw before her; it was those smoky-gray eyes, that unruly lock of jet-black hair, that wide mouth that she had so recently found so irresistible. She flushed crimson as she recalled her lack of control.

Blast him! Blast bloody Max!

But for him she would never have quarreled with Laura. Somehow over the years she had managed to live in relative harmony with this admittedly difficult woman whom she loved so much, and now because of this intruder who, she was sure, gave not a toss for either of them, she and her own mother were squalling like two alley cats. And no Jessie to talk sense into them. That was Max's fault too.

Then she stopped cursing Max and turned on herself. What kind of a gutless, useless wimp was she? She'd better get her act together but quick. The conversation with Max in the car came back to her. His questions had been only too apposite. What were her plans? Her interests? Her talents? When she took a good hard look at it—none. There must be something she could do. She couldn't just drift on like some pampered doll, depending on her parents. And she was no nearer a decision about Gary. She wasn't being fair to him, was she? But to marry him as a cop-out? No. She must find a job, even if it was at the checkout at a supermarket—though she doubted if she'd give the right change. Something . . . anything . . .

She picked a pencil out of the embossed leather container that held pens and pencils of assorted colors, now used only by the temps who came to deal with Laura's fan mail. Star chewed on the end of the pencil and revolved slowly in the huge black leather swivel chair. Time was when she would have tried to solve the problem by making for the fridge and a monumental binge, but even though the temptation was still there she knew that way offered no solution. Suddenly she stopped both rotating and chewing. There was one escape route that could offer independence. Something someone uniquely qualified to know seemed to think she'd be good at. It was worth a try anyway. Propelled into action by this idea she snatched up the A-to-D telephone directory and scrabbled through the pages to the one she had studied only that morning. She ran her finger down the list of names and stopped when she came to what she was looking for: "Costatinos, Dee. Photographer."

Star lifted the telephone receiver and determinedly started to stab out the number.

6

"Twirl . . . and twirl . . . and give it to me . . . Great! You are fabulous, dolink. . . . Come on stronger now. More stronger still! That's it. Fantastic! I want evil now. Evil pussycat . . . No, real mean. Hate me! You are beautiful . . . Fa-a-antastic!"

Dee Costatinos had been commanding, coaxing, forcing reactions from Star for most of the day, all the time clicking cameras at her from every conceivable angle, stopping only occasionally to issue orders to her two assistants concerning lights, reflectors, settings, or whatever. She seemed tireless, and her energy and enthusiasm communicated itself to her model.

Star found that she did Dee's bidding easily, instinctively giving the expression, the reaction, the pose asked of her. Both photographer and model were on that high that comes when two creative people meet, connect, and make sparks. The chemistry was right. Neither of them showed the least sign of flagging. Star felt liberated. Alive. As if there was nothing this woman could ask her to express that would be beyond her. For the first time in her life she felt a kind of ecstasy. It wasn't just the photographer behind the camera, it was the camera itself. Like finding a long-lost lover.

"Mouth open a little, dolink . . . lick your lips . . . Sweet! To me. Sexy! Give me a treat. . . . Perfect. . . . Right, enough." Star looked round, surprised. She had lost all track of time and had no wish to stop. Dee laughed. "Look at her," she said. "She doesn't want it to stop. Like a first real fuck!"

The two assistants laughed. Both in their mid-twenties, attractive, androgynous, one called Katy, the other Jan, they had been tremendously supportive of Star, seeing to her makeup and hair, helping her dress and keeping her relaxed. Katy—or it could have been Jan—said, "Gorgeous, isn't she, though?"

Star grinned, delighted at the compliment.

"Oh, sheet!" Dee made an exaggerated gesture of despair. "I should have caught that smile. Never mind. Plenty more where that came from. I tell you, baby, you were created for this." She indicated the camera. "And I'm not sure it wasn't created for you."

Star could hardly believe what this woman, one of the most brilliant photographers in the world, was telling her—and yet something deep inside told her it could just be true.

"But now relax. Go get dressed and then come downstairs. We must talk."

Star crossed the studio, which took up the whole of the top floor of the rambling Chelsea house where Dee lived and worked. The lower floors, which had been converted into a maisonette, Star had only glimpsed as she climbed the seemingly endless flights of stairs up to the studio. Dee explained, "This way I save on taxis and still have a walk to work."

Jan (or was it Katy?) followed Star to the dressing room to help her out of the elaborately simple chiffon creation she was wearing. Star caught sight of her reflection in the dressing table mirror and it was as though she were looking at a double. Familiar yet strange. Surely *her* eyes were never that bright. *She* never exuded that extraordinary glow.

"Was this really your first session?" Katy/Jan asked, carefully arranging the smoke-gray wisp of a dress on a hanger.

"Yes."

"Well, all I can say is, some people just got it."

"You really think I was all right?" Star asked anxiously.

"You heard what the lady said. And believe me she doesn't hand out comps for free. She doesn't need to, and besides, it's not her style."

Left to herself, Star sat down at the dressing table and started to take off her makeup. How many times she'd sat watching Laura doing this and now it was her turn. Why did the thought make her feel a little uneasy? As though she was doing something forbidden? Perhaps because of their present strained relationship. She was sorry about it—she hated to be on bad terms with her mother. In the end she supposed that she would be the one to apologize—but for what? She'd done nothing wrong. Eventually Laura would come round. Whatever her faults she didn't bear grudges. Determinedly Star stopped thinking about her and went on scraping the pancake off her face. Why spoil this moment? She was just beginning to realize that she did feel a bit tired but she couldn't remember when she'd enjoyed anything so much. If these photographs turned out well, here at last was something she could do. Something of her own.

"You come down from your high now?"

Star looked up to see Dee's reflection in the mirror. She hadn't heard her come into the dressing room. The luminous dark eyes were fixed on her intently and Star, who had posed so happily for this woman for hours, now suddenly felt self-conscious and aware of the fact that she was wearing nothing but bikini briefs.

"Slowly descending," she said. "Almost at splashdown."

Dee threw back her head and laughed—an uninhibited, robust laugh that seemed to involve every part of her. "You are adorable," she said, still laughing. "Okay, dolink. I'm going to take a shower. Come down when you're ready. Katy will fix you a drink."

"Lovely. Thanks."

"You kill me, sweetheart."

And, still chuckling to herself, Dee left the dressing room. Star had no idea what she had said that was so funny. Over her shoulder, Dee called, "You have beautiful boobs, you know it?"

Despite herself, Star grinned. She liked this larger-than-life woman even if she was, as Harry had put it, "odd." She was direct and exuded an infectious energy and enjoyment of life. She had shown no surprise when Star rang her, despite Star's protestations at their first meeting about not wanting to be a model. Dee had given her a date in two days time. "I'll clear everything for the day. We will experiment, okay? Get plenty of rest."

It had been so easy that Star could hardly believe it and had gone to bed full of plans for the next forty-eight hours concerning fruit-only diets and working out at exercise studios. At around six A.M. she had awakened fighting for breath. Her nose was blocked, her throat felt as if she'd swallowed a saw and her eyes were streaming. She knew that she had the mother and father of all head colds.

She sat up in bed, shivered and sneezed. "Jesus, no!" she said aloud, although it came out as "Desus, dough!"

This could ruin everything. You can't start a new career with time off but neither could she show up at Dee's studio with a red nose and runny eyes—and she wouldn't be able to wear her contact lenses.

It was all Max's fault. If he hadn't dragged her off to his blasted cottage she would never have taken her boots off and got her feet wet. . . .

This line of thought would get her nowhere. She remembered Jessie and "The show must go on." She had determined that she would be at Dee's studio the day after tomorrow as arranged and nothing would stop her. If she had a cold then she must just get rid of it.

Suki supplied her with relays of hot drinks and genuine sympathy, which was more than she got from Laura, who did call once on the internal telephone to tell Star to stay in her room. "I shan't come and visit you," she added. "I simply mustn't get a cold." Star accepted this apparent lack of sympathy without question: a cold to an actor is like the bubonic plague to ordinary mortals. Neither of them referred to the previous evening's clash, although Laura could not resist saying in tones laden with meaning that she was hardly surprised that Star had caught a cold. Star let it pass and wished yet again that Jessie was with her. Why in hell had she gone off without a word? She must be found. She searched in her handbag and produced the airline ticket, then reached for the telephone.

"Madge Graham."

The old actress announced her name as she lifted the receiver as though she were presenting herself at court. Yes, she had found Gertie Cozzey's number. Star was delighted and managed to cut the ensuing flow of gossip down to a minimum before finishing the conversation and ringing the number Madge had given her.

The phone was answered by a woman in a state of high-octane fury. "Beryl?" she shrilled and, before Star could speak, launched into a tirade of abuse concerning Beryl's lack of manners, how she'd been waiting for her call for over an hour, and if this was how she was going to behave . . . etc., etc. Eventually Star managed to make herself heard but the woman on the other end was not interested in her quest. Couldn't remember who had sold her the house or where they'd moved to. Star persisted and finally persuaded the excitable lady to write down her name and telephone number and let her know if she found Gertie's new address. The woman complained that she was really too busy to waste time on such things, and now would Star kindly get off the line as she was waiting for a very important phone call.

"From Beryl?" Star couldn't resist asking.

"How do you know?"

"I wouldn't count on her if I were you. Dead unreliable." And she replaced the receiver.

Then she cursed herself for giving way to a stupid impulse. Now the woman would certainly never help over Gertie. Too bloody clever by half, wasn't she? Ah well, just have to manage without Jessie for a while longer and hope that she was okay.

Working her way through boxes of tissues and innumerable tablets of vitamin C, she found her thoughts returning in the most maddening way to Max: going over the time they had spent together, her feelings swinging from angry resentment to sheer physical desire. She was intrigued to read his book but was not going to stir up more trouble with Laura by asking for it back. Anyway, she thought angrily, as I want nothing more to do with him I needn't bother to read his silly book, need I? But she knew that she wanted to.

Late at night, while she was still sniffing and aching, there was a gentle knock at her door and Suki appeared, bearing a steaming mug of some noxious-smelling mixture.

"Drink," she said. "Tomorrow no more ill. You sing like birdie."

More to please the well-meaning girl than with any great confidence as to the efficacy of the medicine, Star swallowed it down. It tasted vile, like rotten raspberries. Within minutes she was asleep.

By morning her head was clear and her nose unstuffed. She felt fine. Suki was vague about just what the mixture contained. "Many good things," was all she would say. Star told her if she patented it and put it on the market, she'd make a fortune. Suki just grinned.

Now Star had only one day to prepare for the photographic session. Her hair, her nails, and horror of horrors—clothes. She must go and buy some.

"Come with me, Suki," she pleaded. "I'm hopeless buying clothes alone."

Suki protested that it was not her day off, but Star assured her that Laura wouldn't mind if she swapped the day. She didn't add that Laura wouldn't even know as they'd be back long before she returned from the studio.

Somewhat reluctantly, Suki agreed to accompany her. They had a great time and the girl proved to have a good eye for what suited Star. They were gone much longer than they realized and came home to a very displeased Laura. Star felt guilty for having made Suki play truant and took full responsibility. Laura was not impressed. "It's about time you grew up. Suki isn't Jessie, to go trailing round doing your bidding. Pandering to your every whim. Why couldn't you go on your own?"

Star had to admit that there was some truth in what

Laura said. From now on she would stand on her own feet. Starting tomorrow with Dee Costatinos.

And now she'd done it. Bit late in the day, but she'd taken that first step. And she'd loved every minute of it. She stuffed her bits and pieces of makeup, hairbrushes, and combs into her tote bag, and went in search of Dee.

The sitting room was almost as spacious as the studio: walls painted cyclamen pink with a wild mural of jungle flowers at one end; overstuffed sofas of black leather, startling black-and-white-striped covers on low-slung chairs. The carpet was dazzlingly white and ankle deep. Dee was wearing a flowing jade-green caftan slung around with gold chains. Her hair was still damp from the shower. Star observed that unexpectedly she was not drinking alcohol but orange juice from an oversize tumbler. She drained the glass and let out a loud grunt of pleasure. She held out the glass to Katy, who replenished it.

"Greatest bloody drink in the world," she said. "Better than any booze. That's rotten stuff. Sometimes I love it—but still rotten stuff. Sit down. Katy will fix you a drink if you want."

"Orange juice would be great," Star said. "I'm thirsty." And suddenly realized that indeed she was.

Dee lay back on the sofa with her feet up, smoking a slim black cheroot in silence. Star drank her orange juice and felt decidedly self-conscious under this unblinking gaze. At last Dee spoke. "Before we go any further there are one or two things we are making quite clear. Okay?"

"Sure."

"First you must realize that modeling is hard bloody work. Today was fun for you. An adventure. But there will be times when you don't feel so good. You got your period, or your boyfriend stood you up. Your grandpappy dies. You got to be able to forget it because if you don't the camera will know it in no time flat and it will show, baby. How it will show. So, number one, complete dedication."

Star nodded. "I do understand. You see, my mother is an actress."

"I know. But she can hide behind the character she is playing. A model has nothing between herself and that wicked eye. Next—your life-style: ballet dancers, nuns, and photographic models live a life of self denial. Booze, drugs, sugar, fat—OUT. Now, your face—divine, but the body . . . good shape but you should lose around ten pounds."

"But," Star stammered, "I just lost weight."

"Not enough. Diet. You know? No food with meals." Star laughed.

"And most of all exercise—anything you like, but lots of it. I want the body hard. It is your style. Muscle is very feminine right now. Sexy. So get yourself to a workout studio. Go running. Swim. Dance. Anything. So long as you keep moving."

"I did aerobics when I was in L.A."

"Fine. Now, sex—ma-aarvelous! But don't be over-doing it! Don't get all crazy involved. Sure, being in love is superb for the complexion but, oh Christ, when it goes wrong!" She shook her hand up and down as though she'd just burned her fingers.

Star swallowed. "I . . . I'm not in love. Not at the moment, anyway."

"Good. If you are a sensible little chicken and work hard, and if you photograph the way I think, you have a career. And good money. Important. You got it you can tell people, 'Get screwed.' You not got it, they screw you. So, do what I'm telling you and you get on top. Right?"

Star nodded eagerly. "Right!"

Dee drew on her cheroot and let out a long, slow

stream of smoke. "I have one particular project could be very fine for you. Danielle are launching a big cosmetic campaign. They want a new face."

"Danielle? Wow! But . . . I mean, would they take me?"

"If I tell them. They have to approve but I decide."

"That would be brilliant."

"It would. Big contract. Money like telephone numbers."

Here was the chance of independence that Star so longed for. She leaned forward and looked intently into Dee's face. "I promise I'll work like a bloody beaver. Do whatever you say, Dee. Honest."

Dee smiled and patted Star's cheek. "Very good. But first we see how your pics turn out," she added with down-to-earth practicality. "Now, run along, little one. I go to a bloody big party."

Star drained her glass and stood up. "I can't thank you enough . . . !"

"Don't thank me. Thank your genes. I think we just call you Star. No second name."

"Fine."

"Oh, by the way. You'll hear lots of stories about me. Take no notice. Sure I like girls better than men— they're a prettier shape. Men bore me with their little pricks and their big egos. Like the song says, 'I am as I am.' But I never let it interfere with business. And you, baby, are strictly business."

As Star let herself into the flat she still felt as though she were walking two feet above the ground. She was bursting to tell her good news to . . . well, who? Suki? She might not understand. Laura? Surely her mother would be delighted that she was launching out on a profession of her own. She was too much of a pro not to be pleased. And, hell, she was her mother.

She could hear Laura's voice coming from the study, probably talking on the telephone. It was not possible from that distance to make out what she was saying but as Star got nearer she heard her mother speaking in a voice that was not her "telephone" voice but was still slightly studied and artificial.

"Kim has become part of me," she was saying. "I'm not sure anymore where she starts and I leave off. I dream her dreams. When she was fighting the big take-over bid from Derbrights, I . . . that is, me, Laura . . . was worrying about it. I think this degree of iden-tification is why people continue to be involved with her after so many years—Kim, that is—to care . . ."

Quietly Star entered the room, stopped, and looked round. No sign of Laura, yet her voice continued. Seated at her father's desk, as though it belonged to him, was Max. On it was a tape recorder out of which came Laura's voice. Max seemed immediately to be aware of Star's presence and in one sweeping movement turned off the tape recorder and swiveled round in the high-backed typing chair to face her. To her surprise Star saw that he was wearing a dinner jacket. The un-usual formality of his clothes seemed to accentuate his masculinity. For a moment she was speechless. Then she stammered, "I . . . I thought Laura was in here."

He didn't reply but sat looking at her appraisingly. She wished she had been prepared for this confronta-tion. Maybe then she would have controlled her reac-tions a little better; stopped the swirling sensation in her stomach, the icy tingle down the length of her spine.

"And what have you been up to?" Max asked as if talking to a dog who had come in covered with mud.

Star was immediately defensive. "Up to?" she re-peated his question, aware that it was a totally inade-quate response.

"You look as if you've been mainlining sunbeams. Or

perhaps," he added with that maddeningly ironical smile she was getting to know only too well, "perhaps you met Prince Charming and fell fifty fathoms deep in love?"

"Neither," Star replied dismissively. "Is Laura home?"

Max ignored the question. "Whatever it is, keep doing it. You look glorious."

To her deep embarrassment Star felt herself blush. A horrible rush of burning scarlet to the cheeks. It made her very angry. She repeated her question. "Is Laura home?"

Again Max chose to ignore it. "Have you read the book?"

"Book?"

"The book I gave you to read." His tone was peremptory. "My book. *Satan's Daughter.*"

"Oh, that book . . . no. I haven't read it."

"Why not?"

"I've been pretty busy . . . mainlining sunbeams."

Max was not amused. "I wanted you to read it. It's important."

Star was puzzled. "How can it be of the least importance to you whether or not I read your book?"

Max looked at her steadily for a moment without speaking. Then, as if coming to a decision, he said, "I intended saying this after you had read it but as time is short I suppose I must explain now."

She waited for the explanation but Max still seemed to hesitate. He got up out of the desk chair and, deep in thought, started to pace the room. Star was disturbingly aware of the compact energy of the man, the scarcely contained animal vitality. He stopped. Turned. Faced her.

"Of everything I've written, this is the book that matters most to me. Now, after God knows how many devious and frustrating convolutions, we seem to have a viable setup for a film. I believe it can make a telling and important movie. Not a million dollar epic, but something that will make people think and care and even, I hope, be entertained—which also matters."

He paused, ran his fingers through his thick black hair, then resumed his pacing.

Star, still bewildered, didn't know what to say. "Well . . . great. I'm very glad for you. But what's this got to do with me?"

Max stopped his tour of the room and stood very still, focusing those unnerving gray eyes on her. "You are the personification of the girl who is the central character. I realize you have no experience but that wouldn't matter."

"But you know I don't want to act."

"You wouldn't have to. You would just have to 'be.' "

"Don't you understand—"

"Possibly more than you do. Like it or not, you're an actress."

"No."

They stood facing each other without moving. Without speaking. Without touching. Then, as if driven by some magnetic force, she was in his arms, his lips were on hers, and she was lost. His tongue hungrily explored the sweetness of her mouth and with every fiber of her being she responded to his embrace. Star could feel his hardness pressed against her and an unknown intoxicating warmth swept through her body. The sensations she experienced were so overwhelming that she felt almost frightened. Not of him but of herself. She was gasping for breath and just about to pull away when a familiar voice called from the living room: "Max? Maxie, where are you?"

"Laura."

Star sprang away from Max's embrace as if she'd just

touched a live wire. She was trembling and swamped by feelings of guilt and something almost like fear. Max, on the other hand, seemed to be completely unfazed by the situation—although he did return to the desk and sit down. He made no attempt to answer Laura's call and, as though nothing had passed between them, repeated his question. "So why haven't you read *Satan's Daughter*?"

Before Star could gasp out any kind of explanation Laura sailed into the room. She was wearing a long dinner dress of deep midnight-blue crêpe, which outlined her figure and showed off her magnificent dark red hair to full advantage. A pearl choker circled her neck but otherwise, as always, she wore little jewelery apart from the diamond ring that winked from a long elegant finger. A long, long fox wrap circled her shoulders and swept down to the hem of her dress. She looked wonderful.

"Oh, there you are," she said to Max, giving no sign of being aware of Star's presence. "We must go or we'll be late."

Max did not even glance in her direction. "Well," he said to Star, "why haven't you read it?" He sounded like a school teacher asking a pupil why she hadn't done her homework.

"Read what?" Laura asked.

"A book of mine," Max replied, still looking at Star, his tone implying that the question had nothing to do with Laura.

"Satan's Daughter?" Laura inquired, studiedly casual.

Max now seemed interested. "Right."

"I've been reading it. Fascinating. What an understanding of women you do have."

"Had I wanted you to read it, I would have given it

to you. I particularly wanted Star's reaction—not yours."

"Did you now? I had no idea you valued her literary opinion so highly." She addressed Star for the first time. "It's in my room if you want to get it."

"I don't." Incensed by this conversation the two of them were having over her head, Star now felt quite cool and composed. "As I have already explained I have no interest in the book. When you've finished it, Laura, will you please return it to Max?"

She turned and started to leave the room. Laura stopped her. "You'll be on your own this evening, Star. You'll have to fix yourself something to eat."

Star stopped and turned, surprised. "Suki didn't say she was going out this evening."

"Suki is no longer here."

"What?"

"I let her go."

"What?"

"I gave her the sack. The push. Fired her—you know."

"Why? She was great."

"I don't like servants who take time off without permission."

"But I told you that was my fault. And she's not a servant."

"She shouldn't have gone shopping with you. I didn't employ her to be your companion."

"Where has she gone to? She has no family here."

"That's really not my concern. I gave her a month's wages. She'll be all right, that one."

"Well, I think it's bloody terrible!" Star blazed. "To throw someone out just because . . ."

"To be honest with you, Star, I'm not too awfully interested in what you think. This is my home, and not only do I choose who works here but I pay them." She did not add that she also paid for Star's keep but this was certainly implied. Before Star could reply Laura added, "And, by the way, could you ask that American boyfriend of yours to go easy on the flowers? The place is beginning to look like a funeral parlor." With a peremptory "Come on, Max. We're late," she left the room.

Star was almost crying with suppressed fury; with outrage at Laura's intolerable treatment of Suki and her display of undisguised bitchiness toward herself in front of Max. She looked at him, her eyes wide with hurt and anger, resentful that he, after what had just passed between them, had not defended her against her mother, and half hopeful that now he would show some sympathy toward her.

His expression was enigmatic, the eyes slightly narrowed and thoughtful as if he had just been watching a scene in a film. But there was no sign of sympathy. No concern.

With a gesture she knew to be childish, Star turned her back on him. Whatever happened she wasn't going to let him enjoy her distress.

"Don't let it upset you," he said, his voice low and strangely soothing. "We must talk, Star," he added.

"Not if I can help it," she spat out between clenched teeth.

Laura called from the hall, impatient, demanding. "Max, come on."

"Go along," Star hissed. "The boss is calling you."

With a sound that could have been a chuckle, she heard Max leave the room and join Laura in the hall. She heard the front door slam behind them as they left the flat. Only then did she realize that her fingernails were digging deep into her palms. Only then did she allow the tears to flow. Not sure exactly why she was crying, whether for Laura's lack of maternal affection, which had always demolished her and apparently still could, or for Max's apparently selfish, superficial use of her, it was hard to tell. Her one overwhelming emotion was the need to escape. To get as far away as possible from both Laura and Max. They could have each other and welcome. She must get out. For good.

Sir Len and Lady Latham did not often give parties. Not the big, swish, hyped-up type affairs that had everything to do with self-promotion and ego trips and nothing to do with the meeting of creative minds and inborn talents. Mostly Len and Ruby entertained in their over-decorated house in London's exclusive St. John's Wood. Their Sunday evenings were famous. Whoever was in town from New York or Los Angeles was there. Whoever was of interest in the current London show-business scene was there. Most of all who was who in television was there. A spurious homely atmosphere prevailed at these Sunday get-togethers, unlike the impersonal mass of extroverts gathered for the glittering occasion at which Harry now found himself: City TV's annual get-together, held in the banqueting suite of London's swankiest Thames-side hotel.

"Mr. Harry Conrad," the footman announced in stentorian tones that Harry felt sure must be heard half-way to Greenwich.

"Harry!" Len greeted him, arms outstretched as if to encompass a long-lost brother. "Wonderful to see you."

Harry resisted the temptation of reminding him it was only two days since they had met and fenced over Laura and her future in *Harringtons*. Instead he smiled broadly and said, "Lennie! How are you?" Then turning to the plump blond figure of Lady Latham, he exclaimed, "Ruby! Gorgeous as ever."

To her credit, Ruby smiled and said, "I know. Curves are in this season."

They laughed, Ruby and Harry. Len didn't smile.
What was funny? He did so wish that Ruby was thin.
Nancy Reagan thin. Thin like the wife of a great and
important impresario's wife should be. Hell, what else
did she have to do with her time and his money?

A new arrival's name was announced and Len
switched the warm-welcome routine away from Harry
onto the newcomer. Harry drifted off into the crowd,
rejected a glass of champagne and managed to acquire
one of Perrier. He looked round at the sea of glitzy,
well-heeled, expensively accoutred, frenetic fantasy
makers, all vying with each other for maximum attention and the lenses of the media cameras. But he could
not find the one he was looking for—Laura.

For the last few years, ever since Vernon had taken
off, Harry had always accompanied Laura on these kind
of occasions. But now that smoothie, Max, had appeared on the scene and Harry had been denied that
privilege. He could have invited any number of attractive, ambitious young women to accompany him tonight, but it would have entailed spending the evening
trailing round while whoever it was did her best to cash
in on the moment and meet everyone useful and influen-
tial among the other guests. That, Harry felt, he could
do without.

Not that he was alone for long. Well liked and well
known in the business, he was soon greeted and kissed
and chatted at, but his eyes didn't stray long from the
door. Waiting. Watching. Not only because he was, as
always, impatient to see the one woman he really cared
for, but also to see how Len would behave toward her.

"Miss Laura Denning and Mr. Donald Maxwell,"
the footman announced, and Laura, looking magnificent and with that amazing trick of seeming to be illuminated by some hidden inner flame, made her entrance. Max followed at a discreet distance.

Len greeted her effusively. "Laura! My favorite actress!" Kissing her warmly on her cheek he then held her at arm's length and gazed at her with deep and solemn admiration. "You look fantastic, darling. As always. Never do you look less than great."

Harry sipped nervously at his Perrier water and thought, Bastard. She's for the chop all right or he wouldn't be this fulsome. Len didn't hand out compliments as a rule. Only when he was preparing someone for the slaughter.

Laura seemed unaware of this and basked in the flattery. Harry disengaged himself from the group he was talking to and edged his way over toward Laura and Max just as they were being royally dismissed from the Great Presence.

Laura seemed genuinely glad to see him, and as she closed in to peck him on the cheek Harry could see lines of strain round her carefully made-up eyes and mouth. He greeted Max with a polite lack of enthusiasm, which Max returned.

Laura and Max were served champagne and the three of them stood for a while, engaged in somewhat desultory conversation. Harry noticed that out of the whole yattering, manic crowd, many of whom worked with Laura and knew her well, none seemed interested in coming to greet her. The word must have got out. Even the slightest suggestion of failure made you about as popular as a leper. Best look the other way and keep your distance, else who knows? It could be catching.

Sylvester Chance and wife Yvonne were going through the greetings routine with Len and Ruby, and then, as more guests were announced, eagerly moved off into the crowded room.

It was quite impossible for them not to notice Laura, and Yvonne, who had always professed the greatest admiration for the star of *Harringtons*, greeted her warmly. Yvonne Chance was thin and very intense, an artist by profession who painted rather bad abstract paintings that to everyone's surprise sold well. She always seemed to have difficulty in controlling her long raven-black hair however many pins or combs she used in the effort, and she dressed as though she had just grabbed the first thing that came to hand in her wardrobe. She now wore an unsuitable Laura Ashley dress with high neck and leg-o-mutton sleeves. There was a small tear at the hem, which she either hadn't noticed or hadn't bothered with.

"Laura, how very nice to see you."

Laura smiled and returned the greeting. She liked Yvonne and felt sorry for her.

Sylvester, who had been aiming to bypass Laura in order to trap other, more rewarding guests, now realized he was caught and, turning to her, said, "Laura, darling!" as though she was the very last person he could possibly have expected to see. He kissed her and told her how lovely she looked, and Laura introduced Max to Yvonne, and they all stood grouped together, apparently quite at ease and with the greatest possible friendliness, talking and joking. Only Sylvester's butterball eyes darting furtively over the assembled gathering of TV notables revealed how eagerly he wanted to escape. Perhaps if he had been a little more aware of his immediate circle he would have noticed who was just joining it.

"Hello, Laura darling. You look fabulous."

Diane Bennet, skillfully dressed in pink chiffon that managed to look both innocent and sexy, kissed the air by Laura's cheek. In tow she had a young actor who occasionally appeared in *Harringtons* and who was a well-known homosexual. Sylvester must have fixed her up with him for the evening while he had to be on display with his wife, certain that Diane would be safe in these hands. Laura smiled, apparently relaxed and gracious, as she greeted them. Sylvester glanced nervously at Yvonne. But if the lady was aware of the liaison between her husband and the delectable Diane, she certainly wasn't letting on. She told Diane how much she enjoyed her performance in the program, and Diane said how much she would like to come to Yvonne's next exhibition. Sylvester laughed rather loudly for no reason and exhibited a kind of amorphous bonhomie. Had Laura not been the victim of this intrigue she would have enjoyed watching Sylvester's discomfort and Diane's mischief-making, but as it was it took all her self-control to remain civil and not throw her champagne over the two of them.

The situation was saved when a determined press photographer hustled Laura and Diane away to be photographed with Sir Len. Harry, like an anxious mother hen, followed them, prepared as always to protect his client's interests: no pushing Laura into the background while Diane hogged the camera. Not that he need have worried. Laura was not going to let herself be pushed. Not by some jumped-up little actress just out of drama school. Not by anybody.

"What a lovely child that little Diane is," Yvonne remarked to Max with every appearance of sincerity. Then added somewhat ambiguously, "My husband has such an eye for talent."

Sylvester let the observation slide, and muttering something about "circulating," took his wife's arm and propelled her away into the crowd, leaving Max alone, anonymous, content to observe these strangers as if he were a naturalist studying some rare and little-understood species.

"Donald Maxwell, right?"

Max was momentarily taken off guard. The tall, dark woman dressed in a black lurex flying suit seemed familiar, but before he could remember where he had met her she introduced herself.

"Dee Costatinos."

"Of course, I'm sorry."

"Why should you be? I like your books," she continued with her customary frankness. "Most especially the one about the witches."

"*Satan's Daughter*?"

"Yes. Terrific. You're a feminist, yes?"

"Am I? Perhaps."

"What are you doing in this *galère*? Not your scene."

"Nor yours."

"You're wrong. I love the sheer phony glitzering of the whole business. I was a slum child. I still get a kick out of all the ostentation. If you've got it—show it. Okay, it's vulgar, but who cares?"

Max laughed. He liked this woman. Liked her candor and the larger-than-life personality.

"I am here," he explained, "partly as amateur anthropologist but mainly to escort my friend, Laura Denning."

He looked over to where Laura was posing for photographers with Sir Len, who had one arm round her and the other around Diane. The very picture of harmonious professional camaraderie. No, Max decided, he didn't like the phoniness, he hated it. Star was right not to want to get involved with it.

"She's a good-looking woman." Dee had followed his gaze and was looking at Laura.

"Very."

"But the real extraordinary beauty is her daughter." Max looked at her sharply. "Star? You know her?"

"I spent the day photographing her."

"Did you now?"

"She has great potential. She is making love to the

camera, you know? And doesn't even realize she's doing it. That is a very rare gift."

"I wonder . . ." Max hesitated.

"Yes?"

"Might I see the photographs?"

Dee raised an amused eyebrow. "I thought it was the mother you were involved with."

Max smiled wryly. "I'm not 'involved' with anyone. But I should be interested to look at the girl's photographs, if you wouldn't mind."

"Give me a ring. Come to my studio."

"Thank you. And . . . I would prefer that Star doesn't know about this."

"Nor her mother?"

Max nodded with mock solemnity. "Correct."

Star tore open the door of the refrigerator and angrily examined the empty shelves. "Why is there never anything to eat in this blasted place?" Eggs. Couldn't live on eggs, and she was hungry. The store cupboard was more rewarding: tins of ham, sweet corn, even baked beans left from Jessie's housekeeping days. She grabbed them from the shelves and, slamming about with the opener, soon had a fry-up of some gooey mass worth God knows how many calories. Ketchup. Doorsteps of bread spread thick with butter. She settled eagerly at the kitchen table and tucked in. Her plate was half empty when she suddenly froze, fork in air, and whispered the dreaded word: "Binge."

This was it, then? The dieter's nightmare. That which leads to all kinds of dread diseases. Suddenly she didn't feel hungry anymore but at the same time terribly wanted to go on eating. Crazy. Just the way to defeat her aims, to spoil her one chance of escape. With an enormous effort of will she scraped the rest of the fry-up into the bin and ran the plate under the hot tap as if to destroy the evidence.

It didn't take a great psychologist to realize that she was reacting to a situation that she found almost impossible to face. She felt anger toward the mother she loved, and love toward a man she despised. It was enough to make anyone go on a binge. All she knew was that she must get away. But how? And where to?

She considered the possibility of various ex-school friends but dismissed that almost immediately. What school friends? She'd got on okay with most of them but none had ever been really close. She could not ring up any of the Sarahs or Carolines and say, "Look—I need a bed and no questions asked." Having a show business background made her something of an oddity—even "fun"—but not "one of them." For the first time Star acknowledged the fact that she really didn't belong anywhere and it wasn't a feeling that she enjoyed. Which led back to Gary and all he had to offer. But it was no use, she couldn't kid herself and she knew that she must stop kidding him. The emotions that Max was capable of arousing in her meant she couldn't even consider marrying someone else. It would be a con. A cheat. No, somehow she must just stick it out here in what she used to think of as her home until she could make a go of modeling.

The prospect no longer appalled her. The session with Dee had built up her self-confidence. If the pics turned out okay and Dee was willing to take her on, then she would give it the works. Forget about everything else. Including Max. Most especially Max. But first of all she must settle things with Gary.

Determinedly she started to stab out his California number—then stopped. What would she say? "Sorry, love, but I've met this self-centered, arrogant S.O.B.

and although I can't stand the sight of him he turns me on, whereas you don't."

She replaced the receiver. It was no use. How can you make a Dear John phone call? She'd have to write to him. She'd be able to explain in a letter. But at the third attempt she realized that a letter was no easier than a phone call. He was a marvelous person and she was going to hurt him. And anyway, was she totally, completely sure that she didn't want Gary? Was a career as a model really so desirable? In the short term perhaps, but as a plan for her whole future? But then wouldn't she just be using him? Not really. No. As soon as she could get away from Max, which was going to be as from now, she would get over all this nonsense and then she might regret having lost Gary. Slowly she screwed up the letter and threw it with her other efforts into the wastebasket. She suddenly felt overwhelmingly tired and decided to sleep on it.

But sleep was something that didn't come easily. However hard she tried she could not help but relive what had happened between her and Max earlier in the evening. Could find no way to stop the excitement that memory evoked in her. Neither cold shower nor warm milk helped to calm her, and she lay in the darkened room listening to a late night phone-in on the radio. But other people's problems did little to assuage her own.

At around two A.M. she heard the front door open and close. She strained her ears, listening for voices, but heard nothing. Laura had come home alone. Within minutes Star was fast asleep.

7

If Star had made up her mind to keep out of Laura and Max's way, they could hardly have been more cooperative. As if by mutual agreement she saw little of Laura and nothing of Max.

Laura had her breakfast in her bedroom and when she returned from work went early to bed. When they did meet they were icily polite. Laura showed no interest in how Star occupied her time, or indeed in whether she was at home or not. She seemed to have withdrawn from all involvement in Star's life—not that she had ever had that much, Star thought with a trace of bitterness.

As for Max, either he timed his visits to the flat for when Star was absent or he had stopped coming altogether. But however much she longed to know, the last person she would ever ask was Laura. No way was she going to give her that satisfaction.

With her customary efficiency Laura had replaced Suki in no time flat. The new housekeeper was English. "At least she can answer the phone, which is more than that Oriental nit ever could," Laura observed. Her name was Mrs. Foskett. She reminded Star of a female impersonator; a sort of malevolent Dame Edna Everage. Big and bony, with iron-gray hair and iron-gray eyes to match, she hastened to inform anyone who cared to listen that she was used to housekeeping in the homes of titled folk, and suggested that the present setup was a big comedown for her. She and Star disliked each other on sight. But she ran the place efficiently and made excellent scrambled eggs, so Laura at least seemed satisfied.

Star still felt badly about Suki's unjust dismissal but realized that it would be useless to try and chase her up as well as Jessie. She had no idea where the girl might be and had no time to try and find out.

Time was something Star now felt she had too little of. She knew what she wanted and was prepared to spend every minute of the day and all her energies getting it. There were more photographic sessions and Dee worked her hard. Any illusions she might have had about modeling being easy were soon disabused. Dee could be exacting, intolerant, moody, and something of a slave driver—but okay, Star knew she was learning all the time and was lucky to have such a fantastic teacher. The first time Dee showed her the contact sheets of her pics Star felt she was looking at a stranger. All those shots—page after page of them. Yes, that was her all right: her features, her hair, her body, but there was something there that seemed almost alien. Yet this was the element that Dee wanted to bring out.

After every session when the contact sheets were developed she would go through them with Star, showing her which were good and which, as she put it, were

"Blotty ta-arrible, dolink. Ee-eek! Look at this, for chrissake. You look like a constipated eel. . . . And this! Horrible! A little typist what has won the pools. No good, dolink. And this . . . !" Star waited for the ax to fall again, but Dee drew in her breath. "For this every last thing is to be borne. Absolute! Now, do you know why this is a constipated eel and this one perfection?"

Star had to admit that she had no idea.

"Because here (the eel) you are pushing and forcing, and here (perfection) you are yourself. Just you and the camera. Like being with a lover who knows how to give you orgasm. Understand?"

Star wasn't sure that she did but she nodded her head. She didn't fool Dee. "I think perhaps you haven't met such a lover yet?"

Star shrugged. "I . . . I, er . . ." She was suddenly embarrassed.

Dee laughed. "If he doesn't show up soon I may have to see to it myself. But I have an idea he might . . . quite soon." She smiled a knowing smile as if she was in on some secret that Star knew nothing of, but felt somehow concerned her. She abruptly changed the subject and returned to the photographs.

After a few more studio sessions Dee took her out on location: in the park, on the river, draped round famous monuments. Once on a wild deserted Norfolk beach. That had been tough. A wicked nor'easter straight from Siberia blew wet sand over everything, including Star. Dee was in a vile mood and insisted on including shots of Star with assorted, highly uncooperative wildlife. Oddly enough the pictures resulting from this agonizing experience were the best yet. Dee studied them carefully. "You have many wild parts," she finally proclaimed. "But you go to a lot of trouble to keep them hidden."

Star felt rather alarmed at the thought of these "wild parts" but knew that Dee was right. She only had to think of Max and they came surging up inside her and all she could do was go for yet another run around the park or take yet another cold shower. Only by packing her days so full that there was not a moment to spare could she hope to wipe out the memory of being in his arms.

The nights were something else again. However tired she was, his image, his scent, his persona was there as though it were part of her. She longed to be free of what she felt to be a kind of horribly undignified subjugation. To be obsessed with someone you despise is truly degrading and she hated him for it.

When she wasn't being photographed she worked constantly on herself. Dee had told her that her face and body were her sales merchandise.

"Like the latest model automobile is for Fords or her dress collection for Zandra Rhodes. It's what you put in the shop window, and it's got to be the best if not better. Okay?"

And the top meant independence.

With almost fanatical dedication Star worked at getting herself in peak condition. A diet of six hundred calories a day, mostly raw fruit and vegetables. Exercising every morning, which she hated, but forced herself to do religiously—quite apart from a couple of hours' running. She gave herself facials in order to improve a skin that was already well nigh perfect and experimented with makeup, learning from Dee's makeup expert, and tried her hair every which way. All this she did with determined objectivity, like training a racehorse for the Derby—a horse that was going to win.

On days when she wasn't working with Dee she went to work out at Body Time—a dance studio/gym. It was here that she met Annie.

Annie Jardine was thirty-two years old, an ex-ballet dancer turned instructor, with the figure of a skinny teenager. A small, birdlike face dominated by huge brown eyes. Long straight hair scraped back into a topknot, revealing a high wide forehead.

"I don't really have features," she said, "just an expression."

In fact, a whole series of expressions, mostly humorous, always lively and intelligent.

Star liked Annie right from the start and the feeling was obviously mutual. Soon they formed an easy, casual friendship. Annie talked readily about herself and told Star how her marriage had come apart and ended in divorce; then how her long-standing relationship with an artist had also ended up on the rocks. "I just have a nontalent where men are concerned. Oh, well, got my cats so what the hell."

Star was tempted to confide her problems but something stopped her. To talk of Laura and Max to anybody except possibly Jessie seemed disloyal and, well, it was sort of a tacky situation—one she was trying hard to forget. But she did tell Annie about her hopes for modeling and how much she wanted to become independent and live her own life. Annie nodded. "Living at home is impossible—however fond you may be of your parents." Star nodded in agreement and left it at that.

Annie was a tough taskmaster. Anyone who wasn't giving full out could forget it. But Star loved her classes. At first she'd had a few aches and pains but she soon learned how to cope with them and found that after working-out she was on a positive high. Also, while she was bending and bouncing to the disco beat she could put Max completely out of her mind. Just concentrate on her own body and her control over it.

After class everyone showered and changed and usually gathered in the bar for fresh orange juice, which

Annie said was a must: "Replaces potassium and other vital trace elements." But on one particular day Star found the bar was practically empty.

"Where is everyone?" she asked Annie, who was perched on a stool behind the bar.

"Wednesday," Annie said as if that explained everything.

"Sorry?"

"Matinée day for most of the kids."

"You mean they work out here and then do two shows?"

"Total dedication, my love. The only way. Slip just a little and you're out."

Star sipped her orange juice thoughtfully. "Too right," she said, thinking of Laura.

Annie topped up her glass. "How are the sessions with Dee going?" she asked.

"Okay, I guess. She's getting some pretty fantastic pics. I sort of find it difficult to relate to that girl in the photographs. She doesn't seem like the real me."

"Still expecting to see Podge?" Star had told Annie about her schoolgirl weight problem.

"Could be." Star grinned. "I sometimes suspect she's still inside there somewhere, fighting to get out."

"Tell her we won't let her," Annie said firmly. "Listen, you in a hurry to get anywhere? Now, I mean."

Star shook her head. "No plans."

"What say I fix us a salad, then?"

Star accepted readily. She had no wish to get back to the increasingly uncongenial atmosphere at home. Without realizing she was doing so, she sighed. Annie, feeding carrots and celery into the food processor, gave her a penetrating glance. "Something wrong?" she asked.

"Not especially. Why?"

"Such a deep sigh. Having problems with Mum?"

"Some . . . and this housekeeper we've got is a real pain."

"Housekeeper? What's a housekeeper?"

"Okay, I know. I'm meant to feel lucky that I have someone to fetch and carry, but honestly, Annie, who needs it? I suppose that's selfish. My mother couldn't do her work and take care of the home."

"Lots of women do."

"She's not like other women. And she does work full out. Talk about dedicated. . . ." She didn't finish the sentence. She was aware of a tone of bitterness and resentment coming into her voice and she didn't want to show these feelings to anyone. Not even someone as understanding as Annie.

There was a pause while Annie switched off the machine and scraped the grated vegetables into a bowl. She frowned thoughtfully. Then she said, "I've been thinking . . . here I am, now that my gentleman is no longer living-in—or even living, as far as I know—with a spare room. So why don't you come and fill the space?"

Star looked at Annie, her eyes bright with excitement. "Move in with you? Honest?"

"If you'd like to, that is," Annie added somewhat tentatively.

"Like to?" Star's voice jumped an octave. "It would be fantastic, Annie. Just brilliant. Oh, but . . ." She broke off suddenly, deflated.

"But what?"

"I'm not earning. I only have an allowance from my father—I know, I know, 'What's an allowance?' but it's not enough to live on in London, and I can't stay with you unless I pay rent."

"So long as you can pay your way and don't make too many long-distance calls . . ."

Star grinned. "If I do, I'll make them collect."

"When the modeling jobs start pouring in you can give me something toward the mortgage."

"Perhaps I could get a part-time job—in a pub or something."

Annie shook her head firmly. "Uh-huh. You're onto a good thing. Stick to it, girl, and no messing about in bad atmospheres getting circles under your eyes."

The telephone rang and Annie lifted the receiver. "Body Time," she sang into the mouthpiece. "Who? Oh, yes, she's right here." She held the receiver out to Star and whispered, "I think it's Dee Costatinos."

"Hullo, beautiful child," Dee's gravelly voice greeted Star. "You get yourself over here, okay." It was an order, not a request.

"But, Dee," Star protested, "I've just done a workout . . . my hair . . . and I only have a tracksuit with me . . ."

"Did I ask what you look like? I got something for you. A surprise. So hurry." And without waiting for an answer or any good-byes she hung up, leaving Star with no alternative but to forgo her salad and do as Dee had commanded.

Annie slapped some salad between two pieces of whole-wheat bread.

"Here. Eat in the taxi."

"Thanks, I will, and to hell with the calories. And, Annie, I'll ring you tonight about the room, or we'll talk tomorrow. I think it's a terrific idea. Just hope you'll be able to put up with me."

"We'll get along fine. Oh, just one thing."

"What?" Star asked anxiously.

"I hope you like cats."

"Mad about them."

"Good. I have three."

* * *

Dee was sitting cross-legged on the floor surrounded by contact sheets. She gave Star the merest glance as she entered the room, then held out an envelope and waved it at her.

"Here. This is for you."

Star took the envelope, completely bewildered. "What is it?"

"You want to know, open it. I'm busy." And she returned to checking through the rows of minute pictures on the sheets.

Star opened the envelope and drew out a piece of paper folded neatly in two. As she went to examine it another piece of paper fluttered to the floor.

"For chrissakes," Dee said without interrupting her work. "Don't throw it around. Not after what we went through on that freezing Arctic bloody beach."

What had fallen to the ground was a check. Star picked it up and examined it. It was made out to her for the sum of two hundred and fifty pounds. She stared at it in disbelief.

"I . . . I don't understand."

"I didn't tell you in case it didn't work, but that session on that godforsaken North Pole was a commission. I showed the agency some of your other pics and they liked the look of you so we all decided to take a risk. Now they are crazy for you." She stressed the "they" as if to infer that she herself was none too pleased. "I say the birds are not bad."

Star let out a whoop of delight and impulsively flung herself down beside Dee and gave her a hug.

"Watch it, dolink." Dee grinned and pinched Star's face as she might a child's. "You know my reputation."

"Yes, I do." Star looked straight at Dee with eyes wide. "That you're a bully and a tyrant and the most wonderful guy anyone could ever want to work for."

Then, without a trace of embarrassment, she gave Dee another great hug.

Dee laughed and yelled, "Katy, come quick. This crazy one is trying to seduce me."

"About time somebody did," Katy cracked as she came into the room.

"There's some champagne in the fridge," Dee said. "Bring it, lover, and some glasses."

Katy dutifully trotted off to do as she was bid.

Dee looked at Star appraisingly from under her heavy lids. "So," she said, "you are now a model. Does it hurt?"

"It feels great. This is the first money I ever earned in my life."

"No fooling. Me, I start earning when I am six. If you call stealing fruits off barrows in the market and selling them cut price to the housewives 'earning.' "

Star laughed. "What did the stall holders say?"

"They never could catch me. I am too smart. I had to be. Not a spoiled little chicken like you."

Star frowned. For the second time that day someone had suggested that she was privileged. "I'm not spoiled, Dee," she protested. "Really not. At least, I don't feel I am."

"Well, if you're not you should be." Dee laughed, so avoiding a conversation that seemed in danger of becoming too serious. She made it a rule never to get involved with her models' personal problems. It interfered with the working relationship and to Dee, that was what mattered.

Star sensed the withdrawal and felt she had made a mistake. Things were going so well; whatever happened she mustn't do anything to put Dee off. "Well," she said, keeping her tone light, "what next?"

Dee considered before replying. "How would a *Vogue* feature grab you?"

Star gulped. "*Vogue*? But, Dee, how?"

"Marcus Fletcher. They're doing a piece on him and his clothes."

"Marcus Fletcher?" Star felt stunned. "But . . ."

"He's a pushy little swisher but he does design some incredible garments. They can overwhelm some girls but they won't overwhelm you, wild one."

"But I've never modeled clothes—let alone Marcus Fletcher's," Star protested.

"Stop squawking," Dee commanded. "If you say you will—then you will."

Star's immediate reaction was to protest at being taken over. She was fighting to become her own person. She wasn't aiming to substitute one kind of dependence for another. But immediately she rejected the thought. She was learning a profession, a skill, and all thanks to this brilliant woman who was prepared to take a risk on her. She was darn lucky to have the chance. It was up to her to make the most of it.

Just then Katy came in the with champagne. Jan opened and poured. They toasted Star's official status as a model and then the four of them sat around, sipping and chatting and laughing, and, rather to her surprise, Star realized how much she enjoyed the company of these highly unconventional women.

Suddenly Dee jumped up. "Enough fun time. I have work to do. And you, little shooting Star, get plenty of rest. You must be fit and strong. In a few days you have fittings with Marcus Fletcher. Then you find out what is hard work!"

As she walked home past the brightly lit shops of the Kings Road, past the swirl of Sloane Square and up the more sober Sloane Avenue toward Belgravia Place, Star felt quite lightheaded. Nor was it just due to the champagne. That slip of paper in her shoulder bag meant more to her than just the fact of the money. It meant that someone thought enough of her to pay for what she did in hard cash. That she really did have a career ahead of her and was not just some whim of Dee's. All this and Annie's offer of a new home meant that at last she could stop being Laura Denning's funny little daughter and could start to be . . . well, Star.

The thought of Laura brought her sharply down to earth and deflated the euphoric mood. The habits of a lifetime couldn't be shed that quickly and the prospect of telling her mother that not only was she launched as a professional model but that she was about to move out filled her with apprehension. Still, it had to be done. With shoulders squared she put the key in the latch and opened the front door of the apartment, prepared to face Laura and tell her everything.

Instead she came face to face with Max.

He stood in the open doorway. They looked at one another in shocked silence for a moment, each deeply aware of the other. Before Star could speak he took her by the shoulders. Gazing intently into her eyes, he said, "Listen to me. Get away from here. Away from all the phony values, the ego trips, the total lack of human empathy. You're a very special person. You must give yourself a chance to grow in a real, constructive environment. I don't suppose I shall see you again, which is regrettable—at least to me. Good-bye, Star."

"Good-bye? But why?" Star whispered. "I don't . . . !"

Before she could say any more Max took her in his arms and kissed her. Star felt the world revolve at twice its normal speed and then fire broke out in the pit of her stomach. Abruptly, without another word, he pushed past her and was gone. She wanted to call after him but felt too stunned to utter. What on earth could have happened to make him speak and act this way? She was physically shaking as she turned to go into the flat. It was then that she became aware of Mrs. Foskett standing in the hall, watchful as a cat with a bird. She must have witnessed the whole thing. "You're wanted on the phone, miss," she said, stony-faced.

With a supreme effort Star managed to control her feelings. "Thank you, Mrs. Foskett."

"And madam said for you to go to her when you got home." Then, unable to keep the relish out of her voice, the housekeeper added, "She seems rather upset."

Star took the phone call in the study in such a state of emotional tumult from her encounter with Max that she could hardly steady her hand enough to pick up the receiver. Her throat felt constricted and when she spoke her voice sounded strained and husky. "Hello," she breathed.

The woman's voice on the other end of the line was barely more audible than her own. "Is . . . is that Miss Merrick?" she asked timorously.

Star said that it was. This was followed by a brief silence, after which the woman nervously cleared her throat. "I . . . that is . . . this is Beryl Benson speaking . . ."

The name meant nothing to Star. Probably some fan of Laura's. They sometimes rang despite her being unlisted. This she really could not cope with right now and was about to make some excuse and hang up when the woman continued, "I believe . . . that is, a friend of mine said you were looking for Mrs. Cozzey."

For a moment the name didn't register and then, "Gertie!" Star shouted. "You know where she is?"

"Well, I've got her new address. She used to be my neighbor, you see. Then yesterday my friend, who bought her house off her, found your phone number that she'd written down, and said you were looking for Mrs. Cozzey so I thought . . ."

Now gaining confidence she went into convoluted details to which Star paid scant attention. Of course—it all fell into place. This must be the tardy Beryl whom Gertie's successor had been so angry with. What a bit of luck! With all thought of Max and Laura momentarily banished, she eagerly scribbled down the address. "And the phone number?" she asked.

"Don't know that, I'm afraid," Beryl said. "Perhaps information?"

Oh well, can't have everything. "Thanks, anyway," Star said. "It was most kind of you to ring, Mrs. Benson."

"Miss," Beryl corrected her. "Miss Benson."

"Sure," Star said for no reason, and thanked her again. She was sincerely grateful. Perhaps Jessie wasn't lost to her after all.

Her first impulse was to try and find out the telephone number. It would be wonderful to hear Jessie's warm, reassuring voice. But it would have to wait. She felt she must go to Laura. Something awful must have happened for her to have let her feelings slip in front of that old battle ax, Foskett. Had she and Max quarreled? Max . . . The thought of him sent her pulse racing again but at the same time she felt anger and a kind of relief to know that he was out of her life.

She found Laura in her bedroom, sitting by the dressing table, furiously shredding sheets of manuscript and stuffing the pieces into the wastebasket at her feet. At first Star assumed she must be disposing of yet another unsatisfactory script, but a glance told her that this was not written in dialogue. It was narrative.

Without looking up Laura spoke through clenched teeth, her voice distorted with rage. "Bastard!" she spat. "Two-timing shit! You try to help someone and they thank you with a kick up the ass. I'd like to kill him, the . . ." She ran out of expletives, which was not like her, and Star realized just how desperately hurt and upset she must be. Obviously Max was the cause of this outburst, but why should he have ever wanted or needed help from Laura?

Star advanced cautiously into the room. "What's wrong?"

"This." Laura held the manuscript on high with a dramatic gesture and shook it like a tambourine. "All the work and effort and care I put in, and he comes up with the most revolting . . . insulting . . . libelous pack of lies—which, I might add, I am supposed to have written about myself. The 'truth.' The great 'self revelation.' With every bloody word he turns me into some kind of raging egomaniac. A ruthless bitch, only concerned with my career and my appearance and my own petty interests. And worst of all"—Star could hear tears in Laura's voice—"what really gets me hopping bloody mad, is the suggestion that I'm a selfish and uncaring mother. When everything I've ever done has been for you."

Star could think of nothing to say. Could only wonder what Max had written—it must tie in with what he'd said just minutes ago when they'd met in the doorway.

"Well?" Laura interrupted her thoughts, voice shrill. "Say something. I mean, you, if anyone, know the truth. Whatever I may or may not have been in my life, I have done my duty as a mother. I have no doubts on that score." She looked at Star, her eyes brimming with tears, demanding her daughter endorse this statement.

But Star found the words wouldn't come—the words she knew Laura expected to hear. "What . . . ?" she stammered. "That is, exactly what did he say?"

"You don't think I'd let you look at this filth, do you?"

"Surely, it can't be that bad—not if you were meant to have written it yourself."

"That's the worst thing about it! I've an idea he never intended me to use it. I think that for some sick, twisted reason of his own he just wanted to hurt me."

"Why on earth should he?"

"Probably because I didn't leap into bed with him."

"You didn't?" The words tumbled out eagerly before Star could stop them. But Laura seemed not to notice. Quickly assuming a casual air, Star said, "I thought . . . well . . ."

"So did everybody. Okay, I wasn't bothered. Doesn't hurt to have something young and dishy in tow. Maybe I did fancy him for a moment but . . . well, there's never really been anyone for me but your father."

Star only half believed this but said nothing.

"No," Laura continued, "it was a purely business arrangement. A collaboration on my book. I can't write so I was to put it on tape and then he'd write it for me. Well, for weeks and weeks he did nothing. Not a word. Then after the night of Len's party he vanishes. Not a peep do I hear. Can't get him on the phone. He doesn't call me. I was really worried. You know how concerned I get . . . how involved with people who are part of my life, for whatever odd reason. I was on the verge of going to the police . . . you know what I'm like, Starlet . . . I sort of over-identify." She broke off, seeming, in the midst of this recitation of her humanitarian attitudes, to have lost track of what she wanted to say.

Star prompted her: "Then what?"

"You may well ask." Laura let out a bitter laugh worthy of the scorned wife in some old-fashioned melodrama. "Suddenly, today, out of the blue he turns up with this. . . ." She ripped the remaining pages of the offending manuscript in half and consigned them to the basket. "And—to show you just what a kinky sadist he is—he sat there and watched me while I read it. When I wanted to stop he insisted I continue right to the end. Bastard!"

Star felt an irrational and almost uncontrollable urge to laugh. But then when Laura looked at her and Star saw the genuine bewildered hurt in her mother's wide green eyes, she could only feel pity. Nobody had ever done this to her before—not even Vernon. Nobody had ever openly questioned her egocentric behavior or her total self-absorption and now she felt it as an undeserved and intolerable insult.

Laura ranted on, railing against Max and against men in general. Star only half listened. Max's effort to make Laura see herself as she really was had been totally wasted. Laura didn't believe a word of it. Again Star remembered what he'd said to her earlier—that she was a special person, that she should give herself a chance to grow. Well, she doubted the "special" bit though certainly she knew she must make her own life. But this was not the moment. How could she say she was leaving with Laura in such a desperate state? And then she realized that once again she was humoring her mother, putting her needs and demands before her own.

Laura suddenly noticed that Star had gone very quiet. That she was not trotting out the customary words of comfort and reassurance.

"Why are you staring at me like that?" she asked.

"I didn't realize I was."

Laura sighed. A deep sigh of fathomless self-pity. "I suppose it was too much to expect you to understand how I feel."

"Oh . . . but I do."

"Thank you, darling," Laura said, completely missing the irony in Star's voice. "You are a great comfort to me, you do know that, don't you? And . . . well, obviously Mr. Max Macdonald or whatever he calls himself was a serious mistake. Good riddance, I say."

Star said nothing.

"I shall forget all about him," Laura continued. "He never existed. I'm glad he's gone. Very glad. I wouldn't have put it past him to try to make out with you. I mean, all that carrying you off to his cottage against your will. . . ."

"You make it sound like an abduction."

"Well, I was very worried . . . for you, I mean."

"Oh, Laura, honestly, you talk as if I were a child. I can look after myself."

"Darling, you must bear with me. I do try not to be the clingy, doting mum, but when everyone lets you down, you hang onto the one person you've always been closest to."

Laura gave Star the full benefit of her wonderful smile, the smile that had always beguiled and dazzled her—but which now suddenly left her cold, remembering a childhood in which a "doting, clingy mum" had certainly never figured.

"Sure," she said without much conviction, and from sheer force of habit pecked at Laura's proffered cheek. Laura seemed reassured.

"Tell you what," Laura said with sudden childlike enthusiasm, "let's spend the evening together watching telly. Just the two of us. Like in the old days."

Star couldn't recall any such "old days" but let it pass. "Okay. Fine."

Laura gave a little squeal of delight. "That will be gorgeous. We'll get old hatchet-face to make us some scrambled eggs. She may be a pain but she does make the best scrambled eggs ever."

"Better than Jessie's?"

A look of such bereft misery crossed Laura's face that Star immediately regretted having mentioned her name.

"Jessie," Laura spoke her name softly. "You know, I still can't believe that she deserted me."

"*She* deserted you? I thought it was you who gave her the push."

"I suppose there were faults on both sides. It was that bloody Max. He mixed it between us."

Star found this hard to believe, but it no longer seemed important to argue about it. Laura shrugged as if determined to shake off thoughts she found painful. "Oh, well, all gin under the bridge now, isn't it? Let's see what's on." She picked up an evening paper and riffled through the pages, looking for the TV schedule. "And let's open a bottle of champagne. There's one in the fridge. About the only thing I'll miss about Max—he did open a neat bottle of fizz. Never mind, it's time you learned. Get it, will you, love?"

Star stood without moving. Anger flooded through her. Suddenly all the years of pandering to Laura's mercurial moods, of bending over backward to please her, trying desperately to gain her love and approval, seemed horribly wasted. Max had stood up to her and refused to be a lapdog and so had been discarded. Well, she too had come to the end of being a little echo, with no identity of her own.

Laura glanced up from the newspaper. "Go on, Starlet. Get the champers."

"No."

Laura blinked in total mystification. "What did you say?"

"I said no."

"Have you gone crazy or something?"

"On the contrary, Laura. I think I've just come to my senses."

"Well, do you think you could come to them over a drink? My tongue's hanging out."

This arrogant confidence in her power to charm anyone into doing her bidding with a joke or a smile left

Star cold. She knew the form too well. "I shan't be having a drink nor will I be watching telly with you."

"Please yourself."

"That's just what I intend to start doing, Mother."

Laura's nostrils flared at the hated word. "When have you ever done anything else?"

"I've spent my entire life trying to please you."

Laura let out a hoot of derision. "Oh, please. Do me a favor. You—the spoiled brat to end all spoiled brats. I suppose I should have known you'd grow up into a selfish—"

"Let's not have the 'after all I've done for you' bit."

Laura flung aside the newspaper and dramatically ran her fingers through her hair. "I was determined you shouldn't have the sort of childhood I had—having to count every penny. I wanted the best for you, and now what do I get?"

"You get a daughter who's a stranger because you made her into one. For Christ's sake, just for once try to be honest about yourself."

"He's been getting at you, hasn't he? That shit, Max."

"No. Of course not."

"I begin to see it now. There has been something going on between the two of you. You're stuck on him, aren't you?"

"No . . . I don't know."

Suddenly Star found herself on the defensive. The moment had been snatched from her and Laura was in command. "I could have taken a lot, Star but not that you should be this disloyal. You thought he was my boyfriend and yet you went behind my back and . . ."

"No. That's not true. I admit I found him attractive, and perhaps he felt that way too, but there was nothing . . . wrong."

Laura looked at Star with something near to hatred in her eyes. "I don't believe you," she hissed.

"But it's true," Star protested.

"I think I'd like you out of here," Laura said, her voice ice cold. "You say I'm such a rotten mother, well, whatever I may or may not be, I'm always loyal to those I love—which is more than you can say. I despise you. I don't want you in my life if this is how you behave. Get out. See how well you manage on your own."

Star couldn't believe what was happening. She'd actually decided to tell Laura that she was leaving and now somehow Laura had taken over and was ordering her out. Before she could reply she was, quite literally, saved by the bell. The telephone bell.

Laura held up a hand in an overlarge gesture of command. "Don't move. I'd hate to ask you to perform such a degrading task as answering the phone." She lifted the receiver. "Yes?" she snapped. "Yes. Speaking."

Star watched Laura's expression change. As she listened to whoever was on the telephone, the cold hard lines of anger dissolved into an expression of near panic. Then, pulling herself together, she said, "Right. Thank you. I'll be ready." She slammed down the receiver. "Christ Almighty, I totally forgot. This is your fault. You and that sod Max. I'm supposed to be going with Harry to a premiere. The car will be here in fifteen minutes to pick me up."

"Don't go."

Laura, who was already halfway to the wardrobe to select a dress, threw Star a look of total noncomprehension. "What are you talking about?"

"I thought we were having an important discussion. It affects both our lives. Tell Harry you can't go."

"Are you mad? This is a big occasion. There's press laid on. Photographers. We're going to a party afterward. I can't miss out on that." She opened the closet door and tore down a black chiffon evening gown. She examined it as if it were a rag and discarded it in favor of an outrageous creation covered with scarlet bugle beads. "Tonight I'm going to make a splash."

"And you still try to tell me that what I feel matters to you?"

"Oh, be your age. Whatever it is that's screwing you up, surely it can wait."

"No, Laura," Star said quietly, "I don't think it can."

"Well, tough titty, kid," Laura said, seating herself at the dressing table and getting down to the business of a quick repair job on her face. "Apart from anything else," she continued, spreading on lavish layers of face cream, "I have to talk to Harry. It can't have escaped even your egotistical attention that things are not well at 'the store.' "

" 'The store,' 'the store' . . . all I ever hear about is the bloody store. What about real life?"

" 'The store' helped to bring you up in luxury and give you a first-class education. That you were too dim and too lazy to benefit from it is hardly my fault. Now get out and let me get on."

Fighting back tears of hurt and anger, Star ran from the room. Half an hour later she had packed her bags and was on her way, leaving behind the place she had always called home.

8

Annie's flat was on the top floor of a tall shabby house off Earl's Court Road. The scruffy-looking street could hardly have been in greater contrast to Belgravia Place nor could Annie's junk-shop-furnished home be less like the one Star was used to. Her bedroom was small and sparsely furnished, but what it lacked in comfort was more than made up for by the easy, relaxed atmosphere of the household and what was to Star the new and exhilarating experience of independence.

There were other first-time experiences too. Things that most other people take for granted as part of every-day life: doing their share of the housework, shopping for food, taking laundry to the Laundromat. Jessie might have taught her to pick up her clothes and put them away, but wash them? Maybe, she thought, Dee had been right to call her a "spoiled little chicken." In some ways she had been, but in others . . . but she refused to think about Laura. It made her too angry and yet at the same time, quite irrationally, guilty. For what? For actually standing up to her? For going her own way at long last? She didn't understand her feelings and didn't try to.

Putting Max out of her mind was not so easy. It was as though an awareness of him was always with her. In everything she did, from the most mundane household task to the most demanding of modeling sessions, somehow there he was. Only by exercising the strictest self-discipline did she stop herself from going to him wherever he might be. In a weaker moment she'd tried to find his London phone number but he wasn't in the book, nor could she track down the cottage. She realized she didn't even know its name. It's not meant to be, she told herself. She had to forget him. And so she did. Almost.

The nights were the worst. When she should have been asleep but instead was gazing out of the window of her little room at the yellow lights of London reflected in the dull slate sky, listening to the strident scream of police sirens, which seemed to be a regular feature of Earl's Court life, then the thoughts she successfully kept at bay during the day came flooding back to haunt her. An overwhelming longing that would not be appeased; to touch, to caress, to hold him close, close. If what had passed between them meant anything to him, why didn't he try to find her? He could quite easily. But he didn't. By now he'd probably forgotten her. Perhaps Laura had been right about him. How could she be sure? At such moments she felt terribly alone. Annie was great but somehow Star still didn't feel able to confide in her. Perhaps afraid to hear what she knew would be Annie's advice: "Forget him. Get on with your life and enjoy yourself."

Jessie? She'd been unable to find a telephone number

for Gertie and there'd been no reply to the letter she'd
written. Nor had there been any reply to another letter
she'd written—but that was understandable. Gary was
probably very hurt by the way she had behaved, and
who was to blame him? She'd been a coward not to
have told him sooner that she couldn't marry him after
all. But she'd had to be sure. Then suddenly she was.
Whatever the future might bring, whether Max was
part of it or not, she knew that marrying Gary would
have been dishonest and horribly unfair. She sighed and
closed the curtain. She got into bed and switched off the
light. She had to sleep. Tomorrow was the all important
session for *Vogue*. A great chance for her. One she was
determined not to miss.

As Dee had said, a lot of women would be swamped
by Marcus Fletcher's creations. They demanded someone of strong individuality and striking appearance to
compete with the outrageous colors, the jungle prints,
the lashings of embroidery, the oversize collars combined with minutest of skirts, the swirling capes, sleeves
that swept the floor, and evening skirts seven layers
deep. They should have been in the worst possible taste
but somehow they were the ultimate in high fashion.
Star adored them. She also took an enormous liking to
their creator as she stood for hours on end while he
supervised fittings.

He was not in the least as she had imagined a top
couturier to be. Looking younger than his thirty years,
he had an almost boyish personality. But let no one be
deceived by the mild manner—he was a perfectionist
who knew exactly what he wanted, and no one got away
with giving him anything but the best. He was delighted
with Star, the way a playwright falls for his leading lady
when she brings the character he has created to life.

"When I designed this," he said, draping a rich jewel-encrusted cloak around her shoulders, "I did it specially for you."

"But you didn't even know me," Star said.

"Which just shows that dreams do come true."

Star was nervous on the first day in the studio with Dee, but the clothes seemed to dictate how she should behave and, as always, Dee knew exactly how to get the best out of her. For nearly a week they worked flat out. They went on various locations, ranging from Dockland to Dover Castle. Star enjoyed every moment of it and felt sorry when Dee finally said, "Okay. Relax. Finish."

Star said, "Now what do I do?"

"Sleep."

"I mean work, Dee. You see, now that I'm living on my own I really need to earn. I can't just . . ."

Dee's brows gathered in a black scowl of disapproval. "You want to advertise cat food then get out of here and don't come back."

"Of course not, but . . ."

"One week you have to get yourself looking fantastic. Every model in London is doing her best for the Danielle contract and you talk shoddy little rubbish about making a few pennies. Listen, I tell you something. You think champagne, you'll drink champagne—you think beer, you drink beer."

"Okay, Dee," Star said meekly. "Point taken."

"So. Go away. Get some air. You look like boil fish."

Dee was right. Less than a week to the Danielle tests. Her reflection in the glass did show shadows under her eyes, and cheeks that lacked their customary glow. A few days in the country or by the sea would do wonders, but where? Then she thought of the perfect solution: Jessie. She was living in the country now, so what could be better than to have Jessie to pamper and pet her and listen to her problems?

Brookmead, Meadowvale Lane, Walston, near Ox-

ford. It sounded perfect. Jessie had to be there. She just
had to.

Star drove the hired car along the M40 with surprising
ease and confidence. It was over six months since she
had passed her test and she'd had hardly any practice
since, but she was a natural driver and found that it
gave her the most exhilarating sensation of freedom. It
was only unfortunate that the route she was on toward
Oxford was the old familiar way out to the television
studios, and she knew that she had only to take the
appropriate turning to reach Max's cottage.

But she wasn't going there, was she?

She stuck to the main road and concentrated on her
driving. Soon she was out in the open countryside. A
lemon-yellow sun shone valiantly in a pale eggshell-blue
sky, though it gave out little heat. She flicked on the car
radio and sang along with the music. "Love me again
. . . Love me . . ." Then Max was back in her
thoughts and she nearly missed her exit to Walston. Just
in time she drew over, signals flashing, into the narrow
side road. A truck driver whose path she crossed did
not seem best pleased. She grinned and waved, and
when he saw her he responded by giving her an appreciative thumbs-up sign.

At first glance Walston looked like the perfect English village. Tiny, cobbled high street with black and
white timbered houses leading to the village green complete with pond, ducks, willow tree, and all. Star
stopped and consulted the scrap of paper with Jessie's
address.

Brookmead, Meadowvale Lane, sounded lovely, but
when she finally tracked it down proved to be a semi-
detached bungalow in housing project of identical, char-
acterless boxes.

Thrilled at the thought of at last finding Jessie, Star

jumped out of the car and hurried up the flagstone path, banded on each side by platoons of brightly colored dahlias, to the front door. When she pressed the front doorbell and the opening bars of "There's No Business Like Show Business" chimed out, she knew she'd come to the right place. She waited then rang the "show business" chime again. The place seemed ominously quiet.

"Malta."

The voice came from the other side of the fence, from Brookmead's Siamese twin, and made Star jump. It belonged to a small, gnomelike, elderly man, dressed in overalls and carrying a paintbrush.

"I'm looking for Miss Raye or Mrs. Cozzey," Star said.

"Yes. I said, they've gone to Malta."

"Not for good?" Star asked anxiously.

"Holiday. They wanted to go to Spain but I said, 'Don't! Malta,' I said. Only foreign place you can get a decent cup of tea. I should know, I was there during the war. . . ."

"Do you know when they'll be back?" Star interrupted before the old gentleman could get launched into wartime reminiscences.

"Don't know exactly. They don't say much. Keep themselves to themselves. But they've been gone over a month . . . no, nearer two . . . I remember because it was a Tuesday and I always—"

"Thank you. I'll just write a note and put it through the letter box." Star scrabbled in her bag for pen and paper. The old neighbor watched her with interest. "You a relative?" he asked, his eyes bright with curiosity.

"Not exactly," Star replied as she wrote: "Dearest Jessie. So sorry to have missed you. Longing to see you. Am staying at—" She hesitated. So much had happened since last she had seen Jessie she couldn't explain it all in a note. She crossed out the last few words and just wrote her telephone number. Then added, "Please ring as soon as you can. I have so much to tell you. Love, Star."

"I'll give it to them if you like," the old neighbor offered, obviously dying to be in on things.

"Thanks all the same but it's okay." Star smiled. She folded the note and pushed it through the letter box.

Politely refusing the offer of coffee and a tour of his garden, Star got back in the car and with a friendly wave drove off, leaving the old gentleman staring after her, his curiosity unsatisfied.

She drove slowly back through the labyrinthine by-ways of the newly constructed housing project, uncomfortably aware of the rest of the day stretching emptily ahead. She felt what she recognized as an absurd sense of letdown at Jessie's absence. As though by rights the old lady should have been sitting waiting for Star to turn up. She also realized that right now there was nobody whose company she really wanted. Except . . . No. Determinedly she pushed the image of Max away. She would get back to London and . . . what? There were a million things she could do. Decorate her bedroom for one—it certainly needed it. Yes, the idea really grabbed her. In her whole life she'd never had a say in how her own room should be decorated. Pretty grisly thought for a grown woman. Right. She put her foot down and was soon speeding along the motorway.

But some thirty miles from London she saw something that drove all thoughts of wallpaper and paint from her mind: a sign on which, among other place names, was one for Barfield. Max's cottage. Max. Her willpower dissolved like butter on a hot plate. The car seemed to develop a mind of its own and apparently with no assistance from her turned off at the next exit and was soon speeding round the twists and turns of country lanes.

In minutes she was bouncing down the rutted cart track toward her goal. The cottage looked just the way she remembered it. The rose-colored brickwork glowed warm in the soft, late autumn sunlight. A spiral of smoke was winding up from the chimney. Star let out a sigh of relief. Max must be home.

Her heart was racing as she got out of the car and walked quickly up the narrow brick path to the heavy oak front door. She lifted the door knocker and gave three sharp raps. She waited. And waited. Knocked again. It flashed through her mind that perhaps he too, like Jessie, was away, but what about the smoke? She knocked again. Still nothing. The tension became unendurable and she turned the door handle and opened the door.

"Max?" she called.

Nothing.

She ventured farther into the house. The fire was burning in the wide inglenook fireplace so he must be around somewhere. She called his name again but to no avail. Then she thought of the study. Of course. She ran into the room, her heightened senses already imagining him, feeling him clasped in her arms, his kisses raining down on her eyes, her hair, her lips. . . .

The study was empty.

The window to the terrace stood open. She went through it out onto the terrace.

Then she saw him.

He was down by the stream, standing statue still, gazing out over the fields. There was something about his stance uncharacteristically dejected. Vulnerable. Star wanted to run to him and throw her arms around him, not only in a physical, sexual way, though that too, but

to hold him close, reassure him, protect him, and . . .
yes, love him.

Before she could speak his name he looked round
sharply, almost as though she had called to him. He
stood motionless, looking at her. His expression, his
whole demeanor changed: the gentle sadness replaced
by the familiar irony. The wide mouth twisted into a
crooked grin. He started to walk the incline toward the
house with unhurried ease. When he reached the terrace
he made no attempt to touch her nor did he show the
least surprise at seeing her. Just stood without saying a
word, regarding her with those mocking gray eyes.

Star found herself struck dumb. The bright opening
lines she had rehearsed on the way disintegrated and all
that came was an involuntary shiver.

"It's getting cold," he said. "Come inside."

He turned and went into the house.

Star followed.

Max produced a bottle of Muscadet and they sat on
opposite sides of the blazing fire, sipping it out of long-
stemmed glasses. But far more than the width of the
fireplace seemed to separate them. Somehow the vibes
were wrong and Star was filled with a deadening sense
of anticlimax. Any dreams she'd had of falling into his
arms or of hearing passionate declarations of love
seemed to stand no chance of fulfilment. Certainly he
behaved with impeccable manners, playing the good
host, but with the cool detachment of someone who
didn't really give a damn whether she was there or not.
He kept the conversation flowing but was formal, almost impersonal, as presumably he would be with any
casual acquaintance who might drop in on him unan-
nounced. It was as though nothing had ever passed between them, as if he had never held her and kissed her,
had not shown concern for her welfare by telling her to
get away from home. She longed to tell him all she had

been thinking and feeling about him, but how could she when he held himself so aloof and behaved with such obvious indifference?

"Let me top up your glass."

His voice almost startled her and she realized that she had been miles away, staring into the flickering flames of the log fire.

"I . . . I think perhaps I'd better go," she said. And did now urgently want to get away. Wished that she had never come.

Max shrugged. "Up to you," he said. And then did not suit the action to the words, but leaned over her and filled her glass to the brim.

She was unnerved by his proximity, and found herself unable to protest. Instead, she took quite a large swallow of wine. He looked down at her, a superior kind of smile twitching the corners of his mouth, but he made no comment and returned to the depths of his easy chair.

"And how were things at 'the store' today?" he asked, coloring the question with a touch of scorn.

Star was taken off guard. "Sorry?"

"I presume you spent the day at the studio, playing the dutiful daughter as always."

Star felt a hard knot of anger form in her stomach. Who the hell did he think he was to taunt and jeer at her? "Then you presumed wrong," she flashed at him, and swallowed another mouthful of wine.

He seemed completely unfazed by her sharp retort and continued to regard her with that air of amused irony that she now knew so well and found so infuriating.

"Why else would you be honoring me with your company?" he asked with mock gallantry.

Star fought to recover her cool. She shifted her position, crossing one long, denim-covered leg with the other. "Actually I was on my way back from Oxford, near Oxford that is, and . . . well . . ." She couldn't invent a reason for the visit but nor would she give him the satisfaction of telling him the truth.

"Oxford?" he interrupted, saving her from further embarrassment. "What were you doing in Oxford?"

"I wasn't actually in Oxford. . . . If you really want to know, I've finally managed to track down Jessie."

"Jessie?" He searched to identify the name then recognized it. "Ah, yes. The funny old lady with the orange hair. She lives in Oxford? Hardly her venue, I would have said."

"As you know nothing about her, I don't see how you can judge where she would be likely to live."

"And did you find her?" he asked, quite ignoring this further outburst.

"No. Well . . . that is, I found where she's living, which as I said is not Oxford—near but not in." She realized she was getting horribly flustered but pressed on. "Unfortunately she's away at the moment."

"You found that very disappointing." This was a statement more than a question.

"Of course I did."

"And what did you do then? When you found she was missing?"

"I was on my way home back to London, but then I . . . well . . . I came here. . . ."

"Ah. So I'm a substitute nanny, is that it?"

"No, it is not!" Star's cheeks flushed angrily at this jibe. "Jessie isn't my nanny. She never has been. She's my friend, my dearest friend, and I've been desperately worried about her. I feel responsible for her. I couldn't just let her vanish without trace and do nothing about it."

"Good," he commented with maddening approbation. "Most commendable. Perhaps you're growing up after all."

Star slammed her glass down on the coffee table so hard that it was in serious danger of shattering.

"You really are the most insufferable, unbearable, arrogant . . ." She didn't trust herself to continue. She had no wish for him to see her totally freak out, understand how mortally disappointed she really felt. With as much dignity as she could muster, she got to her feet. "Thanks for the wine. I'm going now."

She turned and made for the door. With one movement Max was out of his chair and across the room, reaching the door ahead of her. He stood with his back to it to block her way. The expression on his face had changed, the sardonic smile replaced by a look of genuine concern. "Don't go," he said.

Star stood her ground. "I want to," she said. "Let me by."

"No. Stay. Please do."

"Why should I?" she asked, now perilously close to tears. "To have you sneer at me and bait me and put me down?"

"You're overreacting."

"How should I react? I'm not an old doormat, you know. Just because some of the time I give way to other people—doesn't mean I have no pride . . . no feelings."

"I was only teasing."

"No. I don't mind being teased. I've had plenty of that in my life. But there's nice teasing and nasty teasing—unkind, spiteful, hurtful kind of teasing—and I can't . . . I won't take it. Not anymore." Her voice had risen to shouting pitch at the man standing four-square in the doorway, now as determined that she should stay as she was to leave.

She tried to push past him. He grabbed hold of her

wrists and forced her arms down to her sides. She struggled to release herself but his grip was firm and determined. The feel of the strong, hard hands that held her captive sent a thrill of excitement through her body. Star almost resented that he could so easily and quickly arouse this uncontrollable response in her and defiantly returned his penetrating gaze. If in this she hoped to impose her will on him and force him to release her, she quickly realized her mistake: the smoky eyes were now dark-storm gray, the pupils wide and midnight-black; she felt herself lost in them, drowning in the depths of their undisguised passion and desire. She felt almost glad he had so tight a hold on her for her knees felt weak and a strange flood of warmth started deep inside her and soon permeated her whole being.

They stood quite still, caught in the timeless moment. A sense of urgency eddied between them with ever increasing intensity. Not for a second did their eyes cease to communicate the depth of their mutual desire. Neither spoke. Mere words could never have expressed what their bodies were saying with such passionate honesty.

Max lowered his hungry gaze from Star's brilliant, jewel-bright eyes to rest on her lips, which were softly moist and now just slightly parted. Slowly, while still holding her wrists in an iron grip, he leaned forward and zephyr-gentle brushed her lips with his own. This was something not to be hurried over and Star followed his lead, allowing herself to relish the sweet tenderness of his kiss. As his tongue started to probe the inside of her mouth, he released his hold on her wrists and ran his fingers lightly up the length of her arms, over her shoulders and neck and then into the long, flax-soft mane of her hair. He clasped bunches of hair tight in his hands, holding fistfuls either side of her head as his tongue probed deeper into her mouth.

Their two bodies now pressed close and Star could feel the hardness of his masculine desire and instinctively arched her body, pushing her pelvis even closer, sliding her arms round to feel the muscular back, the tight tensed buttocks. Now her tongue slid into his mouth, tentatively at first and then with growing delight, searching and exploring. As their tongues met, warm waves of pleasure broke over and through her. He traced the tip of a finger down the line of her throat. Skillfully he unbuttoned her shirt and his hand glided over the silken softness of her breast. His touch turned her nipples into two little pyramids of desire as he fondled and caressed them. Her hands glided up the length of his spine, gently kneading the muscular strength of his shoulders then on to stroke the delicious area at the back of his neck. Finally she ran her long fingers through the springy, dense black hair.

At last Max broke the embrace but only so that he could kiss her eyelids each in turn, the tip of her nose, the curve of her chin, the perfect shell of her ear, and when he kissed the base of her throat Star felt a fuse light somewhere deep inside her body, ready to catch fire and explode. She held him close, all her senses filled with him: the feel, the smell, the taste of him. And the emotion that had overwhelmed her earlier when she had watched him from the terrace returned, now heightened by his physical proximity.

Now words came tumbling out. "Max, I love you . . . you don't know how much I love you. . . ."

Imperceptibly a change came over him, a tension so slight that Star was not immediately aware of it. He stopped kissing her, stopped caressing, and with only the lightest hold on her shoulders looked at her with sharp intensity, his expression changed, the desire and passion replaced by something near to alarm.

"What did you say?" His voice sounded hoarse.

Star looked up at him, as yet unaware of the turmoil of emotions raging inside him. Her eyes were wide and trusting, full of the glorious knowledge of her love and the certainty that it was returned. When she spoke it was with rapturous joy.

"I said that I love you!"

Max let go of her as if her shoulders had suddenly become two red-hot coals and his hands were burning.

"No," he said. And then again, more forcibly, "No!"

He took a step back from her and screwed his eyes up tight as if in pain. Or as if he wanted to shut out the sight of her.

"It mustn't be. It can't be." He seemed almost to be speaking to himself.

"But why? What are you saying? I don't understand," Star stammered, completely bewildered.

Max turned sharply away and started to pace the room.

"The last time we met I said that I wouldn't be seeing you again. I said good-bye and I meant it." His voice was harsh and a shadow had fallen across his face, the brow darkly furrowed.

"But I don't understand." Star repeated the words, hurt now as well as bewildered. "I'm only being honest with you. And you feel something for me . . . I know you do."

"You know nothing of the kind. You're a beautiful and desirable girl and I should enjoy going to bed with you, but I am not in the market for any emotional entanglements."

"But loving someone isn't something you can just decide about, like whether or not to buy a car or go to the movies . . . it just happens."

"Well, it's not happening to me."

He spat the words out with such vehement finality that Star could find no words, no argument to counteract them. It was unlikely that she would have been able to speak in any case—the breath seemed to have been knocked out of her body. She suddenly felt chilled and shivered.

Max stopped his pacing, went to the window and stood with his back to her, looking out at a sky streaked green with the last vestiges of daylight. Rain was spattering and running in rivulets down the wide expanse of the glass pane. The fire burned low and in the gloom Star stared in utter confusion at the figure silhouetted as if against a lighted screen: shoulders hunched, fists clenched, his whole being tensed as if to ward off some blow. Surely not the behavior of a cool, unfeeling would-be seducer? There must be some other explanation for this sudden withdrawal. Surely it was not so disastrous a thing to have said that she loved him? Then she thought of a possible explanation, one that filled her with icy horror—which she instantly wanted to reject but to which she still had to have an answer. Perhaps Laura had been lying?

"Is it . . . ?" Her voice was barely audible. "Is it because of Laura?"

He did not reply at once, still stood with his back to her, watching the rain now beating savagely against the window.

"What would you do if I said yes?" he asked.

"I suppose I'd have to believe you."

"Then perhaps you'd better."

"Laura told me that there had never been anything between you." Max slowly turned away from the window and without a glance in her direction, as if he were alone in the room, went to the fireplace and rekindled the dying fire, piling on logs, blowing the embers with the bellows until they burst into flames.

Star watched with something near to disbelief. She went and knelt beside him, forcing him to look at her.

"I asked you a question." Her voice was shaking uncontrollably. "I think I deserve an answer. A straight answer, Max."

He looked at her, at the light from the leaping flames reflected green and yellow in eyes as clear and as blue as the deep waters of the Aegean Sea. The brow, smooth and high, the apricot glow of the high cheekbones, the wide soft curve of the mouth. He longed to stroke and caress the silky skin. To kiss that mouth so full of promise.

He closed his eyes as though to shut out her image.

"You shouldn't have come here," he whispered.

"Look at me, Max."

Reluctantly he opened his eyes. For a moment they both remained silent, gazing deep into each other's eyes; not with passion, not with desire, but searching, seeking.

Finally Star spoke.

"It's not Laura, is it?"

"No, Star. It's not Laura. And never was."

"Then who?"

"Why does it have to be anyone?"

He jumped to his feet and moved about the room, switching on lamps, flooding the place with light, breaking the enclosed, dusky atmosphere. He poured himself a glass of wine.

"Is it beyond your comprehension that at this particular moment in my life I do not want to be romantically involved with anyone?" he asked tersely. "Not because I'm in love with somebody else but just because I want to be free of emotional encumbrances. Just be myself. Answerable only to myself. Responsible only for myself." He swallowed down the wine and refilled his glass.

Star regarded him steadily. Unblinking. She considered his outburst, frowning in concentration.

"Supposing," she said, weighing her words, "just supposing that I agreed with you. Supposing I said that, even if I'm in love with you, I wouldn't expect you to be in love with me. And that I would be quite happy to have a no-strings love affair—if that's the way you want it?"

His mouth curved into the shadow of a smile. Not the mocking, ironical smile that she knew so well but something tender and a little sad. "It wouldn't work, Star."

"It would if we wanted it to."

"For one thing, you're too young to sustain this cool detached kind of relationship."

"I'm not too young," Star protested fiercely, "I'm eighteen."

Max ignored the interruption. "And even if, contrary to expectation, you proved to have a sophistication completely alien to your years and character, I . . ." He hesitated.

"What? You what?"

"If we went to bed, Star, how could I help but fall in love with you?"

A rocket of joy took off inside her head and burst into a shower of brilliant light.

"But that would be wonderful," she said, completely missing the note of despair in his voice.

"Wonderful?" he snarled. "You poor deluded child. You've never been in love, have you?"

Star shook her head. It was true. Memories of Gary infused her with guilt. No, she had never been in love. That is—not until now.

"It's like some kind of sickness," Max said bitterly, turning his gaze away from Star and back to the flames, now leaping up the chimney. "Insidious and debilitating —rendering the victim helpless. Incapable of controlling his emotions, his actions. Turning a normally independent, intelligent, functioning human being into a groveling idiot without a will of his own. Love? I tell you, it's the biggest con since the three-card trick. Thanks, but I'm not in the market."

"Who did this to you?" Star whispered.

"It doesn't matter. You want love, little Star, go back to the flower sender in California. I'm sure he has an endless supply. Just don't come knocking uninvited at my door. Okay?"

"Okay!" Star shouted. "I'm sorry if I disturbed your neat little ivory tower. Sorry if I received all those messages wrong. For what it's worth—" She realized she was speaking to his back and gave up. "Oh, what's the use? Good-bye." She slung her tote back over her shoulder and made for the door.

"You can't go," Max said, and she hesitated. Perhaps he had suddenly relented.

"The rain's bucketing down. And it's pitch dark. You can't drive in these conditions."

Star stopped and turned slowly. She felt ice cold with anger.

"So what do you suggest?"

"You can stay here."

"Thanks," she said with deep sarcasm. "Thanks a lot."

"You can't possibly have had enough night driving experience. Not in this kind of weather anyway. No way will I let you . . ."

"*Let* me? Who in the hell are you to *let* me do anything? Or are you joining all the others who think they know how I should lead my life better than I do? I am an adult woman and what I do or think or . . ." Star ran out of words but was so engulfed by rage and resentment that she struggled on. "If I choose to drive in a force eight gale in a snowstorm, believe me, that's just what I'll do."

Max regarded her for a moment in silence. Then,

with a shrug of apparent indifference, turned away from her toward the fire.

Star bit savagely on her bottom lip to keep back the tears and stumbled blindly out of the house.

9

The night was densely black. The rain thrashed against Star's face and wind caught at her hair, whipping it up and every which way across her face and into her eyes. She groped her way up the brick path, now treacherously slippery from the rain, and with an effort managed to unlatch the gate, which, caught by the gale, flew out of her grasp and crashed back against the hedge. As her eyes gradually became accustomed to the dark she could just make out the shape of her car parked up the lane.

Somewhere deep in the recesses of her tote bag were the car keys, and with the rain beating down, soaking her, she searched frantically for them. By the time she found them her clothes were wet through and her hair was sticking to her head like seaweed. She managed to unlock the car door and, after battling with the wind, to climb inside and force the door closed.

At least this seemed like some kind of refuge. She dabbed at her face and hair with a tissue, to no great effect. She now faced the fact that at least in one respect Max had been right: she had no experience in night driving—certainly not in these disastrous conditions. The prospect of fighting through the storm on the motorway filled her with dread. Still, no way would she go back and admit to Max that he was right. Anger boiled up inside her anew at the thought of him and defiantly she rammed the key into the ignition and turned it. It failed to catch. She turned it again.

Nothing.

Only the rain slashing in torrents against the windshield and the windows.

"It can't be," she thought, tears of despair threatening. "At this of all moments—a dead battery! Somebody up there really must hate me."

Again and again she turned the key. No response. Nothing. Dead as the grave. Nothing.

Near despair she rested her head on the steering wheel. The thought of spending the night shut up in an ice-cold car filled her with horror. But so did the thought of crawling back to Max.

Just as she was trying yet again to get the blasted thing started, the car door was flung open. Max stood outside, his hair plastered to his head, rain streaming down his face. He reached in, grabbed her by the arm and pulled her, protesting, out of the car. She didn't move from the spot but stood facing him defiantly while the rain cascaded down on them.

"Sometimes," he shouted over the storm, "Fate takes over."

He gathered her in his arms and kissed her. The touch of his lips on hers released a flood of desire in Star and she responded passionately.

The rain, indifferent, cascaded down on them.

When at last, as if waking from a dream, Max pulled away from her, he said, "I think we may be getting slightly damp."

Star laughed, shaking drops of rain off the tip of her nose and chin.

"Just a bit," she said.

He took hold of her hand and together they ran back into the house. They stood making pools of water on the thick pile carpet, looking like a pair of drowned rats, and laughed. The laughter broke down the final barriers between them and threw them yet again, squelching, into each other's arms.

"You will stay, won't you?" Max asked.

"I don't seem to have much choice."

"I could get you a taxi, although I doubt if anyone would come out on a night like this, or if you insist I'll drive you back to London myself."

Star shook her head, sending showers of glittering raindrops over him. "Oops! Sorry . . . no. I don't want to go anywhere, thank you."

"I'm glad. So very, very glad."

"So am I."

"You must get warm. Go by the fire. I'll find some towels and something dry for you to put on."

He raced upstairs and Star went to the great open fireplace where the logs now burned fiercely; yellow, green, and vermilion flames blazed and reflected in dancing light and shadow throughout the room. Star dropped down on her knees and held out her hands to the welcome warmth.

Max reappeared, his arms piled high with bath towels and robes. He took over. "Get that lot off," he ordered, pointing to her clothes, "and this on." He held out a soft white bathrobe.

Obedient as a child in a nursery, and with the same childish lack of self-consciousness, Star stripped off and stood naked in the firelight. Max gazed at her smooth, long-limbed body with something like awe.

"You are perfection," he whispered.

He picked up an oversize fluffy bath towel and with infinite tenderness started to dry first her arms and then her legs. He kissed each one of her pink fingertips and then the tops of her toes. He moved the towel in sensuous circular movements over her hips and buttocks and with little dabbing movements circled each of her breasts. The rosy pink nipples expressed Star's pleasure by hardening into points. He flicked first at one then at the other with the tip of his tongue, and a thrilled shiver ran through Star's body and over the surface of her skin.

"You're cold?" he asked, knowing too well that she wasn't.

"No, not cold," she assured him, her voice husky, throat tight and constricted, "Really not."

"Your hair is still wet," he said, running his fingers through the long, tangled strands. "I'll dry it for you." He took the towel and started to rub her head vigorously—almost roughly.

Star laughed, protesting, and took the towel away from him.

"What about you? Look at you. Soaking."

The rain had turned Max's casually smooth hair into a tumble of black curls. Star rubbed at his head with the towel and he pretended to fight her off. He snatched the towel from her and said, "You're a bully, you know that?" and laughed, showing even white teeth; he looked like some glorious satyr. Star ran her fingers through his hair and down his muscular neck to the top of his chest. With deft fingers she undid the buttons of his shirt, and exposed the broad, sun-bronzed chest covered with dark, crisp curls. Then she slipped the shirt over strong hard shoulders and muscular arms, pulling it finally over his wrists to end in a bundle on the floor. Her hands glided with wonder over the skin that was sensuously smooth in contrast to the tightly corded muscles beneath.

Max stood up slowly, not taking his eyes off her. Then he turned away, went to the window, and swiftly closed the curtains. He snapped off the lights he had so recently lit and now the room was illuminated only by the warm glow of the fire. He took some cushions from the sofa and threw them on the fireside rug. All the time Star watched him, loving the way he moved, the grace of his muscular body that seemed to be so completely under control.

He stopped and looked down at her as she settled herself back onto the cushions, regarding him with a mixture of trust and desire. With an easy, confident movement that indicated some degree of practice, Max unbuckled his belt and slipped off his trousers and underpants in one.

The sight of the contained power of his naked body and the demanding thrust of his erection, now so palpably evident, gave Star a thrill of excitement.

He knelt beside her and for a long moment made no move to touch or caress her but gazed down at her in wonderment, the gray eyes clouded with desire, glorying in the opalescent skin, the soft curves of her firm young body. She returned his gaze, her eyes bright with anticipation. He leaned forward and wound his fingers round a tendril of her still-damp hair, then pressed it to his lips. He kissed her throat and ran his tongue round the rim of an ear. He teased and tantalized her small rosy pink nipples until they stood hard and pointed, meanwhile stroking the smooth, flat length of her abdomen and the soft, curling triangle of light brown hair. He gentled her legs apart and found the tiny bud that responded eagerly to his expert touch so that soon it was ready to bloom and burst into flower.

As Star gave a moan of pleasure, Max moved above her and as if their bodies had been designed for each other he was deep inside her and, perfectly in tune, they moved rhythmically together, slowly at first, and then as their passion took over, with ever increasing intensity.

Outside the wind beat and slashed the rain against the windows, flooding through gulleys and overflowing gutters, seeming to echo the wild ecstasy of their love. So much pent-up emotion was suddenly released, and as Max thrust again and again Star was aware of a new and unique sensation—starting with a warm tingling simultaneously in the tips of her toes, her fingers, the topmost point of her skull, and running with increasing speed and ferocity on an irreversible head-on course, to clash in a shattering explosion of wild exultation that sent her body into a succession of violent shudders and filled her universe with a frenzied delight such as she had never known nor had ever guessed could possibly exist.

Max held her quite still for a moment but only as long as a pause in a symphony before the orchestra builds up to the great clashing finale.

"My darling, my love. Star . . . Star . . ." He called her name aloud and continued with rising ardor toward his own climax, which Star found as beautiful and fulfilling as her own. Together they subsided, like dancers after a perfect pas de deux. Still holding each other close, still joined as one, they lay in each other's arms stretched out in the front of the fire. There seemed to be no words nor any need of them, only the sound of the wind and the rain now subsiding as though in harmony with their own spent passion, and the gentle crackle of the logs burning low in the fireplace.

Max kissed her lightly, tenderly, and stroked her hair back from her face as one might a child's.

"Sweet Star, the only star in my sky," he murmured, looking searchingly at her as if trying to imprint each of her features on his mind forever.

Star traced the outline of his brow and cheekbones with a finger, gently, lovingly. "That was . . ." She couldn't find the right words to express what she felt.

"I know," he said. "For me too."

"You don't understand . . . I never before . . . well, not like that."

He kissed her again and held her close. Then slowly coming down to earth he noticed that the fire was in danger of going out. "I hate to move, but I have to put some logs on the fire." He smiled, gently disentangling himself.

He soon had the fire blazing again. "And I don't know about you," he added, "but I'm starving."

Star laughed. "I didn't like to mention it but, well, I've hardly eaten a thing all day."

"Right."

Max shrugged on a terry cloth robe and disappeared into the kitchen. By the time Star had showered (carefully avoiding the rose geranium talcum powder) and put on the overlarge robe that Max had given her to wear, he had made a salad and was skillfully cooking omelets.

They ate in the kitchen and Star felt she had never enjoyed a meal so much in her life. They were so easy and relaxed in each other's company.

Star told him about Dee and the modeling, about Annie and her new home. She told him honestly about Gary and how she had realized she could never marry him once she had met Max. He listened attentively and from time to time touched her affectionately on the arm or the cheek. Then Star realized that she had been talking nonstop but only about herself.

"I'm sorry," she said. "I don't usually sound off like this."

"But I want you to. I want you to tell me whatever you have inside. All the things you've been bottling up, keeping to yourself, I suspect, for years."

Star sipped her wine thoughtfully, then with a shrug said, "Not all that much really. Just—I'm not very interesting."

"You, my darling, are the most interesting person in the entire world."

Star smiled. "You are lovely," she said. "At least for the moment I think I'll believe you."

"And see that you go right on doing that."

"What about you?" Star asked, piling butter onto a thick slice of whole-wheat bread and cutting herself a wedge of cheese, completely forgetting any such thing as calories existed.

"What about me?" Max asked, hedging.

"I know that I love you, but quite honestly I don't know much about you."

Max frowned down into his wine glass, which he turned slowly between long sensitive fingers. "I can't promise I'll answer but what do you want to know?"

"Well, for starters, I do believe now that there was never anything between you and Laura. . . ."

"There wasn't. It was basically a purely practical, working arrangement."

"But why? Why on earth should a successful writer like you waste his time ghosting the memoirs of a TV actress—if you weren't somehow interested in her as a woman?"

Star was immediately aware of some kind of withdrawal in Max, as though he had closed a curtain.

"I said that I couldn't promise to answer all your

questions," he said, "only because I'm not absolutely sure of all the answers. But I can see that you deserve the facts about my involvement with your mother." He paused and topped up their glasses. "At the time I met Laura I was at an all-time low. I . . ." He seemed to search for words. "I'd been through a pretty traumatic experience—that's the bit I'd rather not talk about— which had resulted in that affliction that threatens all authors, writer's block. I'd not been able to write a word for months. I felt blank, sterile, dead. I was pretty miserable, bitter I suppose, and feeling thoroughly sorry for myself. We met at a party. I do believe in Fate, you know—if I'd not gone to that party I wouldn't be sitting here now with you, and I can think of no greater disaster befalling me."

Star leaned over and lightly kissed his cheek.

Max took her hand and continued. "Laura, as you know, is an extremely attractive and lively woman. I freely admit that I found her amusing company, but that was all. I was dead, Star. Dead from the waist both ways. When she suggested, right there over the champagne, that I might help her with her book, a suggestion that six months earlier I would have secretly laughed at and politely declined, I thought, What the hell? Why not? I'd never known an actress before, knew nothing of the show-business world, it seemed like a good opportunity to observe this, to me, strange species."

"Like David Attenborough watching monkeys in the wild?" Star teased.

"I'm telling it the way it was."

"Sure. Go on."

"Not much more to tell. On closer acquaintance I realized that Laura was spoiled and egotistical, but because she really had nothing to do with me I wasn't bothered. Not until you appeared. Then I got mad as hell. And at the same time—maybe sparked off by what

I felt—a terrific thing happened: I started to write again."

"Laura's book?" Star asked.

Max nodded. "Maybe I was a bit hard on Laura. I could have been letting out pent-up anger and resentment that wasn't really anything to do with her, but . . . the way she puts you down because she can't tolerate the thought of your growing into a beautiful woman—oh, you must know it, even if you don't admit it to yourself—that's what really got to me. If she'd been able to recognize even the remotest truth in what I wrote about her, I could have felt different, but . . . well, you know how she reacted and that was it."

Star hesitated. "I think it is terribly hard for her, growing older. I suppose she just can't face it."

Max smiled. "How sweet you are. And how loyal."

Star frowned. "What I still don't understand is why did you let everyone think you were having an affair if you weren't?"

"It was not intentional. At least it wasn't for me. To be possessive and demanding is part of Laura's character, I just didn't fight it. I suppose it even amused me. She had no lover or boyfriend at the time, which I think she felt was bad for her image. It suited her to have people think we were a couple. I couldn't have cared less. In a world where nothing seemed to matter, why should that?"

Star wanted to question him further, to know why he had been so demolished. So hopeless. Was it that "madam"? Almost certainly she felt it must have been but wisely did not pursue the matter.

Instead she said, "I'm glad you met Laura at that party too. Even though it did put me through some pretty agonizing moments."

"My darling, I'm sorry. I never meant to hurt you. I

think I just didn't want to face what was happening to
me."

"What *was* happening?"

"When I said a while ago that if we had sex together
I would not be able to stop myself from falling in love
with you, I wasn't speaking the truth."

A shadow crossed Star's face. "What do you mean?"
she asked anxiously.

Max put his arms around her and held her close. "I
was in love with you already."

Star woke to the sound of birdsong and the smell of
freshly brewed coffee.

For a moment she wasn't sure where she was. Last
night's rapture had made her impervious to her sur-
roundings; she had only been aware of emotions and
sensations that she had never before experienced, feelings of such glorious intensity that they had swamped
her whole being, taken over and engulfed her. Nothing
else had any reality for her.

"Max," she whispered, smiling languidly and reaching out a hand. The bed beside her was empty. She
rolled over and buried her nose in his pillow, breathing
in the intoxicating scent of him. Her toes curled with
pleasure remembering all that had passed between
them, and she stretched luxuriously, enjoying the sensation before relaxing back on the pillows.

She looked round the room and realized that this was
not the befrilled, lilac-covered bower she had seen on
her previous visit to the cottage. This room was more
austere and she liked it much better: white painted
walls; simple, stripped-pine cupboards; curtains of
muted blues and greens that seemed to bring the colors
of the countryside into the room. Nor was the bed an
acre wide but a modest four feet. But big enough for
two. Star smiled—quite big enough. She wondered what

the date was. She knew she would remember it always
—it had been the most important day of her whole life.
"Even when I'm really old," she thought, "forty or even
older, I shall remember this."

The sound of the telephone ringing cut through her
reverie. She could hear Max's voice from somewhere
downstairs as he lifted the receiver. This seemed like a
cue for her to stop lying in bed dreaming and to get up
and get on with the day.

A whole wonderful day with Max, just the two of
them alone together.

She opened the curtains and flung wide the window
to a cloudless blue sky and a gentle autumn sun. A
yellow mellow day that totally rejected the possibility of
the wild angry tempest that had raged the night before.
Only some flattened michaelmas daisies, tattered chrys-
anthemums, and a few broken off branches lying scattered beneath the beech tree gave evidence that the
storm had ever been.

"Must get those branches cleared up," Star thought,
and then realized that she was reacting as though this
was her home and the fallen branches her responsibility.
How ridiculous! And yet as she looked out over the
smooth slope of the lawn running down to the stream
and the wide sweep of farmland beyond, she did have an
overwhelming feeling of belonging to the house. And to
Max. Her newfound career, Dee, her problems with
Laura, all seemed a million miles away, belonging to
another world. And she knew in that instant that this
was what she really wanted: total, complete commitment. Quite simply in one word—love.

She threw back her head and smiled up into the sun,
conscious only of the totality of her contentment. Everything was going to be wonderful, she just knew it.
And right now she was going to have her first and most
certainly not her last breakfast with Max. Intimate din-

ners for two were magic, but sharing breakfast . . .
that would be a relaxed kind of sharing, a feeling of
really belonging.

As she showered she could still hear Max's voice on
the telephone. She couldn't hear what he was saying but
the tone was vital and positive. He's feeling good too,
she thought, glad to know that she had made him
happy. As she dried herself on an oversize pink bath
towel she noticed that all traces of rose geranium had
been removed. No more talcum or tablets of soap or
toilet water remained. She felt quite absurdly gratified
at this sign, which surely must mean that he had sev-
ered all ties with the frilly female. Like tearing up old
love letters. Now she and Max were going to make a
new start together: she had finally grown up and he had
finished with a relationship that had been destructive
for him.

She dressed quickly and, stopping only long enough
to run a comb through her long tousled hair, ran downstairs to join Max. His voice came from the kitchen, still
talking on the telephone.

Star wondered who on earth he could be talking to all
this time.

As she got nearer she heard him say, "I tell you I've
got her. Stop looking. I've found her."

A puzzled frown creased Star's smooth brow. Who
on earth was he talking about?

"She is perfection," Max continued excitedly. "Look,
I created the girl so I should know who can play her."

As Star went into the kitchen he smiled at her and
held out an arm for her to walk into. He circled her
waist and held her close as he continued to talk into the
wall telephone. "Sure, of course try Gloria, she's not far
off being right, but I have the one who is dead on target.
. . . Okay, go ahead with her and I'll be with you later.
This afternoon. Right. Just wait till you see her. Three
o'clock it shall be. Bye."

Max replaced the receiver and gave Star a succession of kisses on her forehead, cheeks, the tip of her nose, and finally, with greater warmth, on her mouth. Star responded readily.

"Hey," Max laughed, pulling away from her, "don't get me started again. We have a very full and important day ahead of us."

"We have?"

"Certainly." Max sounded quite surprised. "Didn't you hear what I was saying?"

"Yes. But I didn't know it concerned me."

"Who else could I be describing in such glowing terms?"

Star shrugged. "How should I know?"

"You're just fishing. Come on, let's have breakfast. I'll cook. I do a neat bacon and eggs, but we ate all the eggs last night—so it'll be bacon and toast."

"I usually just eat yogurt," Star protested without conviction.

"Today you need to keep your strength up," Max said firmly, and crossed to the fridge. He got out orange juice, bacon, and butter.

"Here, you can make yourself useful. Pour out the orange juice."

He handed her the carton. Star found glasses and started to pour the juice.

"I don't understand," she said. "What are we doing today? And who were you talking to about me on the phone?"

"My director, Jon Brisson."

"Director? I'm sorry . . . director of what?"

Max stopped, scissors poised in the act of derinding the bacon. "But you know all about it. I told you."

"Told me what?"

"*Satan's Daughter*—the book I gave you to read. You did read it?"

"Well, no, actually I didn't."

"Too many long words?" he grinned, throwing bacon into the sizzling pan.

"No. You see . . ." She was going to explain about the situation with Laura and how her mother had hung on to the book, but didn't want to mention her name at this moment. "I just had so much going on," she explained lamely.

"It doesn't really matter. Perhaps it's all to the good. You won't have any preconceived ideas about the character."

"What character?"

"Abigail. The central character of the book. The young girl accused of witchcraft . . . it's based on a true story."

"Just a moment. I don't want to seem totally dim, but how does this affect me?"

"You're going to play her, that's how. Right, crisp bacon for the lady. . . . Oh, hell, I forgot to put the toast on. Stick a couple of slices in the toaster, would you?"

"Max, what are you talking about?"

"Bread in toaster. Quick."

Star put slices of bread into the toaster, but she wouldn't be sidetracked. "I'm not playing anything . . . anyone, I should say . . . I'm not an actress, Max. You know that."

"I know nothing of the kind. I know that when you are in front of a camera you make love to it."

"Have you been talking to Dee? That's what she says. But—"

"Not just talking. She's a good guy, Dee is, she let me look at some of your pics. They—you—are stunning."

"So—perhaps I'm a good model. I hope I am, but that doesn't make me an actress."

"Wrong. The really great models are all good actresses—at least good film actresses. The theater is something else again."

"Well, I'm not," Star said firmly.

"How do you know?"

"I just do. Anytime I tried I was terrible."

"You're not eating. Go on. You need protein for what you're going to do."

"Max . . ."

"Eat."

Obediently Star took a mouthful and chewed slowly. She could hardly believe what Max had just said—couldn't take it in.

Max ate heartily. He was in a state of almost manic exuberance. Star had never seen him like this before and it made her a little uneasy. Was he perhaps a bit crazy? Why else should he suddenly take it into his head that she should play the lead in his film?

"You'd better get used to the idea," he said between mouthfuls. "Staring from now. This afternoon you're doing a test. No argument. It's all fixed."

Star felt a flicker of anger. "You had no right to fix anything without asking me."

"Of course I didn't ask you! You'd only have put up the same ridiculous argument and wasted a lot of time."

"Listen, Max," Star said earnestly. "I really don't know how to act. When I tried at school I was a disaster. Just terrible. Everyone thought that because I was Laura's daughter I would be great, but I wasn't. I gave up after the first rehearsal and was never asked again."

"I believe you," Max said calmly.

"Then don't set me up to play some big lead part in a film I'm sure means a lot to you. You're just going to make a fool of yourself . . . and me."

"I'm prepared to take the risk."

"Well, I'm not." Star bit into some toast and chewed angrily.

Max seemed unconcerned. "The fact of the matter is," he said, "that it is not failure you won't risk—but success."

"That's ridiculous."

"But true," Max replied with infuriating assurance, helping himself to marmalade. "If you proved to be as good or even a better actress than your mother, it would scare the living daylights out of you."

"You're talking nonsense. Whatever her faults Laura is a terrific actress."

"So you mustn't be one and compete with her! Don't deny it, my darling. I've been watching the two of you at close quarters and I know what I'm talking about."

Star didn't reply. She drank her coffee, averting her eyes from Max's gaze. Something in what he said struck home and she knew it was a sensitive area that she didn't want to touch.

Max continued. "That little girl who stole the limelight all those years ago aroused Mum's displeasure and so you've never risked it again."

"That was nothing. All kids are scene stealers," Star protested.

"Possibly. But you didn't know that at the time, did you? You only knew that you'd done something that Mama didn't like one little bit and you were dead scared that she'd stop loving you."

"I really don't go for all this instant psychoanalysis."

"You don't go for the truth, my love."

"Not so long ago you were telling me to get away from all the false values and everything that was awful about my environment, and now here you are trying to force me back into it."

"I am not 'forcing you' to do anything. If I am trying to persuade you, it is in order to get you away from the shoddy atmosphere in which you were brought up. There is a difference, you know, between the kind of quality film we are planning and that turgid soap opera on which Laura wastes her time and talents."

"*Harringtons* is terrific. It's had top viewing figures for years. Just because it doesn't appeal to a snob, pseudo-intellectual audience doesn't mean it has no quality."

"*Satan's Daughter* will be neither snob nor pseudo-intellectual. . . ." Max broke off. "Christ, I sound pompous and I don't mean to. Star . . . I believe you can act and I believe you are perfect for this part. I'm not just seeing you through lover's eyes—my work means far too much to me for that. Won't you trust me?"

He leaned across the table and took her hand. She looked into his eyes, now so clear and direct. No trace of the old mocking expression. She hesitated. More than anything in the world she wanted to please him but she really didn't want to act. The very thought of it terrified her. "I . . . I was looking forward to our first breakfast," she said wistfully. "And here we are arguing about something I don't even want to think about."

Max considered, then said, "I'll make a bargain with you. Just do the test. Commits you to nothing. Then even if you turn out to be the greatest screen actress since silent movies, I won't hold you to anything unless you feel happy about it."

Star thought this suggestion over very carefully, then said, "You couldn't anyway. Not without a contract."

Max threw back his head and laughed. "Spoken like a real pro. You're going to do all right, my Star." And leaning over the debris of their breakfast he kissed her gently at first and then with increasing ardor.

Star remembered Laura once saying she never made love before going in front of the cameras, it gave you shadows under the eyes. To hell with that, Star thought, and kissed Max right back.

Laura pushed open the immense swing doors of City Television's sumptuous London offices off Park Lane. She walked with determined steps across the thick pile carpet to the receptionist's desk. The girl sitting behind the desk was a good-looking thirty-five-year-old blonde who had been guarding the portals of Sir Len's domain for some ten years. Laura greeted her with the special kind of slightly patronizing friendliness she reserved for subordinates who were useful.

"Hullo there, Judy," she said, smiling warmly. "How are you?"

"Fine, thanks, Laura." Judy belonged to the generation who addressed stars by their Christian names. Did Laura detect just the tiniest hint of coolness in her voice? If so she ignored it. She knew that Len was in his office and she was going to see him or else.

"Good. Would you let Sir Len know that I'm here?"

It was more a demand than a request, despite the charm.

"Of course. Although I have an idea he might be in a meeting. I'll just check." She flicked the intercom. The smile became fixed on Laura's face. Never in all her years with *Harringtons* had she ever been greeted with anything but the red carpet, open arms treatment in this office. What was the meaning of this "I'll just check" bit?

"Hullo, Clare," Judy said into the intercom. "I have Laura Denning in reception. She'd like a quick word with Sir Len."

Quick word. Laura registered this; she'd said nothing about a word, quick or otherwise. What was going on?

Judy continued to listen to Len's secretary on the intercom. Laura could hear the faint quacking but the intercom distorted the words.

"Right," Judy said, "I'll tell her." She flicked off the intercom and looked up unsmiling at Laura. "I was right. Sir Len is all tied up in a meeting and then is leaving immediately for New York, so I'm afraid . . ."

Laura's nostrils flared with anger. Her beautiful mouth hardened into a straight line. Many a director or fellow actor had quailed at these telltale signs of displeasure, but Judy seemed unmoved.

"Would you please get back to Clare and tell her to let Sir Len know that I'm here." Laura's voice was now steely. "I am quite certain he would want to see me if he knew."

"I'm sorry, Laura. It's just not possible. He said that under no circumstances . . ."

"Sir Len told me many many years ago that anytime I wanted to see him he would drop whatever he was doing, even if he was entertaining the Queen. And we both know that Sir Len never breaks his word, don't we,

Judy? So, just get on the blower and tell him I'm here. Right?"

Judy went through the motions a second time with the same results. "Perhaps you'd like to make an appointment?"

Laura stared at the carefully made-up face in disbelief. She was being given the brush. But she mustn't let on to this all-knowing watchdog—or should it be watch bitch?—that she was aware of the fact. For a brief moment she hesitated. Should she beat a dignified retreat or revert to the tactic she'd used all those years ago with Harry?

She made a snap decision, and giving Judy her sunniest smile, said, "I'll just sit here and wait, then. I know he'll want to see me once he knows I'm here. Perhaps you'd be kind enough to convey that message to Clare?"

With this she turned away and, picking up the latest copy of the trade paper *Variety* from the low glass table, settled down to wait as though there was nothing else in the world she would rather be doing.

Judy watched her from behind the barricade of her desk. Clare's message had been adamant: Sir Len had a no-go list and Laura's name had been added to it.

Len did not enjoy scenes. He avoided unpleasantness unless it was likely to result in some kind of advantage to himself, either financial or social. At this moment he was sitting in his office watching a video recording of "Boots Bunnie," the phenomenally successful cartoon series that he had just imported from America. He particular liked "Boots Bunnie" because it did not involve actors. Len didn't really like or approve of actors. In the end they always caused trouble, like Laura stubbornly sitting out there in reception. Why couldn't she read the writing on the wall? God knows it was writ large and clear enough. She was no longer wanted. Her day was done. She was OUT. Why was she forcing him to be unkind? He didn't like being unkind. Wasn't he the most generous and considerate of employers? Everybody's father figure. He'd been good to her all these years so why should she now push him into this corner? Len worked himself up into quite a fervor of righteous indignation over Laura's lack of consideration for his finer feelings.

"Boots Bunnie" came to an end with Boots getting the better of Freddie Fox. Len pressed the remote control button and the picture shrank to nothingness. He sat for a moment, staring at the empty screen, and thoughts of Laura swamped his mind. Was she really sitting out there in reception? Well, it wasn't his fault. She'd become very difficult, everybody said so. And, worse, she had lost audience loyalty. That other girl—Diane—that's who they were switching on for. People should know when they were licked. He reached out and pressed a buzzer.

"Yes, Sir Len?" Clare's voice came through immediately, crisp, bright, always at the ready.

"Is Laura Denning still in reception?" Len asked.

"Yes, Sir Len. She's still there."

Len paused. Considered. Then: "Have Judy give her a coffee, and then in twenty minutes tell her I've left the building."

"Right, Sir Len."

"And, Clare, get me Magda Sherwood in publicity. On my private line."

The studio where the tests for *Satan's Daughter* were being made barely merited the name.

It had once been a parish church but some years back, when the locality had changed from respectable lower-middle class to transient, church attendance had dropped to nothing and an enterprising property developer had bought it up, had it deconsecrated, and turned into a mini film studio where it more than earned its keep by being hired out to minor film companies, mainly for the production of television commercials. Compared to the hi-tech superefficiency of Firbank, the only studios Star had ever known, this was like a one-night fit-up compared to Covent Garden Opera House. But, as Max had explained, this was going to be what was termed an "art picture," which might or might not become a cult success and then appeal to a wider audience. Not the kind of film that backers wanted to risk their money on.

Star sat in the makeup room, which doubled as wardrobe and dressing room. The drab gray dress she was wearing had already been worn by other candidates for the part of Abigail earlier in the day. When Star had protested at the idea of sharing clothes, she was told firmly that that was what she had to wear as it would break the budget to hire a dress for each individual actress being tested. Under any other circumstances she would have walked away, but as she was only going through the whole charade to please Max she decided to adopt a philosophical attitude. Actually, when the simple dress was hooked up and then sewn tighter to fit her tiny waist, she felt an odd change come over her. As though she were already more the character of the poor village girl, Abigail, back in the sixteenth century, than she was Star Merrick here in the nineteen eighties.

"I'm afraid I didn't have time to wash my hair," she apologized to the makeup girl.

"Doesn't matter," the girl said. "No one sees it anyway. It all goes under this little job." And she pulled a severe white cap over Star's hair and proceeded to tuck away any stray tendrils that tried to escape. Far from diminishing her beauty the starkness of the puritan cap seemed to enhance it, emphasising the high cheek bones, the wide-set eyes, the soft curving mouth.

"You get practically no makeup either," the makeup girl said, and looking at Star's reflection in the glass added in a mixture of admiration and envy, "Not that you need it."

As she walked onto the set Star was aware that her knees seemed to have developed an almost uncontrollable action of their own and her heart was pounding so hard that she was sure it would be picked up on the microphone. She made herself walk slowly, very tall and erect, determined to give every impression of cool confidence.

Max was deep in conversation with a tall lean man of about his own age, with a mop of wild brown curls that flopped over his face and tended to fly when he got excited. Star guessed that he must be the director. Max saw her first as she crossed the studio floor toward them, then his companion looked up and stood stock still, staring at her, a hand arrested in midair, stuck in a gesture he'd been making to emphasize some point.

Star came and stood before them and still he stared. Then he said quietly, "I see what you mean."

"I knew you would," Max said with just a hint of smugness.

Star smiled. "Hello," she said, in a voice that seemed to her to come from some far distant place.

Max introduced them, "Jon . . . Star," and then said, "This is where I disappear. I've told Star all I could in the time so now it's over to you." And without stopping to wish her luck or even give a smile of encouragement he walked quickly away.

Jon continued to regard her in silence for a moment and then without preamble said, "At this point we aren't going for any great characterization. It's just not possible without carefully considered preparation to give you time to grow into the person you will ultimately be. What I am looking for now is your own feelings and reactions at a moment of intolerable injustice. . . . You've studied the scene, I take it?"

Star nodded, hardly liking to mention that she'd learned it in the car on the way while Max had done the driving, prompting her at the same time.

"Right. Then let's try a rehearsal."

He took her hand and led her onto the set, which was just a rough backing intended to represent some kind of courtroom. There was a simple wooden stool and Jon made Star sit down, hands folded, head bowed. He knelt down beside her and spoke to her in short, earnest bursts. "The one thing to keep in the forefront of your mind is that you are innocent . . . you are not a witch . . . you are a girl who today would be studying medicine, with a brilliant career ahead of her . . . someone of exceptional diagnostic talents with a genuine gift for healing. You mean to defend that gift. You know it is good and not evil, but the witch hunt is on and they're after blood. You are the victim of prejudice and superstition. Okay?"

Star nodded silently, too scared to utter.

"Right," Jon said, "let's try it. On 'Action,' look up and start to speak. For the moment, stay seated throughout."

Star's hands felt damp and an ominous churning started in the pit of her stomach. But on the signal "Action" she looked up, facing an imagined prosecutor, and despite the constriction in her throat started her speech.

"What you say, sir, with respect, is false. My gifts of healing have been granted me by the Great Lord our God. It is His hand that guides me and never, like you say, the black power of Satan. . . ."

Star stumbled over the next words. "I have sworn and will swear again—" She broke off and snapped out of character. "Sorry," she said.

"Don't stop," Jon said patiently. "Just carry on."

Star couldn't remember where she'd got to. Her mind was blank.

"I have sworn . . ." someone prompted her.

Something near panic started to rise within her. She was filled with the feeling of being somewhere she shouldn't be, of doing something she had no right to be doing. Her tongue had turned to wood and she couldn't produce a sound. Could hardly breath.

"Right," Jon said. "Just relax and we'll run it again from the top." He came and knelt down beside her again. "You're doing just fine. In fact, this time I'm going to run the camera. You just do it your own way. The feeling is all there. Don't worry."

Star shook her head. "I can't do it," she whispered. "I told Max . . . I'm sorry, wasting your time. Don't you see? I just mustn't act."

"Mustn't?" the director asked, puzzled. "Who says you mustn't?"

"Did I say 'mustn't'? I . . . I meant can't." And she remembered what Max had said to her over breakfast. "Mustn't" compete with Laura? She rejected the idea and yet she had just said the word. She was aware of the people around her, of the technicians, the cameraman, all the kind of people she'd always known, and she felt acutely ashamed of the way she was behaving. Where was "The show must go on" and "Mustn't let the customers down" and all the other theatrical sayings that Jessie had reared her on? Her personal problems with Laura were no concern of the crew now waiting for her to get her act together. She tilted her chin in an unconscious imitation of the woman who stood in the way of her even attempting to play the scene, and with the gesture the feeling of panic seemed to seep away.

"Okay," she said. "Let's go."

She bowed her head again and closed her eyes. All

the last minute bustle before a "take" seemed a million miles away. With no great act of will she felt the identity of Abigail, the simple country girl now fighting for her life, take over from Star so that her problems and inhibitions melted away. She heard the one word "Action," and looking up she fixed her gaze on the camera, but in its place there seemed to be a grim-faced man—her inquisitor. She started to plead with him.

"What you say, sir, with respect, is false. . . ." The words came tumbling out as she protested her innocence. "The babe did die but 'twas from the black fever, not from no act of mine. Why ever would I want to harm an innocent babe? I wouldn't harm no one . . . I been given these healing hands to do good in the world. . . ." Involuntarily she rose to her feet, holding out her hands in supplication. "And if the dear Lord don't desert me, I shall go on with my work and nothing nor no one shall stop me." By the time she had finished the speech, tears were coursing down her cheeks.

The director called, "Cut." There was a moment's silence and then Star, still in the grip of emotion, was suddenly brought back to reality by the spontaneous burst of applause that came from the crew and everyone else on the set. She blinked and looked round her, feeling totally bewildered. What a magic sound it was. Then to her surprise she saw Max standing just behind the camera. He wasn't applauding but he smiled at her with undisguised love and pride and, quite uncharacteristically, gave her a thumbs-up sign.

"*HARRINGTONS* STAR SACKED"

Harry blinked in disbelief at the banner headline in the evening paper that Alice had handed him as he walked into his office. He chewed nervously on his unlit cigar and continued to read.

"The rumors that have been flying around show-biz high spots were today officially confirmed—Laura Denning, who has played the character of Kim for more years than some of the soap opera's younger viewers have been alive, is OUT. Her contract is not being renewed.

"The official story being handed out by City TV is that this decision has been arrived at by mutual agreement because Miss Denning wants to extend her talents in other directions. But the fact that the younger and oh-so-sexy Diane Bennet is elbowing her off the screen and out of the ratings is said to be nearer the true reason for Kim's forthcoming demise. Just how the character will be disposed of has yet to be revealed. Personally I will bid her farewell with no regrets. She has more than outstayed her welcome.

"By this I refer only to 'Kim' and not to Laura Denning, who has by her charm and undoubted charisma managed to breathe life into this two-dimensional, totally unbelievable store heiress for so long. . . ."

The piece then ran on to outline details of Laura's life, her marriage, her divorce, and finally—"Recently her name has been linked with that of writer Donald Maxwell, although rumor has it that his interest is centered more on Laura's daughter, the lovely Star Merrick. Well, at least it's all in the family."

Harry threw the paper down on his desk. "Bastard," he said softly, but with great feeling.

"I know," Alice clucked sympathetically. "These reporters."

"Not them. You expect pigs to behave like pigs. No, I meant him . . . Len . . . of all the grimy, underhanded tricks! Call his office! Not that I imagine for one moment he'll be available."

He wasn't.

No, Sir Len was not in his office. No, his secretary

had no idea where she could reach him either now or in the foreseeable future. But of course she would certainly tell Sir Len that Mr. Conrad had called, and he would be sure to return the call.

"Like hell he will."

"Shall I get Miss Denning for you?" Alice asked. "She did call earlier."

Harry hesitated, his bloodhound brow crumpled with worry. This situation was going to need careful handling. He was not really surprised at the turn things had taken, only that Len was capable of sinking even lower in his estimation than he had been already. Laura would be devastated. And who would be there to pick up the pieces? Why, good old Harry, of course. But this time he wanted things to go his way, and if he played his cards right Laura could come out of the whole thing with her pride intact and he would come out of it with —well—perhaps with Laura.

Laura stood staring unseeingly through the gleaming plate-glass window out onto the now bleak-looking terrace. She would have loved a drink, a large neat vodka for preference, but knew it was vital to keep a clear head. The evening paper with the unbelievable item of news about her being thrown off the show lay on the coffee table where she had flung it. The truth of the situation still hadn't completely sunk in, although after the way she had been treated in Len's office it really shouldn't have come as a surprise. The insult implicit in his behavior hurt almost more than the fact of being fired. A tear stole down her cheek. Angrily she brushed it aside. Tears were for failures, not for her. What the hell had Harry been thinking of not to have seen this coming? Not to have protected her? And where was he now that she needed him so desperately?

Harry was in fact at that moment outside the house,

trying to fight his way through the newsmen and photographers clamoring round the entrance.

"You Harry Conrad?"

"Laura's agent. Right?"

"What's the truth about her getting the bullet?"

A photographer took aim at him and snapped, though what anyone would do with the result Harry couldn't even surmise. He said nothing. He was not going to be drawn by any of this mob and continued to push past to the front door. He could see the resolute figure of the porter, Thomson, through the glass door. Thomson peered back at him suspiciously, determined to defend his stronghold against any would-be invaders.

"How does Laura feel about her boyfriend making out with her daughter?"

This got to Harry and unwisely he allowed himself to react. "You print any such filth and I will personally see that you and your rag are sued for slander."

"Great!" the reporter grinned. "Thanks, Harry."

At that moment Thomson, recognizing Harry, opened the door just wide enough to allow him to squeeze through and to keep the surge of newspeople at bay.

"You all right, Mr. Conrad?"

"Thanks, Thomson," Harry said, straightening his rumpled clothes.

Thomson, impervious, made no comment on the situation. He called the lift and opened the door for Harry.

To his surprise Harry found the front door of the apartment ajar. He pushed it open and with a sense of alarm registered how unnaturally quiet it seemed. No sign of Laura, not even of that old harridan Foskett.

"Laura!" he called.

No reply. Christ! Could she have done something crazy? Killed herself or something? Laura . . . my little Laura . . . He hurried into the sitting room, calling her name, then he saw her by the window, silhouetted against the evening sky.

"Laura . . . Laura, baby." He went to her with arms outstretched.

"Where the hell have you been?" she demanded, her voice parrot-shrill.

"I came as soon as I could. As soon as I read—"

"Well, it wasn't soon enough, was it? If you'd been doing your job, none of this would have happened."

"Laura, baby, you're upset."

"Too bloody right I am."

"The way Len has handled this is unforgivable, but you know I did warn you that—"

"You know what else that jerk did?" Laura filled Harry in with details of Len's treatment of her that morning. "Left me sitting in his outer office."

"Why did you go there in the first place?"

"I've always gone to that office whenever I wanted and Len has never refused to see me."

"For Christ's sake, girl, you knew the situation had changed. You knew he was hedging about your contract, that Diane Bennet was moving up the charts and you were moving down."

"Because Sylvester was screwing her."

"Whatever the reasons. I'm not saying there was any justice in it, but those were the facts. The only kind of facts Lennie understands. If you hadn't tried to corral him I could at least have got you out of the whole messy business with some kind of dignity—not to mention compensation."

"There shouldn't be any question of my being out. *Harringtons* without Kim Carson is unthinkable."

"I'm afraid that's not so. You've seen it for yourself in black and white."

Now the truth seemed finally to hit Laura. She stared at Harry, her face distorted with pain. When she spoke her voice was barely audible. "You mean . . . they really don't want me anymore?"

Slowly, silently, Harry nodded his head.

With a sudden, jerky movement, as though the breath had been knocked out of her, Laura sank down onto the sofa. Harry sat beside her, took hold of her hand, and held on tight in an attempt to comfort her. He knew better than to speak. Mere words would mean nothing.

"How?" she asked after a long moment.

"How what?"

"How will they get rid of Kim?"

"No idea."

"Not kill her off . . . no, not kill her . . ." She spoke of the character as though she really existed. As though some sinister gang were planning a murder.

Harry saw that his moment had come and moved in. Gently he slipped a big paw around her shoulder and said, "Marry me."

Laura frowned, as though hearing indistinctly through a thick fog. "Harry, for God's sake, don't you know what this means to me?"

"And don't you know what you mean to me?"

Laura either didn't hear or didn't want to. "I see it all now." She turned wide, frantic eyes on him. "That's why they had her buy that new sports car . . . I said it was out of character. They're going to kill her, the bastards! After all these years." At last Laura allowed the tears to flow. For Kim she could weep, if not for herself. "I should have known. They won't have me back now, Harry. Not even for one lousy episode. They'll kill her off-screen, and there'll be a big funeral, and Diane-bloody-Bennet will be there in black, and . . ." Sobs engulfed her. She buried her face in Harry's shoulder. He put his arms around her and held her close.

* * *

Streaks of gold and flame lightened the night sky, heralding the dawn. Gradually black turned to gray and a dim light slipped past the striped curtains of Max's bedroom. Star progressed gently from sleep to wakefulness. She didn't move but gazed with warm, protective love at the face of the man lying asleep alongside her. He looked so young and vulnerable with not a sign remaining of that sardonic, arrogant creature she had met not so long ago on her mother's terrace. The mouth curved softly, almost smiling, but a gentle, generous kind of smile; the thick black lashes lay in two crescents over his cheeks. Dark unruly curls spread over his forehead. He looked so peaceful, so . . . beautiful was the only apt description, that Star felt completely content just to lie and watch him.

The last forty-eight hours seemed totally unreal to her. She could hardly believe that so much could happen in so short a space of time: to have found the one person she knew she loved and who she unquestioningly believed loved her. To discover—through him—that she really could act after all. To see a future stretching out ahead of her, full of such exciting potential. All the things she had thought were totally out of reach now seemed not just possible but, as near as anything could be, certainties.

After the screen test she had been in a state of euphoria and for the first time really understood why her mother and so many others made such sacrifices in order to act. It was unlike anything she had ever experienced. She knew she was hooked.

"You see?" Max had said. "I told you you were an actress. Perhaps from now on you'll listen to me. I'm invariably right about everything," he added with a mischievous smile. "Come on. We'll go and celebrate."

"But I feel so grotty. I must go back to the flat and shower and change."

"I have a perfectly good shower at my flat. Then, if it really worries you, we'll go somewhere so dark and discreet you can hardly see what you're eating let alone what you're wearing."

Max had a studio flat on the top floor of Chelsea House, a faceless modern block near Sloane Square. It was spacious and well furnished with a magnificent view out over the city and down to the river. It had all the impersonal attributes of a four-star hotel room. Star showered and washed her hair in the highly functional bathroom then, wrapped in one of Max's bathrobes, sat deep in one of the well-upholstered, expensively covered easy chairs. While Max was showering she looked around the room; there seemed to be nothing of him in it. Of his personality. She had an overwhelming urge to get out and go back to the cottage. She didn't feel she wanted Max to make love to her here.

"Is this your own flat?" she asked when he emerged, toweling himself, from the bathroom.

"I rent it," he said.

"Furnished?"

"Yeah. Why?"

"Max . . . I'd rather go home," she blurted out.

He paused, wrapped the towel around his waist, and sat down opposite her. "And where exactly is that?"

Star felt she'd made a mistake. Couldn't really think why she'd called the cottage "home." "Did I say 'home'? I meant . . . well, the cottage."

Max didn't speak. Just sat there looking at her with an expression that was at once tender and unsure. Then he reached out and gently touched her cheek. "All right, my darling," he said. "If that's what you want, we'll go home."

They had lit the fire and eaten a meal of instant something or other from the deep freeze and gone over every point of the test. Then they discussed the whole subject of witchcraft in depth, including the possibility of one person exerting power over another.

Which led to Helen.

"I realize now that I wasn't in love with her," Max said, "but I was truly bewitched by her. To be honest" —he seemed to be reaching inside himself, into some deep reservoir of truth—"I don't think I even liked her. She just had this extraordinary hold over me. Like some kind of addiction."

"How awful," Star said.

"I could deny her nothing. My darling, whatever happens you mustn't ever, ever feel jealous of this. It was, as you say, mostly awful, and I still don't quite understand it. It had nothing of what we have together. And yet I called it 'love.' What a misused word that is. It was not love, I assure you. It was servitude, and who in their right mind wants that?"

Star considered this for a moment—servitude, not love. Her immediate reaction was something near to envy of the unknown Helen who could exact this reaction from him. Then she felt aware of some echo in herself. Some understanding—though of a relationship vastly different: Laura and herself.

"I think . . ." She hesitated, unsure of how to express her feelings. "I know it's not really the same but having someone in your life who sort of takes you over . . . well, I do know that one, don't I?"

Max looked at her intently then reached out a hand and gently smoothed back her hair from her brow. "You are quite incredible, you know that? Who else— what other woman—could ever understand?" He kissed her on the lips. A tender, unerotic kiss. "But we're through with all that now, aren't we? Both of us?"

Star nodded. "I do love you," she said. "I love all

that you are and all that has gone before in your life and all that is to come."

"Amen."

Star kissed him now; cool at first then with increasing passion.

Max said, "Let's go to bed."

Their lovemaking had been free and passionate. Star felt wonderfully uninhibited—glad to experiment and ultimately to take the lead, mounting her lover and allowing herself to experience sensations she had never imagined possible. And to know the joy of making love in a dominant way to someone you adore, to have it within your power to give him the wild delight, the crazed exultation that must lead finally to the enchanting frenzy of shared orgasm.

They had slept, deeply content, in each other's arms. And now as she lay gazing at her love as he slept, she was overwhelmed by an emotion so tender as to be almost maternal.

Max woke quite suddenly. He didn't blink or look bleary-eyed. From one second to the next—fully awake. But he didn't move. He just lay looking at her as she was looking at him. Two lovers cocooned in the warmth of the duvet and their own bodies, neither of them wanting to break the magic spell of the joy of waking up in a shared bed. Of knowing that they had a whole long day ahead of them to spend together in their own private world.

By some unspoken mutual agreement they started gently to explore each other's body, to caress, tease, titillate, excite, until easily, graceful as two dancers in a dream, their bodies merged, giving and taking, playing a limitless variety of chords and harmonies, making heavenly music that rose ultimately to a crescendo as he poured his love into her. Not a word had been spoken. Nor was any needed. Their bodies had said it all.

They lay still engulfed in the sweet smell of lovemaking, then very gently Max disengaged himself.

"I'm hungry," he said.

"Me too," she laughed. "Lovemaking seems to give us an appetite."

Max sprang out of bed and soon Star could hear the shower running and his voice singing decidedly off key but with great gusto. The sound of the flap of the letterbox followed by a thud as either papers or mail landed on the doormat made Star aware that a new day had really begun. She stretched, contented as a cat, and slid out of bed. Soon she heard Max padding down the stairs, heard him pick up the mail (or newspapers) and go into the kitchen.

As she went to take her shower Star decided that she was looking forward to a really hearty, country breakfast. But when she joined Max in the kitchen she was surprised to find that this time he'd not even put on the coffee. He was seated at the kitchen table with some half dozen morning papers spread out on it. Star remembered that he'd told her that he always read as many newspapers as he could each day, to try to keep up with varying attitudes and opinions and hopefully arrive at something like the truth between them. He looked up as she entered the room. Without saying anything he pushed one of the newspapers toward her. Star looked at it, puzzled, then immediately understood: on the front page was a large, rather out-of-date photograph of Laura with a caption that read: LAURA OUT OF STORE SOAP.

"Oh, no," she whispered, and sank down onto the wooden chair opposite Max.

"Oh, yes," he said grimly. "They've really gone to

town on her . . . and on us." He pushed the papers across the table toward her.

"Us?"

Star looked at the other papers. They all carried the same story with varying degrees of sensationalism: the up-market journals reporting in more modified terms, calling Laura by her own name and not that of the character she played, and making no reference to her private life apart from the fact that she was once married to Vernon. The slush-to-gutter tabloids stressed her advancing years and declining popularity but most of all they dwelt on details of her private life: the loss of her "lover" Max to her teenage daughter. This was covered by being accredited to rumor but the smear was there nevertheless.

Star felt a wave of nausea sweep over her.

"It's . . . horrible," she stammered. "How can anyone write such filth?"

"That's not the worst," Max said, his voice harsh with anger. "That sewer scraper 'Walter Ricky' has really excelled himself. Listen to this."

He rifled through one of the murkier tabloids, past other features of varying inaccuracy and tawdriness, until he found the page that featured the notorious "Ricky" column. There was a picture of Laura displaying much cleavage—a photograph that had obviously been imaginatively gone over by the art department— and another pic of Max and Star taken on that long-ago night when they had first danced together at Renata's Club.

"The banner reads: LAURA DITCHED BY LEN AND LOVER."

"I . . . I don't think I want to hear this," Star protested, barely able to whisper.

"You'd better know. I suppose it does concern you." He continued to read aloud: "On the day that Sir Len

Latham, boss of City TV, fired fading—if not faded—
Laura Denning, star of the too-long-running soap
Harringtons, her ex-boyfriend, Donald Maxwell, was
screentesting her beautiful daughter, Star Merrick, for
the lead role in the film of his best-selling horror novel
Satan's Daughter, thus adding insult to injury following
Max's switch of affections from mother to daughter.
Donald Maxwell, born Maximilian Macdonald of Austrian origin, has caused a serious rift in the mother/
daughter relationship. They are no longer on speaking
terms following a violent quarrel over the sexy scribe. I
wonder who 'Satan' is in Laura's book right now? Whoever it is, my guess is that the lady will have a good
supply of pins and knows exactly which wax image to
stick them into."

Max lowered the paper, his face expressionless, only
the stormy gray of his eyes expressing his feelings.

Star found she couldn't speak. She suddenly felt
rather sick. Max folded the paper and slammed it down
on the table. "Now, listen to me. This guck has nothing
whatever to do with us. You had to know but now you
must put it right out of your mind."

"How can I?" Star asked, agonized.

"If you see a pile of dog shit in your path, you don't
stop and examine or comment. You just hold your nose
and walk past."

"I suppose you're right. But they won't let us alone,
you do know that?"

"If we refuse to get involved they'll soon get bored,
and in a week's time they'll find some other poor sod to
pillory."

"The worst thing is the distortion. I mean, I couldn't
really deny what they say. . . . I *did* quarrel with
Laura and in a way it was about you. I *did* do the test,
and we do love each other. . . ." Tears filled Star's
eyes. "This rubbish makes it all sound so sordid."

"That's the object of the exercise, isn't it? Right. Now let's put it where it belongs."

With one expansive gesture Max gathered up the newspapers, crossed to the wastebin, and stuffed them inside.

"Now," he said, "for something really important: breakfast."

"I'm not hungry."

Max ignored her and set about grinding coffee, making toast, squeezing orange juice. He gave it his full attention, did not even glance at Star hunched up in her chair in stunned silence. Neither spoke until Max handed her a glass of orange juice and said, "Here, instant vitamin C," and Star said, "Thank you," rather formally. The sweetness of the juice did seem to help. She started to come alive again. She stared down at the empty glass, turning it round and round in her hands.

"Poor Laura," she said finally.

"She'll survive," Max said.

"She won't. *Harringtons* is her whole life."

"Then it's time she filled it with something a bit more edifying."

"Being pushed out like this—you don't know what it'll do to her."

"I think Laura subscribes to the school of thought that believes that any publicity is good publicity."

"Getting the sack? Your daughter swiping your boyfriend?"

"In case it has slipped your mind," Max said with dangerous calm, fishing boiled eggs from a saucepan, "I was never her boyfriend—not even her friend."

"You know that and I know it . . . because you said so, and I believe you. . . ."

"Thanks," Max said dryly.

"I do," Star said with almost too much emphasis.

"Okay. So?" Max placed egg, toast, butter on the table in front of her. "Eat," he commanded.

"I don't understand you. How can you be this cool, this uncaring? All right, you weren't emotionally involved with her, but you allowed people to think you were having an affair even if you weren't. You spent time with her, lived with her. . . ."

Max chopped the top off his boiled egg in one decisive slice and started to dig in with his spoon. He took a mouthful and then buttered a slice of toast. "I thought I had explained the situation and that you understood. However, let's make it quite clear: I only took on the somewhat bizarre assignment of being Laura's 'ghost' because I was going through a period near suicidal despair. You know why."

"Helen," Star said, picking at some dry toast.

"Helen. I am not proud of the episode. It seems in retrospect as though I had a severe attack of some dread disease . . . something over that I had no control and that almost did me in. I'm not excusing myself but I took on the job with Laura as just that—a job."

"To get over Helen?"

"And to get over a monumental writing block."

"So Laura helped you?"

"Indirectly—and strictly unintentionally—yes, I suppose so."

"Then why do you hate her?"

"Do I hate her? Not really. I only hate what she has done to you—because, in case you don't realize it, I love you."

Star held her hand out to him across the table. "And I love you too. So much."

They sat for a moment looking at each other in silence. Then Max said, "So. We stay here, right? I'm unlisted and any of that putrid pack who might try to hunt us down will be baying outside my London flat—

as presumably they are outside Laura's. We just stay put
here and get on with our lives until the whole mucky
little cloud blows over."

Star shook her head vehemently. "No," she almost
shouted. "I must to go Laura. I must."

"Don't be absurd."

"I know you were around her for a while and to you
she seemed just an egotistical actress, but I know what
losing *Harringtons* will mean to her. Kim, the character
she plays, is part of her."

"Always seemed quite crazy to me."

"That's because you're not an actor."

Max regarded her thoughtfully. "And you are." It
was a statement, not a question.

"Yes, I guess I am. Yesterday when I was in that
studio I wasn't me . . . not all the time anyway. I was
Abigail. I suppose if that feeling doesn't come to you
then you aren't an actress. And whatever she may or
may not be, Laura is just that. And losing Kim . . .
who she's been all these years . . . well, I can tell you
that her feelings about you and me are as nothing compared to losing Kim. Losing 'the store.' "

Max chewed on a piece of toast. "As you say—poor
Laura."

Star missed the irony in his voice. "You do understand?" she asked, so wanting him to.

"Up to a point. I think there's a difference between an
actor identifying with a role and being taken over by it
to the point of schizophrenia. But we won't argue that
now. I don't honestly see how you can help her. Your
presence will just rub salt in the wound. She's got Harry
and various other hangers on."

"I'm her daughter," Star protested. "I must go to
her. Support her."

"And lay yourself open to those muckraking pigs?"

"There's something you have to understand, Max,"

Star said softly. "Have to accept. Come what may, infuriating as she can be, I do love my mother."

"And I love you—more than you know. I can't stand
the thought of you being hurt."

"That's a risk I must take."

Max looked at her as she sat across the table from
him, her eyes wide with childlike concern. Feelings of
tenderness and frustrated anger fought for supremacy
as he realized how tied the girl still was to the woman
he knew to be incapable of caring for anyone but herself. But what right had he to tell a daughter how she
should feel toward her mother? He sighed. "Right
then," he said, quite matter-of-fact. "You're car's okay
now. I had the mechanic come to fix it yesterday while
we were in London."

Star reached out and took his hand. "I do love you,"
she said. "Just don't forget it. Not ever."

As Star drove through Knightsbridge in the direction of
Belgravia Place she went over yet again in her mind
how she should handle the reporters who most certainly
would be swarming around Laura's front door. She
would stick to "No comment," smile politely, not be
provoked into showing her true feelings, and if absolutely unavoidable pose for one picture. Must be sure to
have her key to the outer door ready so that she could
get in quickly without having to stop and search for it in
her handbag. She would leave her overnight bag in the
car so that no conclusions could be drawn as to where
she was living. She was dressed in the same casual
clothes she had worn to go on her search for Jessie—
what seemed like years ago now. She had tied her hair
back severely with a scarf and wore glasses. She had
tried hard to play down her beauty, though without
success—a fact she did not realize.

Along Sloane Street, into the succession of side

streets, and then, with heart racing, she turned the car into Belgravia Place. The square was filled with parked cars—but no more than usual. Then, as she drew near to number forty-eight, Star blinked in disbelief. The porticoed entrance looked as discreetly quiet as always. Not a reporter loitered. Not a photographer hovered. Just Tiger, the tabby cat, sitting in his accustomed place on the top step. Star felt an unreasonable sense of anti-climax at the normality of the scene. Something close to resentment that, after all, Laura should be deemed so unnewsworthy. But most of all she felt relief that she wouldn't have to deal with brash, possibly offensive newshounds.

Still, as she went up in the elevator she fought off feelings of apprehension. Feelings she had experienced years ago when she knew she had aroused Laura's dis-approval for one reason or another. "Just stop it," she told herself sternly. "You're an adult, for God's sake, so behave like one."

Laura might not be home. Perhaps she had gone into hiding, which would explain the absence of reporters. Star half hoped that this was the explanation, which would delay the confrontation with her mother.

As she let herself into the flat, Star was surprised to hear Laura's voice coming from the direction of the sitting room. It was not her natural voice but more like the tone she used for public appearances or on stage.

"I'm a professional person myself," she was saying, "so I appreciate that you have your jobs to do, and this is why I thought it would be easier if we had this little get-together to give you the facts instead of you having to do a lot of inventing. . . ."

Star followed the sound of the voice to the sitting room. She stopped in the doorway, hardly believing the sight before her eyes.

The room was crowded with reporters, photographers, radio reporters slung with tape recorders and microphones. A television cameraman was aiming a handheld camera at Laura as she spoke. Not for the first time in her life, Star was filled with admiration for the cool way Laura could take a bad situation and turn it to her own advantage. The way she now sat on a sofa, with every sign of being completely in command, slender legs crossed, dressed elegantly but somewhat demurely in a simple high-necked jersey dress in her favorite shade of green—the one that reflected her emerald-colored eyes and made them seem even more startling than usual. Seated alongside her on the sofa was the faithful Harry, gazing at her in adoration. Looking round the assembled company, Star saw that everyone present seemed to hang on Laura's every word. Seemed to be positively hypnotized by her. Clearly Max was right—Laura had no need of her. Mum was doing fine.

Star was just about to leave as quietly and quickly as possible when Laura's voice rang out, "Star, darling! Oh, this couldn't be better."

Star turned. Laura was standing with arms outstretched toward her. Star smiled a little weakly. She knew she was trapped. Had no option but to go to her mother and play her part in whatever charade was about to take place. Laura flung her arms around her daughter and Star dutifully responded, thinking how clever it was of Laura to take the wind out of any grubby sails that might be unfurling. Cameras clicked as the smiling mother and daughter embraced each other. Still holding on to Star's hand, Laura pulled her down beside her on the sofa.

"So what's all this about us quarreling?" Laura laughed.

Star smiled and shrugged.

"You see?" Laura continued to the scribbling, snapping assembly. "You really did get that one wrong, didn't you?"

"What about Donald Maxwell?"

"What about him?" Laura asked ingenuously.

"Your name was associated with his, and now—"

Laura held up an imperious hand. "I'm not going to say we were just good friends"—this got a laugh—"although it may have appeared that way for a while. The fact is that Max was helping me to write my autobiography. It was a purely business arrangement. Certainly there was never any kind of personal involvement."

"What about—?"

Before the question could be asked, Laura was in with her answer. "Of course I knew that my darling girl and Max were a bit 'that way' about each other, and being a good modern mother I also knew that it was none of my business. If they can be happy together, then fine. Now, if you don't mind I'd like to make an announcement. . . ." Laura smiled lovingly at Harry and with her spare hand reached out and took hold of his. "The reason that after all these years I am bowing out of *Harringtons* is sitting right here beside me. Yes, Harry Conrad, who has looked after my professional interests for so long, is now committed to looking after my personal life. We are going to do that old-fashioned thing and get married."

More clicking of cameras, more frantic scribbling on pads coincided with the appearance of three white-coated waiters bearing trays of glasses filled with champagne, which they proceeded to hand round to the eager, ever-thirsty media people.

Laura continued. "Of course I shall not give up my work completely, but my first priority will be looking after my husband."

Star saw the expression of deep joy on Harry's usually lugubrious face and hoped that he would be able to take Laura on a full-time basis. Certainly it did seem a solution to the present crisis and she gave Laura full marks for the way she had handled it.

They posed for loving, family-type pictures. Star said "No comment" several times when questioned about Max and the possibility of her playing in his film. Eventually all the champagne was drunk and the company dispersed, leaving Star feeling exhausted. Laura was on a positive high.

"Well," she said lightly, deliberately understating, "that all went quite well, didn't it?"

"You were magnificent," Harry said reverently.

"Great," Star said, although her feelings about the whole display were mixed. Certainly Laura had got the better of a tricky situation but wasn't it all rather . . . she searched for the right word . . . rather undignified, and certainly insincere? Not for one moment did she believe that Laura had suddenly decided that she'd rather be Mrs. Harry Conrad than anything else on earth. It was a straw that had been clutched at in desperation. She found it incredible that Harry could be taken in and seem elated as a kid on his first date. Still, perhaps it might work. Perhaps Laura knew what she was doing and had finally realized what a sweet guy Harry really was. She sincerely hoped so and gave Harry a kiss and a hug.

"Congratulations, Uncle Harry."

"And what about me?" Laura pouted. "Don't I get any congratulations?"

"Of course." Star brushed Laura's proffered cheek with her own. "I hope you'll both be very happy," she added.

"Of course we will," Laura cooed.

Harry wanted to take them both out to lunch to celebrate but Laura begged off. "This whole thing has totally demolished me, darling," she said, passing a weary hand across her brow.

Harry, affectionate and understanding, took his leave. Afterward Laura looked steadily at Star, the bright little-girl smile with which she had said good-bye to Harry wiped from her face. She didn't speak and Star could think of nothing to say. The hired waiters were still clearing up the debris of the champagne and canapes. Star watched them for a moment.

"Where's Mrs. Foskett?"

"At the bottom of the river with a stone around her neck—at least I hope she is. Cow! It was she who . . ." Aware of the waiters, who might easily be runners for some gossip columnist, Laura interrupted herself. "Come into my room." It was a command in the old, old style and Star bridled. She had no wish to be involved in any post mortems.

She only wanted to get back to the cottage, back to Max. But she, too, saw the waiters giving them surreptitious glances. No way was she going to argue with Laura in front of them. So she followed her, determined to make her getaway as quickly as possible.

Laura kicked off her shoes and settled herself on top of the bed, piling up the collection of lacy pillows at her back. She patted the edge of the bed to indicate that Star should take the place that had always been hers in the past whenever Laura could spare time for her but which at this moment Star chose to ignore. She sat on Laura's makeup stool.

"Well, Star," Laura said, her voice heavy with sarcasm. "To what exactly do I owe the honor of this visit?"

Star tensed but was determined not to swallow the bait. "You were saying something about Mrs. Foskett?"

"Bitch. She was selling juicy tidbits about us to the press. I chucked her out."

"Who have you got now?"

"I don't imagine you came here to discuss my servant problem."

"No. I came . . ." Star hesitated. "I came because I thought you'd be feeling desperate about *Harringtons*."

Laura looked down at her hands. Suddenly the bright, hard expression was replaced by a frown of real unhappiness. Star saw that her mother was fighting back tears. On an impulse she crossed and sat on the edge of the bed and took Laura's hand. Laura held on tight and for a moment neither of them spoke.

"It was the way it was done," Laura said at last, her voice husky with emotion, and went on to tell Star just how shoddily she had been treated.

"That's foul," Star said indignantly. "After all you've given to them. I am so sorry, Laura."

"It's a pretty shitty business. I've always known it, which is why I hoped you'd never go into it. And now it seems you're going to anyway."

"I think so," Star admitted.

Laura looked at her daughter sitting there on the edge of the bed, so young, so amazingly beautiful, and a wave of such envy and resentment passed over her that she felt almost physically sick. The moment of closeness vanished—the feeling of something approaching affection smothered by overwhelming jealousy. Why was she, after all her years of hard work, being thrown on the scrap heap while this inexperienced child was being handed success on a plate? She withdrew her hand from Star's.

"You shouldn't do it. I don't want to be hurtful, Star, but well, let's face it, you just don't have the talent, do you?"

Star shrugged. "I don't think so either, but after the test the director and—"

"Our friend Max has been filling your head with this nonsense, I suppose," Laura asked venemously.

"Let's leave Max out of this, shall we?"

"So. It's true, is it?"

"What?"

"You know very well 'what.' You're having an affair with him."

"I am in love with him."

"Oh, Starlet, no!" Laura wailed. "You don't know what you're getting yourself into."

"I am an adult and—"

"No. You think you are, but you're not. You're a child. My child! And I can't stand by and see you destroyed by a man like that."

"He's a wonderful man," Star protested.

"What? A man who is capable of worming his way into a woman's home, doing his best to get into her bed, and then—"

Star sprang to her feet. "That's a lie. I won't hear anymore."

Laura ignored the interruption and pressed on. "Then because I wouldn't, has his revenge by writing venomous, insulting lies about me. And then"—a sob rose in her throat—"seduces my daughter!"

"Seduces? That's disgusting. I tell you we love each other, and I won't let you or anyone else spoil that."

Star turned and made for the door.

"Star, wait!"

Laura's voice was desperate, pleading, and despite her impulse to get as far away as possible Star stopped, her hand on the door handle.

"Star, look at me."

Slowly she turned back and faced her mother. Laura's eyes were filled with concern, whether genuine or not it was hard to decide, but the look of anguish seemed sincere. "Please listen to me, baby," she pleaded. "Whether you believe it or not I do only want what's best for you. And that's certainly not Max."

When Star did not respond Laura continued, a harsher tone coming into her voice.

"You think he's so great?" she spat out the words. "I suppose he has mentioned the fact that he is married?"

Star ran down the front steps of the house into Belgravia Place and was immediately accosted by cameramen and reporters, including a miniskirted Amazon who thrust a mike into her face.

"That right that you're living with Donald Maxwell?"

Star stared at the girl blankly. Couldn't immediately think where she could have sprung from. She felt so stunned by what Laura had told her that all thoughts of reporters had fled and she couldn't imagine why anyone should be asking such a personal and horribly painful question. When the situation clicked into place in her mind she was outraged at the intrusion.

"What the hell's it got to do with you?" she said, and pushed past in the direction of her parked car.

Cameras clicked, the photographers delighted to catch her off-guard. The woman reporter trotted after her. "You're news, Star," she said. "And news is my business."

Star searched frantically for her car keys in the depths of her bag. She cursed herself for playing into their hands by reacting emotionally—by reacting at all.

"Come on, Star," the reporter pleaded. "Give me a break. Woman's angle. Did you and your mum really quarrel over him?"

Star didn't reply. At last she found the elusive key and with fingers suddenly thick and clumsy fought to unlock the car door.

"If you won't talk to me, I'll have to use my imagination, won't I?"

"You probably will anyway," Star couldn't resist retorting. She slid into the driving seat and banged the door closed after her. Reporters continued to rap on the window and photographers went on snapping as she started up the engine and made her escape.

Her one thought now was to get to Max as fast as possible. To have him put his arms around her and reassure her that Laura had been lying. Of course he wasn't married. He loved her and wouldn't deceive her even by omission. She knew it. They would have a calm, sensible discussion and sort the whole thing out. Though she was sure there was nothing to discuss. If Max were married he would have said so . . . wouldn't he? Of course he would. She pushed doubts furiously aside. There was no reason for him not to. It didn't make sense.

She bumped the car down the lane and saw that the Porsche was not standing in its customary place outside the front gate. But smoke was trailing up from the chimney in a straight, unbroken line into the clear, windless sky of late afternoon, which meant that Max was around but must have gone out for some reason.

She parked the car, and as she opened the garden gate noticed that the FOR SALE sign had been taken down.

Did this mean that the cottage had been sold? Or had Max changed his mind and taken it off the market? She did hope so—she had developed such a sense of belonging to the place. She couldn't bear the thought of strangers living there. The front door was unlocked so she opened it and went inside.

"Max?" she called.

There was no reply. Obviously he was out. She subdued the feeling of anticlimax and crossed to the window, half hoping that she might see him as she had on that other occasion, standing down by the stream. She stood by the window and looked out at the view she had grown to love: the calm gentle sweep of countryside worthy of a Constable painting. And as she stood there she became conscious of an odd sensation: the conviction that she was not alone in the house. It was the smell she noticed first. A faint but familiar scent of rose geranium. Then she heard the footsteps on the stairs. Light footsteps descending. Certainly not Max's firm, masculine tread. Then Star turned and saw her and knew immediately that this was Helen.

About her own height and build with the same long, sunstreaked hair. It was easy now to see how the housekeeper had mistaken her identity. But there the similarity ended. Aged about twenty-five, with huge brown eyes in a small heart-shaped face, a small tip-tilted nose and a mouth that had something babyish about it— coming to two distinct points on the upper lip and then taking a downward curve at the corners. A mouth that seemed both sexy and petulant. She looked frail and vulnerable wearing a frilly, diaphanous negligee, which she held close around her thin body as though it could provide some kind of deeply needed protection.

They stared at each for a moment in silence. Then, rather as though she were making conversation at a cocktail party, Helen said, "Nice view, isn't it?"

Star continued to stare at the girl in total bewilderment, something approaching shock. What was she doing here? And how come she was dressed—or rather undressed—as she was? It was only a matter of hours since she—Star—had left the place. How come this one seemed so well installed? So completely at home?

"I'm Helen," the girl continued when Star didn't speak. "And I suppose you must be the one all the fuss is about in the papers?"

"I'm Star Merrick," she managed in little more than a whisper.

Helen made no comment but came slowly into the room. She picked up a packet of cigarettes from the table and lit one. She blew out a long slow stream of smoke, regarding Star all the while with the same curiosity people usually display on seeing an unusual exhibit in a museum. Finally she said, "You seem very young."

Star bridled. She resented the tone and the implication. "I suppose I am quite," she said noncommittally. She felt horribly at a loss. The woman seemed to be regarding her as an intruder in the place that Star had so quickly and easily made her own. She was aware of feeling gauche and awkward. She could think of nothing appropriate to say.

Helen sank down slowly into one of the deep armchairs, carefully crossing her thin, thin legs and arranging the yards of filmy chiffon around her. "I think," she said with very precise articulation as though measuring every word, "I think it would be best all round if you were to leave immediately. Before Max returns."

"But I've come here to see him," Star said, defending her position in the face of this unexpected attack from one whom she now saw as her enemy.

"I appreciate that," Helen continued in the same cool staccato manner. "And I'm sorry—really, I mean it, because you are, as I said, very young, that Max seems to have led you to believe that he was available. He isn't, you see. I live here. This is my home. Surely you must have realized that he was committed? I mean, one look around upstairs must have told you. . . . I assume I am right in thinking that you did go upstairs?"

Star could not reply. Just continued to stare at Helen with a feeling of near panic clutching at her throat.

"It's really very naughty of Max. I suppose I should be used to it by now but he just never can resist; the minute my back is turned there's someone installed and I have all the bother of throwing out forgotten personal possessions. . . . Did you know you left your hairbrush behind, by the way?"

Still Star didn't move. She felt quite paralyzed.

"And they get younger all the time," Helen continued. "I keep saying I've had enough but after all this time I know that he'll always come back to me in the end, so best to let him have his fun with his dollies. I know it doesn't really mean anything to him although at the time, for five minutes, he talks himself into believing that it's the love of his life. I understand the one before you was your mother? I'd have thought her a bit old for Maxie—he really is rather into teenyboppers."

"I don't believe you." The words seemed to say themselves before Star could check them.

"I'm sure you don't. None of them ever do. He has got a very convincing line, and especially with you if he saw you playing Abigail. That would have summoned up all his Pygmalion urges."

"Just tell me one thing. . . ." Star choked out the words. "Are you Max's wife?"

Helen smiled a slow, rather sad smile, opened the great brown eyes even wider, and said, "What do you think?"

All Star wanted then was to get away. She turned and

ran out of the house, slamming the heavy front door behind her. She got into her car and, with harsh grinding of gears, turned it around and drove like mad down the lane, practically wrecking the suspension as the car bounced and rocked from one pothole to the next.

Halfway down the lane she saw Max's Porsche coming toward her.

As soon as he saw her he stopped his car, sprang out, and waved for her to stop, whereupon she accelerated and, swerving onto the edge of the road and practically into a ditch, sped past him and away, leaving him waving frantically after her, shouting words that she could not hear.

She drove back to London in a kind of stunned daze, only just managing to keep control of both the car and herself. Somehow she found her way back to the Earl's Court flat where, to her relief, she found that Annie was out. She could at last give way to her misery, to her feelings of utter despair. She went to her room and collapsed on the bed. Only now did she give herself permission to cry. She couldn't. Her eyes remained dry. Not a sob, not a sigh, passed her lips. The pain she felt became physical and pressed on her chest and throat with such strength that she felt she must surely pass out from it or else explode—but still there was no release. Max, her Max, so dear, so loving, so . . . everything, and the only man she could ever want, was a cheat and a liar. Every part of her seemed to ache as though she were suffering from a kind of fever. She rubbed at her arms and legs to try to get some relief and was sitting thus, curled up, arms clutched across her breast, rocking back and forth, when Annie came in and found her.

From some hidden source she produced a bottle of brandy and gave Star a good slug, which warmed her, and though it didn't bring her round to her normal self at least she was able to communicate.

At first Annie assumed that Star was upset about the publicity in the papers, and it was not until Star managed to gulp out what had happened with Max and Laura and Helen that she caught on. Her reaction was predictable.

"You mean you found out this man is a bastard? Well, I have news for you, darling, he's just normal. They're all bastards. Listen, kid." Annie took Star's hand in her own. "Forget him. You are just starting out on one hell of a successful career. I know it. Dee Costatinos wouldn't spend five minutes of her time on someone she wasn't sure of. You're going to be tops. For chrissakes, don't blow it for some two-timing Romeo. He's not worth it. None of them are. You have all kinds of talents there inside you. Glory in them. Use them. Be your own person."

It made sense, didn't it?

Still Star spent an agonizing night hoping that the telephone would ring and it would be Max telling her it was all a hideous mistake and that he loved her and only her. Around five in the morning she fell into a troubled sleep only to be awakened at seven by the alarm.

Today was the big test session for the Danielle contract. Jeesus! Zombielike, Star submitted herself to makeup and hairdressing. Danielle had provided their own makeup artist and hairstylist and they worked on Star as though she were a potential exhibit for the Royal Academy of Art.

The Danielle representative, an ultrachic woman in her mid-thirties, watched the proceedings with a critical eagle eye. The success or failure of the whole campaign rested on her shoulders and she wasn't taking any risks. When makeup and hair were complete she regarded Star with ruthless scrutiny then pronounced judgment. "Perfect," she said. And the session was under way.

But if the Danielle rep was delighted with Star, Dee was not. She knew something was wrong and was swift to suss it out.

"Wassa matta wid you?"

"Sorry?"

"What's this boil fish look?"

"Sorry?"

"Stop being bloody sorry and give a little, huh?"

They tried again, Star really doing her best to give Dee what she wanted. After an hour Dee stopped and walked away.

"No more," she said.

The Danielle lady was bewildered. "But she's terrific. Great. What's wrong?"

Dee did not immediately answer. She lit a cheroot and signaled to Katy to "save the lights." Eventually she turned to the P.R. and said, "It's better we wait. Everybody has flat days, slime days, nondays, and today that is what our Star has got. I'm sorry. I know she is the model for you but not today. Today I am the photographer, you are the client, but this"—she glared at Star—"is not the model. Unless we have all three going at once I get no pictures, Danielle sells no cosmetics, and we might as well all stay home and knit."

Standing in the small arena in which she had been posing, Star felt deeply humiliated. The one concept with which she had grown up was not "love thy neighbor" or "honesty is the best policy" but "the show must go on." She had just committed the ultimate sin; the show hadn't gone on and all because of her.

The Danielle lady and her two makeup artists withdrew, bowing to Dee's dictum. Dee herself had disappeared in a cloud of black disapproval. As soon as Star had changed into her outdoor clothes she went in search of her. She found her in the sitting room, sunk into the vast leather sofa. She barely glanced up as Star entered.

"We must talk," she growled.

Star sat next to her on the sofa and for what, to her, seemed an age, Dee said nothing. Just sat staring in front of her.

"Have I been perhaps wrong about you?" she said at last. "Are you just a spoiled little girl playing a game of being a model?"

"No, Dee. Really I'm not."

"Then why the bloody hell you suddenly make like a dead camel?"

"I . . . Well, something happened yesterday."

"That rubbish in the paper? You let those worms upset you?"

"No . . . well, that too. . . . But you see . . . someone I care for a lot . . . That is—"

"Please, spare me. I don't want to know. Not my business. You want a psychiatrist or an agony auntie, go someplace else. Here, you come to work."

"I'm sorry. I was trying—"

"Trying? Who wants trying? I want a model who is at least living."

"I really am sorry."

"Sorry doesn't make up for the waste of everybody's time and money, and my talent, which comes very expensive. How would you think if I got everyone together and say, 'Sorry, not today. My lover left me last night. No pictures.' You think I am fucking amateur and you would be hitting right on the nail."

Star didn't speak. Just sat with her head bowed.

"Okay." Dee said after a pause. "Go now. And come tomorrow all in one piece and alive, please. Or else—I don't kid you, babe—out!"

* * *

Star saw the envelope in the pigeonhole for Annie's flat as soon as she let herself into the main entrance hall. For some unknown reason she knew that it was for her. And one glance at the bold, strong hand told her who it was from.

She didn't open the letter at once but propped it up on the mantelpiece while she made herself a mug of coffee. Then she sat sipping, and staring at the envelope, trying to guess at its contents. After what Dee had said perhaps it would be better not to read the letter. Not even open the envelope. But then again, perhaps it might hold some logical and completely acceptable explanation and everything would be fine.

There was only one way to find out. She opened the envelope and knew from the horribly formal beginning that she wasn't going to like this one bit.

Dear Star,

I feel I owe you an apology. It was wrong of me to allow my feelings for you to overrule my common sense. Wrong and stupid. For one brief moment I deluded myself into thinking that you were a mature, intelligent adult when I should have known that you are, in fact, a retarded, unreasonable child.

I have no intention nor, as it happens, any need to justify myself nor explain the situation that you imagined you found here yesterday. After all that had passed between us I would have thought you could at least have had some modicum of faith in me instead of jumping to erroneous and overemotional conclusions. I suppose with your upbringing this is hardly surprising. Clearly you are not ready to enter the sort of relationship that I was fool enough to hope we could have. I am sorry. You can have no idea how sorry.

Max

Star sat for a moment, staring down at the letter in numb disbelief. Then, as emotions started to seep through they were no longer of pain and desolation but of anger. Of outrage that he should have the nerve to play the injured party. To accuse her of lack of faith! To write in this patronizing, pompous, priggish way. *He* was deluded? If anyone was deluded it was she who had allowed her feelings, her emotions, to gallop away with her. She hated to admit it but Laura had been right about him.

She'd been an idiot, and the knowledge of that fact was almost harder to bear than the realization that this was not, after all, the great love but only a brief affair.

Star tore the letter in half, then across again and yet again, and then threw the scraps into the wastebasket. Doing so relieved her feelings, but as her anger subsided a bleak sensation of bereavement started to creep back. Tears welled in her eyes. "No!" She shouted the word out loud. She dug her nails into the palms of her hands in the effort to gain control. She was not going to give in. She'd played the wrong number, backed the wrong horse, but she wasn't going to let it destroy her.

Suddenly she had an image of Laura as she sat facing the press with a confident smile, beautiful, composed, not a hair out of place; completely in command when Star knew that underneath she was still reeling under the crippling blow to her self-esteem. Okay, when you can't be happy at least don't give others the satisfaction of seeing it. But how the hell did Laura pull it off? The only way she knew how. Laura was an actress, and when necessary she went right on acting in real life. If Max had done nothing else (Oh, but he had—though she wouldn't allow herself to dwell on that right now), he had shown her that she could act. So, from this moment on she would quite consciously act at being self-confident and self-contained. The affair would be as nothing to her, and Max of no importance. She was in charge. Her own person. She knew it would be difficult to fool Dee but she was determined to have a damn good try.

She succeeded better than she could have imagined possible.

The sense of outraged pride and righteous anger sustained her through the second Danielle test with surprising force. The hurt child was left cowering under the bedclothes and the dedicated career girl took her place.

Dee was delighted. "Now you fire with all your cylinders, maybe you make a model."

"You bet I will," Star replied, and set about achieving her goal with total dedication. When she was not working at the studio she gave all her time to keeping "the product," as Dee called her body, in good shape. Working out at Body Time and long runs in the park not only kept her fit and slim but also exhausted her sufficiently so that when she got to bed she slept and didn't waste energy crying into her pillow. If memories or secret longings played her false in the small hours of the night she read thrillers or listened to all-night radio. She bought tapes of relaxing exercises and found that mind really could win over poor weak matter, and that even the enemy, insomnia, could be conquered with enough perseverance.

As newsworthy subjects both she and Laura were soon discarded by the press, much to Star's relief. A scandal had broken, involving a cabinet minister and a prostitute, a story that consumed the front pages and gossip columns, pushing Laura and Star and Max to a couple of lines somewhere on an inside page, and then to nothing. Max had been right about that one. Now, Star thought, she would really be able to forget about the whole thing. But it wasn't that easy. However hard she "acted," however well she convinced others and much of the time even herself, deep, deep inside was that hard nugget of pain. That longing that would not be denied.

If Annie knew what Star was going through she was tactful enough to leave the subject alone. Star didn't talk of it so she didn't either. Not until one evening when they were eating whole-wheat quiche and salad in front of the telly, watching a play in which a young actress appeared playing a smart, streetwise girl who still falls for a man and gets pregnant. It was a performance of great skill and sensitivity. Funny, tough, and touching all at the same time.

"Brilliant!" was Star's verdict.

"She is, isn't she?" Annie agreed. "Her name's Tracy Wilmot. She was at the National last season. Played Ophelia. Fantastic reviews she got. As a matter of fact . . ." Annie hesitated and frowned intently down at her empty plate before she continued. "There's something I've been meaning to tell you. . . . I heard it, you know, through the grapevine."

"What? What did you hear?" Somehow Star felt she wasn't going to like it, whatever it was.

"She's been cast for the part of the witch in that film —the one you were going to do."

Star felt a sharp stab of jealousy, of resentment toward this actress who had taken the part that should have been hers, but she wasn't going to show it. She just said, "Well, of course I don't like it but no way was I going to play it now . . . so, can't think of anyone who'd be better."

"I felt I had to tell you. I wouldn't have wanted some bright newshound suddenly springing it on you."

"Of course, thanks. Actually, to be honest, I suppose they're right to take a real professional actress. Oh, I guess I could have done it with a great director but I wouldn't have really known what I was up to."

"You'd have done fine."

"You know what, Annie?" There was a note of suppressed excitement in Star's voice that made Annie look up sharply. Star continued, "I suddenly know exactly what I want to do . . . I want to act. I mean real serious acting. Go to drama school. Do the whole bit."

"Great."

"If I get the Danielle contract I'd earn enough to live on and pay for my training. I wonder which academy I should go to? The Royal Academy of Dramatic Arts is supposed to be good. Or the Guildhall." Star was now completely carried away by her enthusiasm for this new plan, her eyes shining, her cheeks flushed. "I can't wait to get going," she said.

"Hang on," Annie laughed. "First you have to do an audition . . . and before you do the audition you must prepare for it. You'll need some coaching."

"Yes, I suppose I will. Just because I got away with one film test doesn't mean I'd get into RADA. Oh, Annie, I'll just die if I don't. I do so want to be good. As good as—" She was just about to say "Laura" but somehow found that she couldn't. Instead she substituted, "As good as that Tracy Wilmot."

"You'll be better. Now," Annie said, "I've a copy of *Contacts* here somewhere." She started to search through the pile of magazines on the coffee table then triumphantly produced the little magazine that provides show-business people with all the practical information they need: lists of managers, agents, touring companies, repertory companies, and acting schools.

"We'll write to the lot. At least you can get the application forms," Annie said, getting out paper and pen.

"What about finding a coach?"

Annie frowned for a moment, then with one of her exuberant gestures she held a hand aloft. "I know just the guy!"

Star grinned. "I knew you would."

* * *

Jeremy Grant was an ex-actor in his mid-fifties. "Ex" not because he was a bad actor but as a result of a car accident that had put an end to his career. But what might have been the theater's loss was a considerable gain for young hopefuls like Star. At their first interview he was forthright to the point of being offensive. Her voice, her breathing, her projection, her deportment— all terrible. "You wouldn't be heard beyond the first row of the stalls. All right for television but not in the theater, dear. That chap in the back row of the gallery has paid for his seat, too, and deserves to know what the play is about."

Star was quite unfazed by his assessment of her. After Dee she was used to hearing home truths. "Okay," she said. "That's why I'm here. To learn how to reach that guy in the back row. And to get into acting school."

This presented problems. She was too late for most of the spring-term auditions but Jeremy told her of a new school that was opening where she might, with luck, get in. "The standard is going to be tremendously high," he said. "Not one of those fly-by-night places that take just anyone. Dame Peggy Smith is going to be the patron, and she wouldn't lend her name to anything but the best."

Star was impressed. Dame Peggy Smith? One of the greatest actresses of the day. And one who, to Star's shame, she had never seen act. She kept this information to herself but went to see Dame Peggy in her current interpretation of Cleopatra at the National. If she hadn't been hooked before, she certainly was after that.

At last she seemed to have a sense of direction. She landed the Danielle contract and continued to work with Dee but her greatest interest was now in acting. She saw every play and film that she could get to, began to be able to judge both drama and performances. And she worked with devotion at her voice exercises, at her breathing. At what it means to approach and understand a character.

"I see you as Viola," Jeremy said, and together they studied *Twelfth Night* and Star realized that Shakespeare was not the tedious bore she'd thought him at school but sheer magic.

Viola's unrequited love for the Duke struck a chord deep within Star. She could identify only too easily. For all her newfound aims and objectives, her self-realization, her overextended work schedule, still the longing for Max remained. She hoped that one morning she would wake up and find that her first thoughts were not of him. That she might be free again. That Max would be just a memory. Something that belonged to the past. After all, that's what he was. Sometimes the thought of him almost tore her apart and she felt she had somehow to find him. To make it all right again. The way it was. But then with a supreme effort she would banish him from her mind.

The New London Academy of Drama held entrance auditions at the end of November. Star took her place among the dozen or so other would-be actors and, barely able to control feelings of apprehension that verged on stark panic, waited her turn. Then the moment came. That unforgettable moment when for the first time in her life she stepped out from the shelter of the wings onto the blinding exposure of the stage. Then, as in the film test, she forgot Star and became the character she was portraying. It was not she but Viola who said she would "make me a willow cabin at your gate, And call upon my soul within the house . . ." The rest of the audition seemed easy: the contemporary excerpt from a Tom Stoppard play, and the improvisation, which she positively enjoyed.

Jeremy seemed moderately optimistic about the outcome. Almost enthusiastic—for him. "I think perhaps you might make an actress after all," he said.

Then came an agonizing wait until just three days before Christmas she received a letter that she was too scared to open. "You look," she said to Annie.

Annie tore open the envelope. "You're in!" she shouted.

Star snatched the letter from her, and yes, "Dear Star Merrick, We are happy to inform you . . ."

The two hugged each other.

"You're on your way," Annie said. "You're going to have your work cut out, mind. Modeling as well. What does Dee say?"

"That we stay very selective. Which is what she wanted anyway. I don't mind hard work. I know I'm just so bloody lucky."

Annie shook her head. "You make your own luck," she said, "and that's just what you've done."

Star folded the letter and thoughtfully put it back in the envelope. If what Annie said was true then she certainly hadn't played it right with Max. Not much luck there. At this moment she would have given anything to share her good news with him. It seemed somehow empty to be pleased just on her own behalf. Come to that, there was no one to share it with. No Jessie. No Laura. She could call her father in L.A. but she was never able to talk to him, he was always so busy, and anyway he'd say that acting school was a waste of time when she could be earning top money in television soap out there with him.

"Penny for them?" Annie said.

Star looked up, startled out of her reverie. "Some pretty unproductive thoughts actually. I think I'll go shopping," she said with a touch of defiance.

That great mecca of shoppers, Harrods, was ablaze with Christmas decorations and packed with people fighting to complete their Christmas shopping. Star bought a super track suit for Annie and a long, long red silk scarf for Dee. And that, she realized, was her Christmas shopping complete. Nor, she reflected as she wandered round one lavishly stocked department after another, had she made any plans for Christmas Day. Annie had invited her to go to Newcastle with her to visit her family but Star felt she would be intruding. Perhaps accept Dee's invitation? But, apart from work, she didn't really belong there either. So where did she belong?

Then she saw the brooch. It was jade, or something that passed for jade, in one rough-hewn chunk. Perfect for Laura. Her green. Star stood staring at it and felt how very much she wanted to see her mother. To be friends again—however difficult it might be. Perhaps even admit that Laura could have been right about Max. She supposed she must have been crazy, but knew that was not true. She had simply been in love. But that was in the past. Laura was her mother after all, and Star felt sure she'd be pleased and proud that her daughter was going to be an actress.

She bought the brooch, had it gift-wrapped, and half an hour later was outside Laura's flat, ringing the front doorbell. There was a long, long pause and she was about to try again when the door was opened by a harassed-looking middle-aged woman wearing a crumpled white overall.

"Yes?" she asked, her tone implying that she had been interrupted in the performance of some vitally important task.

"Miss Denning? I'm . . ."

"Miss Denning's giving no interviews," came the oft-recited statement.

"I'm her daughter."

"Oh." The poor woman seemed nonplussed. "Then I

suppose you'd better come in." She closed the front door, and as Star stepped into the hall asked almost irritably, "Do you want to be announced?"

Star smiled. "I don't think that will be necessary."

"She's in her room."

Star resisted the temptation of pointing out that all the rooms were Laura's, even that balloon-covered one that had once been hers.

As she walked past the familiar portraits, the luxurious furnishings, the low-slung sofas, she thought how different it all was to Annie's bright, unpretentious flat and decided that she preferred Annie's. This was designer living—not for real people.

Star knocked at the door of Laura's bedroom.

"Yes? What is it?" Laura snapped in a tone that indicated frayed nerves and temper. A tone Star remembered only too well. She opened the door. The sight that faced her brought her to a standstill. Laura's normally immaculate, meticulously controlled environment looked as though it had been hit by a whirlwind: wardrobe doors stood gaping, their contents piled high on the bed; open drawers spilled over onto the floor; even the holy of holies, Laura's dressing table, was a disaster area. Laura, wearing a silk slip, was sitting at the table, concentrating on brushing mascara onto her eyelashes. She glanced up at Star briefly and, showing no sign of surprise, returned to the job at hand.

"Hullo, Star," she said as though they had met that morning.

"What happened?" Star gasped. "You been burgled or something?"

"No. I'm packing."

Only then, as she looked around to find a space to put down her parcels, did Star notice the open suitcases.

"Good you could come by," Laura said, screwing up the mascara wand and putting it into her makeup case.

"I need all the help I can get. That moron the agency sent me is worse than useless. She's been hours ironing a couple of frocks."

"Where are you going, then?"

"Of course you don't know, do you?" Laura said as though her ignorance was some deliberate act of willfulness on Star's part. "It's all happened so fast—honestly, I hardly know what's hit me."

"What has?"

"Starlet, I really haven't time to chat. But of course you should know. It's just fantastic. Unbelievable. I'm going to Hollywood. . . . At last it's actually happened."

"You mean to work?"

"Of course to work. I wouldn't go otherwise. It's no place for unemployed actresses."

"That's terrific. What is it? And when do you go?"

"If I can ever get packed, I leave from Heathrow in exactly four hours' time." She held up a stunning coral-colored dress and examined it critically. "What do you think? Bit tatty, huh?"

"No. That looks great on you. Take it."

"Right. Stick it in the big case, will you?" She threw the dress in Star's direction and indicated a brand new Vuitton suitcase already half packed. Without hesitating Laura had slipped back into their old relationship of glamorous mum and obedient nonperson child as though none of the recent events had ever happened. For a moment Star felt a wave of rebellious anger but then, controlling the emotion that once she did not even allow herself, she could only feel amused. It was almost reassuring to note that come what may Laura's ego was strong and healthy as ever. Star carefully folded the coral creation and put it in the case.

"So, what will you be doing in L.A.? And how did it happen?" she asked.

"You will never believe," Laura said, and her voice sounded excited as a child telling a Christmas tale. "It was Vernon."

"Daddy?" Star was so surprised that she spoke the forbidden word.

"Vernon. Yes. A couple of nights ago he rang. I nearly freaked out. I couldn't imagine why he would ring me, and then he said he'd got this new soap set up ready to go and there's a great part in it for me. . . . Well, you know, since Joan Collins and Stephanie Beacham, mature British actresses are all the go. So—who knows—I may never come back."

"Well, if that's what you want. . . ."

"And you know, I have a funny feeling that Vernon and I might just get back together."

"But," Star protested, "what about Harry?"

"What about him?" Laura scrutinized a dress with disapproval. "You can have this if you like," she said casually. "It only needs cleaning."

Star ignored the offer. "I thought you and Harry were getting married."

"Don't tell me you believed that?"

"Of course I did."

"How can anyone be that naïve?"

"And I was under the impression that Harry believed it too."

Laura shrugged. "Too bad. Look, I had to find a facesaver in a hurry and he was it."

"Laura, how can you do that to him? You know how he's felt about you for years and years," Star blazed, now really furious.

"He'll get over it."

"Maybe he will. Maybe he won't. That doesn't alter the fact that you just used him."

"Think of all the money he'll be making out of me.

Ten percent of what I'll be earning will make my 'store' money look like mouse droppings."

"Have you told him yet?"

"Listen, I really don't have time for this interrogation. You flounced out of here weeks ago for absolutely no reason, and now—"

"No reason? You have a very short memory, Laura. You deliberately tried to ruin everything between me and Max."

"I only hope I succeeded. Now please go and let me finish packing. Where the hell is that bloody woman?" Imperiously she pressed the bell to summon the housekeeper.

Star stared at her in horror. The words that had tumbled out of her in anger, which she didn't even really believe in, now seemed to have some element of truth to them.

"What you said about him," she said, her voice hardly more than a whisper, "about Max being married . . . was that something else you invented just because it suited you at that moment?"

"I don't know what you're talking about. For God's sake, Star, I have a plane to catch. A whole new career in front of me. Probably the most important thing that ever happened to me in my life."

"What about me?"

"And you, of course, you know that."

"That's not what I mean. If you lied to me about Max being married then you ruined the most important thing in *my* life."

"I refuse to continue this ridiculous conversation. Where the hell is that woman? I shall miss the plane."

Star went to the door and turned the key. She took it out of the door and, holding it up high, faced her mother. Her voice was quite matter of fact, calm. "Yes, Mother. I think you well may miss the plane."

"What the hell do you think you're playing at? Give me that key."

"No. Not unless you answer my question."

"I have put everything about that jerk out of my mind. If something I said made you finish with him then I am delighted. Now open that door."

Star stood her ground. Laura made to snatch the key and missed. There was a knock on the door. Star and Laura stood facing each other in a silent battle of wills. The knock was repeated and a voice said, "Miss Denning, are you there?"

"I could send for Thomson to force the door," Laura hissed at Star.

"You could. But I don't think you will. Not the sort of publicity you want just now."

"Don't you threaten me."

"Just taking a leaf out of your book, Mother. Much as I despise it."

"Don't call me that!"

"No. I suppose I shouldn't. You certainly don't behave like one. Not the one I tried to believe I had for years. Now, do I open this door or not?"

"Okay. You want to ruin your life, that's your affair. You want me to say he isn't married? Okay, then—he isn't married. Happy now? But, Miss Clever Cloggs, if you're so convinced I lied before to suit my own book, how do you know I won't be lying now just to get the bloody door open?"

Star knew her ploy had failed. Laura was right. She couldn't be sure of this woman. She never had been and never would. The knock was repeated on the door, more urgently this time. Slowly Star put the key in the door and turned it. She opened the door and the housekeeper practically fell into the room. "You rang, Miss Denning?"

"Yes. For God's sake help me with this packing. The

car will be here in a minute—whatever happens, I mustn't miss that plane."

Laura continued to give orders, flinging garments at the poor flustered woman to pack. Star gathered up her parcels. She looked down at the small box that contained Laura's present. She placed it on her mother's dressing table.

"I bought this for you," she said.

Laura looked up, surprised.

"Christmas."

Laura's eyes filled with tears. She went to Star and flung her arms around her. "I do love you, Starlet, in my own crazy way. You know that."

"No, I don't. But it doesn't matter now."

The telephone rang. Laura scooped up the receiver. "Yes? Okay, I'll be down right away . . . I must go, Star."

"Sure. Good-bye, Laura. Hope things work out the way you want them to."

Star was near to tears as she walked quickly away. She clenched her teeth to stop herself from giving in. Laura was out of her life now. And Max? He wouldn't want to know, would he? Not after all that had happened. If she could only see him. Talk to him. Then perhaps . . .

The telephone was ringing as she let herself into Annie's flat. She dropped her parcels and ran to lift the receiver. Her heart was racing, accelerated by desperate hope.

"Hello," she said, breathless.

"Star?"

She recognized the voice at once and then the dam burst. Tears held for so long in check ran unbidden and uncontrollably down her cheeks. Only with the greatest difficulty could she gasp out, "Jessie!"

12

"You look lovely, pet," Jessie said proudly, holding Star at arm's length. "Doesn't she, Gertie?"

"Lovely," Gertie agreed enthusiastically.

Jessie gave Star another hug.

"You look great too," Star said. "I love the hair. Really suits you."

Jessie had changed almost beyond recognition. The dyed red hair, the rouged cheeks, the painted mouth—all had gone. In their place snowy hair and a suntanned face devoid of makeup. "Thought it was time to bring down the curtain," Jessie said. "Hang up my tap shoes and be my age. Can't tell you the relief."

Over a lunch of succulent roast lamb followed by apple pie and cream, which Star ate with gusto and to hell with dieting, she told them about her modeling and her acting plans.

"Not surprised," Jessie said. "Always knew you'd go into the business."

Then the sisters told Star about Malta and how they planned to go and live there. They'd only come back in order to pack up and sell the house.

"Not sure I shall like that," Star said. "You being so far away."

"You'll come and stay whenever you like," Jessie said.

"For as long as you like," Gertie added.

As if by some unspoken agreement, Laura's name was not mentioned. Not until lunch was over and Gertie had discreetly retired, muttering about doing something in the garden. Then, when just the two of them were sitting by the fire sipping coffee, and only then did Jessie broach the subject.

"I read about it in the papers," she said briskly. "We get them in Malta—a day late but never mind—about your mother and *Harringtons.* Can't say I was really surprised. I told her, must be a year ago. 'Get out,' I said. 'You can't go on playing the same part forever.' The public was bored with the character. Not Laura's fault. But she wouldn't listen. Stubborn and willful as always. She ought to go back on the stage. That's where she was at her best."

"Actually—she's gone to Hollywood."

"Oh? Doing what?"

"A new soap. Something Vernon has set up."

"Vernon? Good. Perhaps now they'll both stop mucking about and get back together where they belong."

"Perhaps."

"Wasting her time chasing after a chap half her age. . . . Oh, I forgot . . . was that true what was in the paper, ducky? About you and him?"

Star evaded answering. "Didn't you like him, then, Jessie? Was that why you left?"

"No. I'd been planning to leave for ages. Soon as I saw you off on your own with no more need of me."

"But . . . I thought Laura told you to go."

"That what she said?" Jessie shook her head in mild exasperation as though over a naughty child. "She just can't stand it if someone thinks they can manage without her. She begged me to stay but I'd made up my mind—I wanted a life of my own before it was too late. But I told you all this in my letter."

"What letter?" Star asked, puzzled.

"The one I left for you with Laura. Don't tell me—"

They looked at each other for a moment in silent disbelief, surely not even Laura could be that mean. Neither of them wanted to believe it even now. "She must have forgotten to give it to you. Mislaid it, most like. She can be very scatty sometimes," Jessie said—ever loyal.

Star was not so convinced but didn't want to destroy Jessie's remaining illusions about Laura. She nodded and said, "Sure. She had a lot on her mind."

"As if I'd go off without a word to you."

"No, of course not." Star smiled and reaching over squeezed the old lady's hand. "I . . . that is . . . you were saying about Max . . . that he wasn't the reason why you left."

"No, nothing to do with him," Jessie said firmly. "Funny sort of devil, but to tell the truth I rather liked him. What I didn't like, and I'm not telling tales out of school, because I told her straight out, was the way she carried on over him. He made it quite clear there was nothing doing, anybody could see that, but . . . well, he's a dishy number and Laura wanted to show him off. I hated to see her making a fool of herself. Yes, I suppose that is what we quarreled about. Though, like I said, it wasn't the reason I left."

Star stared down at her coffee cup. She didn't want

Jessie to see the relief she felt. Max hadn't lied to her about Laura . . . and now she was convinced that he hadn't lied about anything. It had been Laura making trouble. Her own mother who had lied. Somehow she must find him. Must tell him how sorry she was to have doubted him. She realized that Jessie had stopped talking and was regarding her with a quizzical expression.

"And now you've fallen A over T for a bloke that's as complicated as a monkey-puzzle tree?"

Star didn't deny it. But to her surprise she felt reluctant to talk about him. She had so often wanted Jessie's advice but now she didn't seem to need it after all; didn't want to hear any arguments that might try to put her off. She knew exactly what she wanted. As if guessing her thoughts, Jessie said, "Be a handful, I'd say, but not for me to tell you how to live your life. You're grown up now, love. You're going to have a successful career. You must do things your own way."

"I do seem to get things wrong a lot of the time," Star said ruefully.

"Bound to make mistakes, everybody does. But, ducky, when you do, have a good cry and then no regrets. Remember, an actress never loses out on anything life throws at her. She can put it in her work."

Star nodded, thinking of Viola and how her experience with Max had helped to interpret her.

"I always say it wasn't the things I did I regretted," Jessie said with a smile. "Only the things I didn't do."

On an impulse Star jumped up and kissed her old friend. "Thank you, Jess."

"For what?"

"For being you."

Gertie came in offering fresh coffee, which Star declined. They all agreed that it looked like snow and Star had better be on her way.

Jessie said, "I expect you're all booked up for Christmas, but if you want to come we've a spare bed."

"I might just do that, Jessie. Can I . . . can I let you know?"

"Of course. Now then, time to get the show on the road."

Star spoke the familiar words with her and they all laughed.

As Star drove away she could see Jessie reflected in the rear-view mirror, still standing by the garden gate, waving and blowing kisses. Star waved her hand out of the open car window in reply as Jessie's image got smaller and smaller and then vanished for good. She suddenly felt very alone and rather cold. A light sleety snow started to fall. She closed the window and switched on the windshield wipers. She made her way slowly through the lanes and byways that would lead her eventually back to the motorway. By the time she reached it she had made up her mind. She moved into the fast lane and stayed there.

She parked the car in the lane under the bare branches of a gnarled old oak tree and sat for a moment without moving, torn between wanting desperately to go to Max and an urge to turn the car round and get away as fast as possible. No, she was here now. She must see it through. Suppose Helen were still here? Suppose after all he had gone back to her? Supposing . . . for chrissake, woman, stop messing about. Get that show on the road.

She left the car in the lane in case she wanted to get away without being noticed, and went the rest of the way on foot. The sleet persisted and it was getting dark. She felt chilled but there was excitement too at the thought that in just a few moments she might see him again. As always the sight of the cottage gave her a thrill of pleasure though now, in the dreary gray of an early winter evening, it looked a little bleak, huddled down into itself behind the hedge. No light shone out in welcome from the windows, no cozy spiral of smoke telling of a warm hearth waiting. Then, as she reached the garden gate, she saw that the estate agent's sign was again in place. Only this time it proclaimed in bold letters just one word: "SOLD."

Star stared at the sign in disbelief. Sold? She felt bewildered, deprived. In spite of Helen she still had proprietary feelings about the place. It had been the scene of the greatest joy she had experienced in her life and she felt outraged that Max should have sold it without consulting her. Okay, that was unreasonable, but after all they had shared how could he let anyone else live there? She was about to go back to the car when she saw that one last rose still bloomed on the rambler by the front door. She opened the garden gate and walked up the brick path. The rose was dangerously full blown, its petals damaged, almost drained of color, a ghost of a flower. With the utmost care Star broke off the stem and held the fragile bloom up to her face. It still retained the faint, sweet smell of summer. The raindrops that clung to the petals transferred themselves to her cheeks like tears. She found a tissue in a pocket and lovingly wrapped it around the rose. Then gently she placed it in her bag. If she was behaving like a Victorian heroine she didn't care. She had to have something of the place to keep and to remember always.

She turned to go back to the car, but yet again changed her mind and walked slowly round the side of the house and into the garden, just as she had done on that first visit, which now seemed light-years away and yet so close.

The garden had been tidied up but this only seemed to add to the air of desolation. She crossed the lawn and was glad to be wearing flats and not those spike heels that had caused so much trouble that other time. She smiled sadly at the memory. Wonder what happened to that toad, she thought as she reached the stream and stood gazing out over the fields that lay sleeping in the gathering dusk. Snow was falling in earnest now and she imagined how beautiful the place would look covered in snow. She could almost see the sweep of countryside under its white blanket, the filigree branches of trees gleaming silver. Would the stream freeze over? They would sit by the roaring fire on winter evenings, just she and Max, safe and warm. And they'd trim the tree for Christmas and kiss under the mistletoe.

She shivered and realized how damp and chilled she felt. Snow was clinging to her hair and eyelashes. No use standing here dreaming impossible dreams and catching pneumonia, she thought, and started to climb up the soggy slope of the lawn back to the house.

When she reached the terrace she couldn't resist the urge to look through the window into Max's study. Not that she could see much. However, she could make out his furniture still in place: desk, chairs, just as she remembered them. But it did seem as though the bookshelves were empty. Perhaps he'd sold the house, furniture and all. Just taken his personal belongings and gone abroad or something. So intent was she peering through the window that she didn't hear footsteps creeping up on her and so was all the more startled when a flashlight was beamed onto her.

"Who's there? What are you doing here?"

The voice was unmistakable—Max.

She turned and the light fell on her face.

"You . . ." he breathed, his voice barely audible.

For a long moment they stood facing each other in silence. Star, blinded by the light, could only just make out the shape behind it but the drumming of her heart told her only too well that her ears had not deceived her and that Max actually stood so close that just by reaching out a hand she could have touched him. But she made no such move. She couldn't. Her vocal cords seemed to have died on her too.

"What the hell are you doing here?" he asked roughly.

Here was her chance. Her wish had come true. Incredibly, from out of the snow and the gloom, Max had actually materialized. Now was the moment to say what she'd come to say. But she couldn't seem to form the words and the moment was gone.

"Is that your car in the lane?" Max asked in the same harsh tone.

"Yes," Star replied in a hoarse whisper.

"You should have left the parking lights on. I damn near ran into it."

"I'm sorry," she said, icily polite.

"You'd better not try to turn in the lane. You'll only end up in the ditch."

"I do know how to do a three point, thanks."

"No. Bring it to the front of the house and I'll guide you. I don't fancy spending the rest of the evening digging you out."

He turned abruptly, and without waiting for her strode off. Star found the dark even more intense after the glare of the lamp, and keeping her eye on the bobbing pool of light followed in his footsteps. He stood by the open door of the car, holding it for her with an air of mock courtesy. Now, in the light from inside the car, she could really see him. Her every impulse was to run to him and hold him close and tell him how she loved him, how she always would—but the cold, hard expression on his face made it impossible. She could see that all the old arrogance was back in force. Star stumbled toward the car, trying to carry off this miserable situation with as much dignity as she could muster. Determined now that she must drive away from the place and from Max forever. But when she joined him she was instantly aware of the power of his physical proximity. Of her intense need of him. She hesitated and made no move to get into the car. With an irritable gesture, Max held out his hand.

"Give me the keys," he said. "I'll turn it round for you."

"I . . . I'm not leaving," she finally blurted out. "I came here to see you."

"Well, now you've seen me. Please go."

"Can't we at least talk?" Star was horrified to find herself pleading with him.

Max did not reply at once and they stood within embracing distance yet with a fathomless gulf of alienation dividing them.

"I don't think we have anything to discuss," he said curtly.

"That's not true."

"I suppose you did receive my letter?"

"Yes. I did."

"And I assume you read it?"

"Yes."

"Then I'm right, aren't I? There is nothing to talk about."

"I think there is," Star persisted. "Okay, maybe I did overreact, I'm not sure, but even if all the things you said about me were true I still think I deserve some kind of explanation."

"Oh, Star, Star, what good would it do?"

"I don't know for sure—I might even hear things I don't want to hear. If I do, well, too bad. But I've tried just walking away, Max, and it doesn't work. What happened was too important for me to leave a lot of loose ends. If it can't be, then at least I want to know why."

Max stood looking at her, his gray eyes opaque, then with a shrug he closed the car door. They walked back to the house in silence. Inside, the place felt cold and unlived in and Star guessed that Max had not been there for some time. Perhaps it was fate that they had both come here at the same moment? Star was careful not to voice this thought—in fact not to voice any thought.

"Cold in here," Max observed. "Mrs. Crompton must have turned off the heating."

He disappeared into the kitchen and Star heard the sound of the boiler igniting. In a moment he returned, carrying a bottle of red wine and glasses. "This'll warm us up." He opened the bottle, poured the wine, and handed her a glass with no attempt at conversation.

Star sat on the sofa, sipping the wine, and watched while Max set light to the fire that was laid in the fireplace. Soon the logs caught and flames blazed up the chimney. He picked up his glass and sat at a safe distance from her. Still they did not speak. Star was determined to let him take the lead and finally he did.

"So, you want an explanation? I must tell you I'm not much into justifying myself, especially when there's no cause. However, if it gives you the impetus to go away and get on with the job of growing up, I'll give you the facts as I see them." He paused and frowned down into the deep red glow of the claret in his glass. He drank and then continued, "Helen, whom you met here, is highly attractive, intelligent, frequently amusing, and, yes, passionate. She is also unstable, promiscuous, and a compulsive liar. I had the misfortune to meet her and become totally infatuated with her."

Star had to fight hard not to flinch at this information. She had asked for it so she had to take it.

"Go on," she said, with unnatural calm, determined not to betray her feelings.

"When we met she told me she was married and was in the middle of a divorce. She regaled me with tales of a cruel husband who had apparently perpetrated every known abomination on her, and said that all she needed was the love of a normal, healthy man with whom she could share her life and her home. So, we found this place and I allowed myself to get lost in the fantasy of nest making and all the other romantic rubbish that goes with the illusion of love. She filled me in with other fictions about her life . . . no need to itemize them here . . . then I found out that her husband was a mild enough chap whom she in fact deserted and who then started divorce proceedings, citing me as the wicked wolf who broke up his marriage. So, after many scenes and much hysteria, she admitted that she had lied and I, like a fool, accepted this as one slip on her part and the divorce went ahead." Max shook his head and passed a hand over his eyes. Star felt a stab of guilt at making him relive something that obviously caused him so much pain. She wanted to hold him in her arms and say that all that was behind him now and that what mattered was that she loved him. But clearly it was not all that mattered, was it?

Max got up and started to pace the room, almost as though he had forgotten Star was there. "She lied about such stupid things—unimportant, mundane things—that it was impossible to understand why she felt compelled to do it. I think it was some private battle she was fighting in which she needed to score point. Every time I found it more bewildering, and gradually I began to realize that this was not a woman I was living with but a very mixed-up child." He went to the table to replenish his glass. Star saw the tension in his neck and arms; she also saw and understood why he had reacted so violently when she seemed to behave irrationally. He'd had his fill of little girls and wanted—no, needed—a woman.

"Then, out of the blue," Max turned his gaze back to Star, "she bolted. Left without a word, taking practically nothing with her. I was frantic. I went to the police in the end and had to suffer the indignity of their cross-examination. They made me feel that I had had some highly suspect part in this mysterious disappearance and were just on the point of digging up the garden when I got a scruffy little note sent from Spain. Madam had found her 'soul mate' and our whole thing had been a terrible mistake."

He laughed. A rough, bitter sound that made Star wince.

"Max," she said softly. "I'm so sorry."

"Why the hell should you be?"

"Because it hurt you so much and I don't think I can bear for you to be hurt."

He stood by the sofa, looking down at her. The cold gray eyes softened. "This is what I can't take, Star. The knowledge that caring seems to mean pain. As soon as you care for someone you are left defenseless. All the protective skins are suddenly stripped away and you are vulnerable as a newborn babe."

"I think you've had a sort of extra-bad trip—it doesn't always have to be like that. I just don't believe it."

Max came and sat beside her on the sofa. He sat staring into the fire and for what seemed an interminable time he didn't speak. All that could be heard was the sound of the wood crackling in the grate.

"Anyway," he continued, his voice steady, his composure regained, "I managed to get it together and I swore—swore on anything and everything that I had ever held dear—that I would never, ever get caught again. And, sure enough, I did manage to coast along reasonably well. Except that I couldn't write. Which darn near killed me. That's where I was when I met Laura . . . the rest you know."

Max took a swallow of wine and stared into the fire. Nothing in his expression betrayed what he was thinking or feeling.

"Why did she come back?" Star asked quietly. "Helen, I mean."

"The Spanish idyll hadn't come up to scratch, it seems. She wanted—or said she wanted—us to pick up where we had left off."

"How . . . how did you feel about that?"

"You can ask that?" He turned on her, his eyes black with anger. "This is what I mean, Star: if two people have what we had how can there be any room for doubt? You should have known that she was an intruder. A mischief maker. How could you have questioned my love, even for a moment?"

"But I did believe that you loved me," Star protested. "Or I thought I did, until . . . it was Laura. She said you were married, and then I come here and find this woman in a dressing gown who seemed totally at home, and when I asked her she more or less said that it was true—you were married—so I just sort of panicked and ran away."

"Laura lied and so did Helen. I'm no more married than you are. Never have been."

"So Laura really did say that just to ruin things between us."

"To be fair she might even have believed it. Or talked herself into believing it—because I always refused to discuss my private life with her. I was determined not to get involved in any way. Still, it was a wicked, vindictive act to try and ruin our love. If only you'd had some faith in me."

"Max, can't you understand that I grew up in a world where people change partners the way they change their cars? For as long as I can remember my father had a succession of girlfriends. I hated it, Max, I still do. I believe that if two people love each other they shouldn't cheapen that love with shoddy little affairs on the side."

"If you'd stopped the car out there in the lane . . . asked me straight . . . trusted me."

"I know. And I regret that so much now."

"Without trust, Star, complete and total, no relationship can stand a chance."

"I feel the same, but it's something I've never known. Something that was always looked on as being ridiculously romantic. Oh, don't you see? We both want the same thing. And we both want each other . . . don't we?"

"I wish I could believe that."

"I love you, Max." She spoke the words with such simple sincerity that he could no longer doubt her. "And, yes," she continued, "I only want complete commitment."

"How can you be sure at your age? You're still so young."

Star shook her head. "I've done a lot of growing up lately. I expect we'll both change as we go along but we'll change together."

He made no move toward her. Just sat looking at her with a burning intensity. For a long moment he said nothing and then, in a voice almost devoid of expression, he said, "Will you marry me?"

Such immense joy exploded inside her that Star could only barely whisper, "Yes."

Then Max was beside her and they held each other as if they would never, never let go. And his lips were on hers and the kiss spoke more than a million words could ever have done. That from here on in they were one and could take whatever life threw at them because it would be shared. When at last Max released her she looked as though a light had been switched on somewhere deep inside. Everything about her seemed to effervesce and Max laughed with pleasure at the sight of her.

"We should have some champagne."

"I don't need it."

"Just as well, I haven't any."

They both laughed and hugged each other again. And just as it seemed that everything must be perfect Star remembered something that made the smile fade. A small shadow fell across her face.

"Just a minute . . . there's something we must discuss first."

"Oh? What?"

"Well . . . it's about my acting."

"Look, you don't have to if you don't want to."

"But that's just it. I do want to."

"Then what's the problem?"

"I'm going to drama school. I want to learn to be as good as I possibly can. I'm serious about it, Max."

"But that's wonderful."

"Are you sure? I mean—how can I be a really good wife if I'm involved in an acting career?"

"I hadn't visualized you sitting at home darning my socks. We'll be partners."

"But I've seen what it can do to someone. . . . I, well, I don't want to live only for my career the way Laura always has."

"I will now make you a solemn promise," Max said, his eyes twinkling. "If ever you start to show even the faintest resemblance to Laura, I shall personally take you over my knee and give you a good spanking."

Star laughed. "And you really don't mind if I act?"

"But I wanted you to, remember? Nobody else will ever really be Abigail for me."

Star nodded a bit wistfully. "Yes, I'm sorry to have lost her. But it may be for the best. If such a chance comes again I'd like to be sure I know what I'm doing."

"You'll be a wonderful actress and an even more wonderful wife."

"Oh . . . but where shall we live?"

"Here."

"But it's sold."

"It was, or so I thought. The sale has fallen through. That's why I came here—to see the estate agent."

"I'm so glad. I should have hated to leave it."

"Right. From this moment on Lamb Cottage is withdrawn from the market. I want it for myself and my beautiful wife!"

"It's called Lamb Cottage? I never knew." Star smiled at him affectionately. "Must say, darling, I can't imagine a less appropriate name for a home of yours."

Max laughed. "I know. But that's always been the name, so who am I to change it?"

"We're going to be so happy here, I just know it."

Max looked thoughtful. "I wonder if we can get a special license and be married before Christmas?"

"What does it matter?" Star said. "So long as we're here together."

Her eyes shone with excitement. "We'll have a tree and holly and a turkey and mince pies, and I want to buy you the most fabulous Christmas present."

"This is the only Christmas present I want," Max said, taking her in his arms. "The best I've ever had or ever could have."